Tracy Farr is a writer who used to be a scientist. Melbourne-born and Perth-raised, she lived for five years in Vancouver before moving to Aotearoa in 1996. She's lived on Te Motu Kairangi Miramar Peninsula in Wellington, where *Wonderland* is set, for nearly thirty years. Her debut novel *The Life and Loves of Lena Gaunt* was longlisted for Australia's Miles Franklin Literary Award, shortlisted for the Barbara Jefferis Award and Western Australian Premier's Book Awards. *Wonderland* is her third novel. She's co-curator of the live literary series Bad Diaries Salon and its sister project, *Bad Diaries Podcast*. Find her at tracyfarrauthor.com

Wonderland
Tracy Farr

THE CUBA PRESS

For my father

This book is copyright apart from any fair dealing as permitted under the Copyright Act, and no part may be reproduced without permission from the publisher.

© Tracy Farr 2025

Tracy Farr asserts her moral right to be identified as the author of this book.

Edited by Siân Robyns.
Cover design by Paul Stewart and Tracy Farr.
Book design and typesetting by Paul Stewart.
Set in Sabon LT Pro 10.5/14

Cover image: *Wellington's Wonderland at Miramar 'The Water Chute'* by Zak (Joseph Zachariah), 1907. Te Papa, PS.003399. Modified from original.

A catalogue record for this book is available from the National Library of New Zealand.
Kei te pātengi raraunga o Te Puna Mātauranga o Aotearoa te whakarārangi o tēnei pukapuka.
ISBN 978-1-98-859593-1

Published with the support of the Laura Solomon Trust and the New Zealand Society of Authors.

¶ NZSA THE NEW ZEALAND SOCIETY OF AUTHORS
TE PUNI KAITUHI O AOTEAROA (PEN NZ INC)

Printed in Aotearoa New Zealand by Your Books, a division of Excel Digital Limited, a Toitū net carbon zero certified organisation.

THE CUBA PRESS
Level 6, 138 Wakefield Street, Te Aro
Box 9321 Wellington 6141
Aotearoa New Zealand

*'Once upon a time there were three little sisters,'
the Dormouse began in a great hurry ...*
—Lewis Carroll, *Alice's Adventures in Wonderland*

*Fame is an astonishing mirror, sometimes faithful,
sometimes distorting like the convex glasses of an
amusement park ...*
—Ève Curie, *Madame Curie*

The Mataura Ensign, Thursday, December 21, 1911

FIVE DUELS
Professor's Separation

Paris, December 20, 1911

Five duels have been fought over Madame Langevin's separation suit against Professor Langevin, Madame Curie being cited as co-respondent. The court granted a separation.

Mme. Curie is the eminent French scientist who in conjunction with her husband, the late Professor Pierre Curie, discovered Radium. The Swedish Academy of Science has awarded this year's prize for chemistry, valued at £7773, to Mme. Curie.

In 1903 she received jointly with her husband her first Nobel Prize. After the shocking and untimely death of Pierre Curie, killed by a carriage on a Paris bridge in 1906, a large majority of his colleagues recommended appointing his widow as his successor. This gifted woman, the only one of her sex who has ever received this high honour, is now a full professor in the venerable Sorbonne.

Mme. Curie is known as a woman of very simple tastes. All who have seen Mme. Curie at work in her laboratory, or listened to her lectures, have been impressed by her undemonstrative zeal, and her aversion to sensational effects. The current scandal will surely test her legendary abstraction from external disturbances.

The Evening Post, Friday, April 19, 1912

MME. CURIE MYSTERY
Where in the World is She?

Paris, March 29, 1912

Marie Sklodowska Curie, the Polish scientist more widely known as Mme. Curie, whose once untarnished reputation as scientific savant has been for some months shaken by scandal, is once again the subject of rumour and mystery. Mme. Curie was last seen in public in January of this year, when she left the hospital in Paris in which she had been secluded for more than one month, suffering from a reported 'kidney ailment'. A separation suit widely reported as naming Mme. Sklodowska Curie as co-respondent has been settled in the courts in Paris. Her whereabouts are currently unknown.

Prelude

OUR FIRST MEMORY
Triplets

Here is a story. We can tell it to you. We saw it with our own six eyes. We heard it with our own six shell-like ears. We held it in our own six hands, so we can tell you (oh yes!).

The start of this story is the day the Lady came.

No, the start of this story is the start of us, and Wonderland.

Our first memory is of the sea. Salt scent womb water, the iron taste of birth. Our mother croons songs—birdlike, incomprehensible—from her own mother's faraway home, while Charlie, our father, drinks whisky and shouts his thanks to God.

Our next first memory is of holding hands. We three, holding hands in the womb, all together. Then—whoosh! Into the light! Ada goes first, as Ada always will, slithering into the world at a quarter to midnight on the eve of the new year. Oona is next, forever in between, born on the middle stroke of midnight, as the old year cedes to the new. And Hanna, dear Johanna, is last of us to land, waiting for the new year, new day, a January baby. Our mother always says that we slipped out of her like broad beans from the pod, pop pop pop, slick as you like, unstoppable once we started. When our father first saw us, he made the sign of the cross—spectacles, testicles, wallet and watch—whether in thanks at our safe delivery, or to ward off the witchery of our triple likeness, we cannot know (though we like to think it was thanks).

Our third first memory is of the scent of apples. We three lie in a wooden apple box lined with flannel and newspapers, there in all our newness, on the first day of the brand-new year. Our hands reach to connect, Ada's thumb in Hanna's mouth, Oona's hand on Ada's cheek, Hanna grasping Oona's pointing finger in her fist.

Mrs Reddy delivers us, and it is Mrs R who has the forethought to mark us as we make our appearance.

'Three little girls, Saint Katie Sheppard help them.'

Mrs Wilma Reddy wears the suffrage colours (Votes for Women!) in a rosette at her breast, in support of her not-yet-enfranchised British sisters. She unpins the ribbons to fix them to our ankles, green for Ada, white for Oona, violet for Hanna, fixing our colours for life. We have those scraps of ribbon still. Our mother, Matti, kept them.

In the now of then, we look up towards the shape of our mother. We three are our own little selves, lying in our apple box, the space between us blurred.

We cannot remember (how could we?) the womb. We cannot remember the apple box, or the incubators we were moved to that first day (the three of us, behind glass, as alike as little dolls), or any of our earliest days and years at Wonderland. And yet, we do. We do remember them, even if those memories are not entirely our own. We remember the apple box, the incubators. We remember the scratch of the white linen masks that disguised our mother and Mrs R. We remember sucking gritty milk from rubber nipples on glass bottles.

And we remember the world around us, and above us.

We remember Mr Halley's great comet that shone in the sky, and our father's plan to sell gas masks to save us all from its poison, and a word we heard then, *perihelion*, like the name of a flower. We remember (though perhaps it hasn't happened yet) the whale, beached at Lyall Bay, and the children playing on it and around it (until it began to wobble and stink). We remember—though it happened before we were born—the day the hot air balloon landed with a crash, and we remember thinking that a hot air balloon, as it deflated, might look like the shape of a whale on a beach, or a teardrop on its side, going nowhere. Like this:

So, yes, we remember the events of our shared lives, and of lives before our own. Some are in softer focus, hazy, as in a dream. Others we see with such crystal clarity—as if shone like coloured light shifting on a bare white wall—that we can summon and relive them in an instant.

There could be no mother of tiny triplets better prepared for the care of us than our own dear mother, Matti, a graduate of the medical school in Dunedin in the dying years of the old century. Despite her class-topping marks, the only position open to Dr Matilda Rumble (as our mother was then) was in the womanly field of obstetrics, and she took to it with the gusto she had applied to all her studies. That same gusto took her north and east, across the Pacific Ocean by ship, then across the great expanse of America by train, to New York City, to see for herself the startling new inventions she had read about—baby incubators saving the lives of tiny earlyborns, sealing them snug as bugs in glass cases, for lifesaving medical care.

Matti arrived in New York with a letter of introduction to Dr Martin Couney. When hospitals had refused to risk his new technology in their conservative institutions (leaving tiny too-soon babies to slip away, *God's will, amen*), the enterprising Dr Couney had taken a showman-like leap. He famously took his fabulous contraptions to the carnival sideshow instead—the miracle of life as amazing an attraction as any of the freaks and frights and sights on show—and used the entrance fees to fund the babies' care. And so, Dr Matilda Rumble found herself assisting Dr Couney in the Living Infant Incubator at Coney Island, every day donning white coat, white stockings, white lace-up shoes, a white paper cap over her straight dark hair, busily tending babies behind the viewing glass, ignoring the punters who (ignoring the signs) rapped on the glass with their knuckles. Matti spent two years saving tiny lives under the rattle and scream of the Coney Island roller coaster, learning everything she could from Dr Couney and the very many babies in their joint care. Then she took the train west across the country, and then the ship south across the sea, all the way back to New Zealand, with three glass incubators and all their fittings packed into wooden crates, a bag stuffed with papers and lists and treatment regimes, to set up her own model baby hospital. Her challenge: to find an accommodating carnival of her own, back home.

That's how Dr Matilda Rumble first crossed paths with our father, Carnival Charlie Loverock, and he wooed her with his big hands and loud voice, and his grand dreams of Wonderland amusement park, Miramar's Mecca of Merry Souls. He promised a place for her Infant Incubators, and that was that. Before she knew it Matti had a bun in her own oven, and a ring on her finger, in that order.

The bun was three buns, though she did not know it at first. She grew bigger and bigger, as each day the grand opening of Wonderland—complete with Wonderland's Wonderful Infant Incubator, waiting empty, quiet and ready—grew closer. Her timing, as it happened, could not have been better. She popped us out, pop pop pop, while the paint was drying on the colourful façades and plywood hoardings of Wonderland's wonderful buildings and many attractions, and the stage was set for its official opening.

And so we became Wonderland's first residents, first act, and first show.

Here we are, whisked out of our apple box. Now we lie in the little glass cases of the incubator, we three sleeping beauties in our snow-white linens, safe and snug and warm and cared-for, side by side by side.

It's our first performance, our first stage, where we earn our keep from an early age. We are three weeks old when Wonderland opens, on the holiday weekend in January 1905, and we are among the star attractions. Our father—Carnival Charlie Loverock, his dreams as big as his belly—stands on a rostrum, a megaphone at his lips, and spruiks as the punters come through the grand Wonderland gateway.

'See the tiny triplets—can you tell them apart? Tuppence to see the tiny triplets! Identical, as if one was copied from the next. Proof of God's hand, if ever you needed it.'

He crosses himself (just in case) as he pauses for breath.

'See the latest in Medical Technology, for the Scientific Management of Infants. Direct from America!'

Amehdika is the way he says it, *Ahhh-MEH-Di-Kah!*

'The Wonderful Infant Incubator, only here at Wonderland, the one and only medical baby incubator facility in the Whole! Southern! Hemisphere! A scientific novelty! See the future today! Only at Wonderland!'

We three pippins in our little glass cases are the future! Babies in boxes, glassed-in nurseries! Timed feeding from bottles filled with scientifically formulated liquids, measured by the fluid ounce. Our mother tends us, dressed in her trustworthy, doctorly whites, assisted by Mrs R, who has re-rosetted her unsupported bosom (Votes for Women!).

'Truly bringing the Wonder to Wonderland!' our clucky father shouts, meaning it with all his big, proud, well-intentioned heart.

~ ~ ~

We are tiny babies who become tiny children, small but in perfect proportion. Our mother says we're survivors.

'Those first days, you were only just in this world. Your father could hold each of you in one hand—all three of you in both hands.'

She holds her own hands out, cupping them around tiny remembered us.

Yes, we are tiny, and people think us frail, when they see us, in need of protection. But we're fine like tungsten filament in a blown-glass bulb, and we burn as bright.

In Wonderland's Wonderful Infant Incubator, and later in the Tiny Toddler Tea-Time Nursery, we three learn to be on view, on stage, always aware that we are gazed upon. When we hold a tea party, we instinctively know to pull up our chairs, one of us at each side of the table, leaving the fourth side to the viewing window, so the punters might imagine themselves sitting down to tea with us, sipping sugar water from tiny china cups.

Skip forward. Now we are five. We have graduated from improvised tea party pieces to our own scripted act, staged, rehearsed. We've become Wonderland's Own Three Little Maids, Pacific's Triple Star. In an approximation of Japanese dress—Ada in green, Oona in white, Hanna in violet, with paper fans to match—we step and bow in perfect time. Our faces are only lightly powdered, so that our alikeness (*It's Uncanny!* the posters for our show insist) is on display.

> *Three Little Maidens all unwary*
> *Come from the baby nurse-er-ary*
> *Tell us apart now, if you dare-y*
> *Three Little Maids are we!*
>
> *Three Miramar Maidens, all identical*
> *Born in Wonderland's Baby Hospital*

Not an illusion, real or optical
Three matching maids are we
Three matching ma-a-aids are we!

We are matching. But we are not pretty, we Three Little Miramar Maids. We are skinny scraps, with faces too sharp to ever be pretty. We'll be called *handsome* when we're older. We'll even make ourselves seem beautiful. And the camera, capturing us in still or moving pictures, will always love us.

But not now. Not yet. We're getting ahead of ourselves, time in a muddle again.

Skip, skip, skip. Now we are six. We can Three-Little-Maids in our sleep, it's all so familiar, so tested and true—the costumes, the makeup, the music, our slippered feet stepping on the limelit stage. The punters still love us, so our father tells us, but once we start school, we only play weekend shows, as our mother insists.

Skip again, skip forward, until now. Now we are seven, and Wonderland is closed. After unseasonal rain and flooding washed out the holiday weekend—the Biggest Wonderland Weekend of the Summer, as it was billed—and then the big earthquake buckled the tramlines, stopping the trams to Seatoun and Miramar, our father shuttered the ticket office and padlocked the Wonderland gate. Just for the season, he tells us. Just until the trams start running again. Just for the winter. Just until summer. Just just just until then (until when?).

We cross our fingers behind our backs in hope that maybe, just maybe, we'll open for the Winter Gala.

Not now, no, not now.

Not yet.

Now we are seven, are six, are five. We're one two three, at sixes and sevens. Time is so tricky to catch.

The thing is, sometimes we remember backwards, and sometimes we remember forwards. To put it another way, sometimes we remember the past, but other times we remember the future. We don't claim to understand this, or how it works. It seems to defy the laws of science, and space, and history. But we do know that memory is not a simple straight line from then to now, inching forward with each tick of the clock, each circuit of the Earth. Memory folds back on itself, forms knots into which we cannot see, knits patterns and shapes from simple strings, leaves gaps, leaves holes.

We can remember back to the time before our birth (we told you so). And we can remember forward to the time long after the autumn and winter of the Lady's visit, when Wonderland is gone, when there are houses where the Helter Skelter spiralled and the water slide once slid, when nothing remains of Wonderland but memories, impossible memories. We remember a time to come when Miramar (*the Hollywood of the South Pacific*, someone will call it, but the name'll never really catch on) is dense with people and houses and cars and trucks and buses and shops, and then a time more forward still, when the seas have risen, and Miramar is an island once more (as it was before the olden-days earthquake thrust it up).

We imagine alternate histories, other memories, might-have-beens and maybes.

This is a story of some such memories, and imaginings.

We'll begin again at a different beginning.

Miramar

Autumn 1912

LADY BLOODY RADIUM
Triplets

We are seven years old when the Lady comes to stay.

She steps carefully, slowly, down the gangway of the ferry *Duchess*, squinting into the soft glare of pale May sunshine, a leather satchel in her hand, close by her side. At the bottom of the gangway she stops, lifts a long-fingered hand to her throat. There she is (swoon!) with her high brow, her grey eyes, the flyaway of her hair, the fairest skin we've ever seen, her little mouth pursed with care and caution. In the autumn sun, she almost seems to glow.

We leap up from our spying spot in the dunes, brush the sand off ourselves and each other. We stand, holding hands, at the edge of the land, where the wooden wharf ends and the road to Worser Bay begins.

Our mother received the first of several letters and telegrams last month from her old and very dear friend Ernest Rutherford (the Great Man of Science, far away across the ocean), asking our mother to welcome the Lady, his famous scientist friend. Though we are (so everyone says) Good Little Readers, we could not have deciphered his spiked and spidering words even if our mother had handed us the ink-thick pages (she did not). We listened, instead, to our mother read the letter to our father, and to our father harumph as he always harumphs (though we do not know why) whenever a letter arrives from the Great Man of Science. We heard our mother read *not for long*, and *the woman's a genius*, and *she and her poor health and spirits could not be in better hands than your own*. We heard *scandal* and *witch hunt* (though we thought witches were just in books and tales). We remember hearing *daughters*, and daughters are some of our favourite things. We remember the finish of the letter, *I remain your dear old friend, Ern, in your debt once more. My best wishes to you and Charles—and of course to your hat-trick of daughters. Chuck them under their three chinny chin chins from me.*

And so—our chinny chin chins thoroughly and Ernest-ly chucked under, and the front room more recently made ready for our guest, to the sound of our father's harumphing and bloody Ern-ing and underbreathmuttering—our mother caught the ferry into Town this morning to meet the Lady's ship. All day we sat in our classroom, impatiently scratching slate and spilling ink under the watchful eye of our teacher, Miss Grimshaw. As soon as school finished, we ran down the hill and around the bay, to lie snug and sandy in the dunes and beach grass by Seatoun Wharf, waiting for the first sight of the ferry chugging its steamy way, bringing our mother and the Lady home from Town.

We watch now as the other passengers file off the *Duchess*, splitting and spilling around the Lady who stands, still and waiting, pale and strange, at the bottom of the gangway. Our mother appears, the last to disembark, struggling a large leather valise down the gangway towards the Lady on the wharf. She places the valise beside them both, then takes the Lady's hand, and pats it with her own, leaning closer to the Lady as she speaks. They both nod, then their hands separate, and they turn to walk towards us down the length of the wharf. Almost all we can see of our mother, who walks behind the Lady, is the great leather case that bangs against her leg as she lists to port for balance. They reach the end of the wharf and stop, a little in front of us.

Our mother says, 'Girls, there you are! Madame, may I present my daughters, Ada, Oona, Johanna.'

She points with her free hand as she says each of our names, and each of us nods as she does so. (We do not curtsey. We keep our curtseys for the stage.) The Lady nods at us in return.

'Our house is a very short walk from here, just a few minutes around the bay. I can manage your valise. Perhaps the girls might carry your satchel—'

The Lady smiles, and shakes her head, and says some words that make no sense. Our mother smiles at her, and answers with the same strange sounds. This must be what our mother calls *another language*. What words have been said? We imagine them as objects floating past us, unreachable.

'Come, girls,' our mother says. 'Rally, rally!'

Our mother walks in step with the Lady, while we skip behind them, keeping up easily, for they walk more slowly than grownups usually do. The Lady holds our attention, though we can only see the back of her, the shape of her, the pace of her. She is shorter than our mother. They are both equally slim. We watch the Lady's skirt flatten against each of her legs in turn, hear the skirt's shush as she walks. Our mother and the Lady continue to talk, in the language we do not understand. We hear the hum of it, the soft hiss of it, the rise and fall.

Then the Lady slows, and stops, and our mother stops, too, and turns to her and says some language words. Our mother eases the Lady's satchel over her own shoulder, and takes the Lady's arm, and we all walk on, until—only a minute or two later, though time has stretched, and it feels like longer—we reach the door of our little house, in Worser Bay, by the sea.

'Out from under my feet, girls, and leave our visitor be!'

We'd thought we might be a Very Great Help in assisting our curious visitor to settle in, but our mother shoos us out of the way when we try to help her unpack, so we retire to the back step with our knucklebones (Ada had them in her pocket from Morning Play at school), grabbing an apple and a handful of digestive biscuits on the way. We sit on the doorstep taking turns clicking the knucklebones onto the concrete, scooping them into our palms, click, scoop, Onesies, Twosies, Threesies, Fours, and Alls (though only Hanna has mastered Alls). We pass the apple between us, the crisp sweet of it chasing the dusty biscuit crumbs. We eat the apple down to the core, and then to pass some more time (and because our mother keeps shooing us every time we try to spy), we eat the core, bite bite bite, not one bit afraid of growing apple trees in our bellies.

The front door crashes, and we hear the boom of our father's voice, then hushing from our mother, and then huffing and blowing from our father, and there he is, as large as life and twice as marvellous, and he scoops the three of us up in his arms and asks us about our day as he walks with us (Hanna balanced on one enormous boot, Oona on the other, and Ada with her fingers tucked under his belt and holding on for dear life) around the side of the house, past our lovely old horse, and across the road to the beach, where we run and jump and somersault in the sand under the proud gaze and loud encouragement of our father, until we are tired enough for our tea.

We cannot hide our disappointment when the new, strange Lady does not appear at tea-time. She has retired, our mother says, tired from travel, and besides she is unwell. Our mother takes her a bowl of broth on a tray. Later, when she brings the tray back to the kitchen, the bowl is still full, the broth cold, a slick of fat on its surface.

In the night of that day, we three nest together in our bed, squirming like baby mice, keeping each other warm. We poke our mouths from under the blankets and breathe dragonsbreath into the cold moonlight. We listen to our mother and father move and murmur in the kitchen, keen to hear what they have to say about the foreign Lady (though our mother says we mustn't call her that, but must call her *Madame* or *Professor*).

We hear the scrape of chair legs against floor, then our father opens the door from the kitchen on his way out the back to the WC. Oona makes a hissing pissing noise through her teeth, and we all titter with the cheek of it. Our father says *By crikey, you ratbags!* as he ambles through, not even pretending to be quiet. We hear the WC door open, hear his stream hit the porcelain, hear his piddle go on forever, and we titter even more. When he returns, he curses *bollocking thing!* as he trips on the uneven paving in the dark of the back yard, and we echo it at him—*bollocking thing!*—as he comes in through the back door. He comes to our bed, gathers us all in his arms. He smells of beer and tea.

'My little ratbags! Who needs the privy, one last time?'

But none of us does.

He kisses us and tucks us in and returns to our mother in the kitchen, leaving the door unlatched to drift open, just so, just enough for us to hear their night-time speaking, the scratch of our father's chair on the kitchen floor, the teacups' rattle. Their voices are lowered. Every now and then a word, a sentence, rings clear, but there are too many gaps for us to learn their proper meaning.

Ah, there, our father's voice rises, 'And for how long?'

Our mother's voice is soft in reply, like lambswool, nestling, murmured, and we cannot hear its words.

'By Christ!' says our father, 'Bloody Rutherford has a cheek, assuming you'll honour and obey his whims and commands! I've said it before, I'll say it again, this time he's gone too far. We're not a bloody hospital, nor a charity. And a hospital is where she should be, no matter who she is.'

Our mother says, 'Charlie, Charlie, she's a woman in distress and need, I could hardly turn her away,' shushing him, both their voices softening, lowering.

Our father's voice rings out, 'Lady Bloody Radium—'

Our mother hushes him once more as she shuts the door, blocking out their noise and light and the rest of their talk.

Oona grabs the words first
lady bloody radium!
repeating them to fix them. Then Ada says it too
lady bloody radium
and Hanna hums her name
lady radium-hum-hum
as we snuggle together, the three of us, and fall asleep to the muffle and mutter of our parents' voices from the next room, and the wind worrying across the bay. The sound of the Lady's name sings in our dreams.

We wake together in the dead dark of night, the wind dropped to nothing, the world strangely still. We listen to the house, listen for our parents' voices, but all is quiet as quiet can be. Without a word, we scuttle out of bed—all warm and flannel-soft, smelling of sleep—and, linking hands lightly, we slip through the kitchen and down the hall.

At Ada's nudge the door to the front room opens, just enough for us to slip through. Cold mirrors off the bare window. Silvered moonlight slips the outside into the room. Lady Radium sleeps, the quilt drawn up to her chin. The table beside her is busy with papers and notebooks, pencils, a paring knife, a glass with a stain of liquid in it, a metal syringe in an enamel pan.

The Lady stirs, her fingers clutching the quilt tighter to her face. We three clutch each other, in motionless silence. We dare not breathe, lest we wake her. Side by side by side, still, we stand and stare. In the fabulous moonlight, the Lady's fingertips—her blunt nails, her milk-white, blue-light skin—reflect the night's cold glow.

SMOKE
Matti

A mothering flutter in her brain wakes her. *The children are up.* Matti Loverock slides out of bed, into slippers, across the floor and into the hallway. There, there, their nightdresses ghost the dark doorway of the sick woman's room. Matti goes to them, bundles them, hushes them, hustles them aside, and—looking through the doorway, noting even breath, the rise and fall of bedclothes—closes the door gently, quietly, on the sleeping woman. To their room, to their room, no words to encourage wakefulness, just murmured meaningless sounds, motherese, mother-ease, and her arms around her daughters, mother-henning them towards bed, and sleep, their sleep, her own sleep.

Once they're settled, as she turns for bed in the dark, her hand reaches into the pocket of her nightdress and turns over and over the body-warm tin. Her finger traces words she knows by heart, stamped into the tin's lid, *Grimault's Indian Hemp Cigarettes for Asthma! Cannabis eases tightness in the chest and gives relief from gasping breath.* A smoke would help her sleep. It's been quite a day, after all.

She sits at the kitchen table, removes a cigarette from the tin and strikes a match to light it, breathes in deep and holds it holds it holds it, the deep sweet must of it. This woman's arrival has not been what she expected. Not at all. The woman is weaker than Matti thought she'd be, sicker than she'd gleaned from Ern's letters. Barely strong enough to walk from the ferry to the cottage, though perhaps she should have anticipated that. And yet, they made it. Matti can manage this. She can mend this. Yes. She can mend this. Matti has French, which helps, though her French feels rusty, only barely serviceable. Ern's trust in her—his favour asked—is something she wants to meet, to match. To earn, ha ha. She raises her smoke vaguely northwards in salute, *to Ern*.

Ern is one of her oldest friends. Since their school days in Havelock, when she was the cleverest, Ern not-quite-so, of the children in Mr Reynolds' upper school class, Matti—the only child of elderly parents—had gravitated to the bookish, boisterous boy and his many siblings. When Ern went off to Nelson College, Matti and Ern started writing letters. They've been writing to each other ever since. Letters, so many letters, closely scrawled on fine-leaved onionskin, have crossed the world between them.

Matti shivers. She reaches for the dark wool shawl she's learned to keep in the kitchen, its familiar weight and texture a comfort on these restless, smoke-filled nights. She draws it around her shoulders, pushes her chair back from the table, stands. *I should check on her*, she thinks, though she knows the carefully measured medications she administered will keep the woman sleeping, pain-free, until morning. She presses the back of her legs, her rump, against the cooling stove. Her left arm holds the shawl across her abdomen, left hand supporting the elbow of her right arm, her smoking arm, and then, in practised sequence, she pushes her spectacles up her nose with the thumb of her right hand as her index and middle fingers, cigarette lodged between them, slip down to her mouth and so, and so, she draws smoke in deep, calming.

Charlie sleeps. She can hear the rumble of his snoring even through the walls. He'd sleep—snoring, without stirring—through the world ending, she's certain.

He was stirred tonight, though, stirred almost to anger. It feels unfair of him to raise objections now, when the woman is in the house, for goodness' sake. To be honest, though, she'd expected more resistance to the impending arrival of their visitor; anything related to Ern has an uncanny power to rile her usually gentle man. But Charlie has been distracted, she knows, by Wonderland and its complications. So only now it bubbles to the surface, this—this what? Is it jealousy? She supposes it is. There's nothing to be jealous of, not with Ernest. Not now. She thinks of a summer, before Ern met May, before Matti met Charlie, before before before. No, nothing to be jealous of. Nothing at all. Sweet Ern, her dear old friend, who would do anything for her, and for whom she would, likewise, do any asked thing.

She'd mollified Charlie tonight, responded to each of his raised concerns with patient explanation. *Not for long, until she is well, she needs my care.* He is most concerned about money, though he cannot bring himself to say this in so many words. She can manage it, though. Matti can manage it. Matti always manages.

She pushes herself away from the stove and prowls the small house, trailing sweet smoke, easing doors open with care, closing them with hand-dumbed clicks. The sick woman sleeps in the front room, lulled dormant and pain-free by morphia, chlorodyne and exhaustion. Matti's daughters sleep in their room at the back of the house, just off the kitchen, their three dark heads mussled and jumbled together, nesting in bed, inseparable. How quick they are to tumble from waking into sleep, she thinks as she kisses them, each of them, naming them one by one: she kisses her firstborn, Ada, their leader; she kisses sharp Hanna, Johanna, their reckoner; she kisses dear Oona, their father's favourite, who lies between her sisters, holding the space, a voice for all three.

Matti is the only one awake in the house. And she *is* awake now, thoroughly awake, completely awake, alert. Her nightworking schedule disrupts sleep, even on nights—like tonight—when she is not needed at the hospital. Restless, she opens the back door, breathes in chill air. The wind soughs up the hill behind their house, the hill blanking the sky black so all she can see is absence, night. A cat appears from out of the dark, mewling, plaintive, threads itself around and between Matti's ankles. *Hello, who in the world are you?* Matti greets the cat; or perhaps, Matti thinks, the cat greets her. Matti bends to pick it up, the black cat in the black night disappearing against the dark wool of her shawl. There, there, the cat purrs, trembling its throat at her chest. Matti gently pours the cat from her arms, dissolves it back into the night. There is reading she can do, there are patient notes to review; there are Charlie's red-stamped bills to go over—while he sleeps, dearest man, oblivious—then to put back where he left them, neat, before morning. Work, any work, is better, for Matti, than fitful sleep. She opens the stove, riddles ashes, wakes the fire. The kettle will take an age to boil. Another cigarette, then, while she waits, and works. She strikes a match and sparks her smoke, pulls the cord to light the overhead lamp.

Matti wakes before dawn on the daybed in the kitchen, her brain furred and mouth mucked from too much smoke and not enough sleep. She lies for a while, concentrates on pulling air into her lungs, holding it, pushing it out, deep, deeper, deepest. She lifts aside the thin blanket and slips her arms into one of several coats her sleep-dumbed, smoke-lulled self must have pulled down in the night from the hook on the back of the door. Feed the fire, fill the kettle, let the day begin. She bends close to the open stove, brings coals to life under the pot of overnight-soaked oats.

She straightens, wipes her hands on the cloth by the fire, pushes her hair from her face, turns and is startled by the slight woman who's appeared, silent as the grave, in the kitchen doorway. *Like creeping bloody Jesus, Charlie would say.*

Matti fusses towards the woman, who insists that she is feeling much better, *thank you, I apologise for my lack of social graces yesterday.* She offers to bring her tea in bed, but the woman says, no, she would prefer, if Matti does not mind, to sit with her, in the kitchen. Matti settles her at the table, *of course, of course*, offers tea, a cushion, both declined. Slipping into doctor mode, Matti finds herself reverting—without thinking—from the simple French that is all she can muster in conversation, to English, for the precision it affords her. She lifts her hand—*if you don't mind, Madame Professor, I should just check*—towards the woman's forehead. The woman nods then bows her head, just slightly, as if in prayer. Matti rests her hand on the woman's brow. She registers dry heat—too hot, but not alarmingly so, and at least not clammy—and nods. *And might I?* she says, and reaches for the woman's hand, feels the pulse pulse pulse of her as she counts, her eye on the sweep of the hand on the clock on the mantel, the beats under her finger moderate and regular, not the flighty flicker of last night's measure. *Good, good*, Matti nods again, and she releases the woman's hand, lets it rest on the table.

Thank you, the woman starts to say, again, as the door is flung open and the children bowl in, tumbling to a wide-eyed stop at the sight of the strange pale-skinned woman who sits in their father's chair at the head of the table.

'Good morning, my darlings,' Matti says to the girls. As she turns to pour tea into the good china cups, bothering—which she wouldn't on any other day—to place each cup on a saucer, she watches her daughters watching. They sit in a line on the long wooden bench, staring, mouths open in wonder, like the bank of painted plaster clowns, always unsettling, in Sideshow Alley at Wonderland.

'Porridge is nearly ready. Now, say good morning to Madame Professor, girls,' Matti says, and she thinks, *and close your bloody mouths*, as Charlie blusters in through the back door, beaming, wind-flushed, stamping like an old horse.

'Morning, all. Madame.' He tips an invisible hat at their visitor. 'Now, is there any porridge for your hungry husband, Matilda mine?'

All last night's concerns and objections seemingly forgotten, or at least set aside, Charlie takes Matti's hand, twirls her in his best dancefloor move, kisses her on the cheek, then dips to pull a too-short kitchen stool up to the table and lowers himself to triplet height. He casts his eyes towards the woman sitting in his accustomed chair, and Matti catches the bold stage wink he winks at their daughters, who wink leerily, inexpertly, back at him. Matti shakes her head, smiling, as she slides bowls of steaming porridge across the table. The children lift their spoons, but she clicks her tongue, and Charlie and the girls stop, their spoons held in the air. Matti hovers the porridge pot in the woman's direction.

'Are you sure? There's plenty.'

'Tea is all I need,' the woman's voice crackles, as if on a gramophone recording.

Matti nods at her daughters, and they start to eat. Across the table, the sick woman lifts the teacup neatly to her mouth, sips silently, then returns the cup to its saucer without the slightest tinkle. Everything is contained, precise, measured in her movements. Her right hand rests, palm upward, on the table's floral oilskin. Her thumb rubs a circle against the tip of her index finger. She looks into the distance, not into Matti's eyes but over her shoulder, away. There's a tight smile on her face, a light sweat on her forehead.

Charlie scrapes the last spoonful of porridge from his bowl, 'Eat up, girls! Quick-smart, it's time you were outside in the sunshine!'

Spoons ring on china; bowls pile in the washtub, bell against each other. The girls take turns at the washstand. As they dry their hands and inspect each other's faces for tracks of night-time spit or breakfast porridge, the sick woman rises, slowly, and stands with both hands resting on the back of the chair.

'I'm feeling, I think. Still. Tired. If I might, oh—'

The woman starts to fall. Matti and Charlie reach her together, and lift her as she murmurs, *so sorry so silly I shouldn't*, and they all murmur, and Matti and Charlie stand with her, supporting her, and walk her to the front room, ease her onto the bed. Matti hurries back into the kitchen, lifts her medical bag from the shelf. The three children are still by the washstand, frozen in tableau, Ada holding Oona's drying hands between her own, Hanna's hand lifting to tuck Ada's hair behind her ear.

'Our visitor needs quiet, off you go, outside. Good girls.'

Matti turns to the front room, passing Charlie as he returns to the kitchen, and she hears him shouting, 'Out, girls, out!' She imagines him settling into his chair, pulling his newspaper out of nowhere and unfolding it, shaking it, folding it again and placing it between his elbows, settled on the table in front of him. Dear, predictable Charlie.

His distant voice rumbles—'Go on! Off you go, ratbags!'—as Matti moves through the front room, across creaking floorboards, the swoosh of her skirt and of bedclothes, the brush and dulled tap of the soles of her shoes on thin carpet. She leans over the woman on the bed, mops her brow, lifts a glass of syrupy liquid to her lips, whispers in the woman's language, *there, there.*

All day Matti comes and goes, carrying glasses and pills, a syringe and rubber tubing, a dark glass bottle, damp cloth and soiled bed linens. She brings the woman broth in a two-handled cup. A sugar cube. A boiled egg sitting proud in striped china. Grated apple, sweetened with honey, in a cut-glass dish. She boils a syringe in a pan on the stove, leaves it to dry on a cloth on the kitchen table. She steps past her daughters sitting on the back step playing knucklebones, to empty the woman's chamber pot in the privy, steps past them again to return it, clean, to the woman's room. Rinse and repeat.

That day passes, and the next, upturned, uncertain. Matti sleeps, both nights—though barely sleeping, mostly listening for sounds of stirring, or unrest—on the daybed in the kitchen. Finally, on the third day, the woman seems more settled, stable. Matti breathes, relaxes, starts to anticipate her own return to work, the return of their house to a kind of normal. She writes to Ern, just a scrawled half-page. *She is safely arrived, installed chez-nous, and settled. Already her health improves.* She does not ask what on Earth he was thinking to send the woman, so sick, across the seas. And she does not write the thoughts she can't quite grasp: that she cannot see in this small, sad, sick woman the genius Ern promised; that she is, for now, simply Matti's patient. Not yet herself. A series of symptoms, sickness written on the body, that Matti can read, to which she can respond. *This is what I do*, she thinks. *I heal. I mend. This is who I am.*

Matti seals the letter, rubs sticky gum from the tips of her fingers. She thinks of the callouses and corns she's observed on the sick woman's fingers, the skin that flakes as if burned or otherwise damaged. Her work, Matti thinks, the chemicals, they're harsh. The skin is white in patches, as if deadened, or dying. The activity of radiation? Perhaps. Matti's own fingers—worn, though not like those of the other woman—press together, the pads of index finger and thumb rubbing in circles, mimicking the behavioural tic she has observed in the other woman. She thinks of Charlie's long-ago lost finger, that fragment of her husband that she has never known, like the missing piece of a puzzle. She thinks of Charlie's nine remaining fingertips, feels the trace of them on her skin.

Matti is dressed and ready to leave for her night shift at the hospital for the first time since the woman has been with them.

She pulls the blanket up under her daughters' chins and kisses them goodnight. As she turns to go, the girls cannot contain their curiosity. *Who will look after her*, Ada asks, and Hanna adds, *when you're at work. And will she die, poor thing*, Oona almost cries.

Matti gathers her three daughters in her arms, and inhales their soap-clean smell, and she can almost smell her own tiredness from the coming and going of that day, and the days and nights before. She tells them that their visitor is sleeping, now, and she will not die, though she is sick. She tells them that their visitor needs quiet, and kindness, and medicine. She reminds them that her dear friend Ern—*you know him, my famous scientist friend Ernest, far away*—has entrusted this visitor to their care, and that their visitor is far, far from home, across the world from her own dear daughters. Can she trust them?

She can. Of course she can!

Can they be her eyes and ears, and helping hands?

They can! Of course, they can!

And she kisses them again, pulls up the blanket to tuck them in tight, then closes the door on them. Matti resists the urge to disturb the sick woman, to check her again. She knows she is settled, and safe. She goes to her husband, reading the paper at the kitchen table, and kisses him goodnight, then she walks into the outside, and the night.

Matti wheels her bicycle down the side of the house, towards the road that hems the bay, delaying the moment of mounting, enjoying the crunch of shell grit under boots and tyres. She matches her strides to her breath, fully oxygenating her lungs. She is bone-tired already, with a night's work still ahead of her. She had caught a single still moment in the middle of the afternoon to sleep, while the girls were at the beach, while Charlie disappeared off to the office at Wonderland as he does so often, his unpaid bills stuffed in a canvas bag with his account book, its figures—as she well knows—inked red more than black. He had kissed her absently before he left, his hand on her shoulder as she lay on the daybed in the kitchen, his lips brushing her forehead, the smell of him calming, familiar.

The wind whips across the harbour now, and she shivers although she is dressed for the weather and does not feel the cold. The streetlights stringing the road's edge—their new electric hum strange, still—turn her into shadow, and light her shadow's way. As she mounts her bicycle, across the road the front window of their house illumines. There, Matti sees their visitor, her shape in silhouette, for just a moment, and then the light goes out. Matti's hand raises involuntarily, as if to salute, then she drifts her fingertips to her lips, blows a dry and silent goodnight kiss to her family, and—why not?—to the woman in the front room.

Their cottage is dark now against the hill, but she knows its shape in her brain and her bones. Her dog-tired, dead-tired bones. Bones that will benefit, loosen from cycling through the tunnel and across the flats and up and over the rise to Newtown. As she bicycles, she'll prepare for the night ahead, empty her mind as she fills her lungs with the night's cold air, ready herself for the long waits, the stretches of careful attention, and the moments of urgency that each baby's emergence might demand of her.

Matti checks that her bicycle lamp is steady. She pushes off with one boot, wobbles to upright, and pulls away from the kerb and out into the centre of the road, towards the Seatoun tunnel.

CABINET OF WONDERS
Triplets

The sound of a bicycle bell ding-ding-dinging down the road, closer and closer to home, wakes us. We leap from bed at our father's familiar morning call—*Rally rally rally, ratbags!*—and slither bedwarm into our knickers and vests, then run through the house and stop in a pile by the front door to step our feet into cold canvas slippers. We open the door, and there is our mother, propping her bicycle against the verandah post, home and weary after her long night shift at the baby hospital in Newtown. She bends to kiss each of us in turn, then straightens to kiss our father last and longest. We watch her pause at the Lady's door, listening, but not opening it. Her doctoring bag looks heavy in her hand, unbalancing her.

On the first few days of the Lady's visit, our routine was abandoned. But today it's business as usual, starting with the calisthenics that our mother and father insist on, for health and vitality. We step off the verandah, past our mother's big black bicycle, and sing our way into the day. We sing an exercise song

wind! rain!

sun! fog!

calisthenics, whatever the weather!

as we march across the road to the beach, through the low dunes, and onto the flat of the tide-wet sand. Our father is close behind us, his long-ago-wrestler's belly (now pie, pork and beer belly) barely contained by his neck-to-thigh black stretch woollen swimsuit. Look at him! The fluff of his chest, the wire of his legs, the ham of his arms! And look at the three of us! What a fine advertisement for modern life we make, our sleek strong limbs, brown to the edge of our vests, our lily-white torsos underneath.

We warm up, reaching for the sky, touching our toes. We spread our arms and legs, and in that shape of stars we jump.

'Breathe deep, ratbags!' our father puffs at us. 'Assimilate the ozone!'

As our father struggles and huffs and star-jumps, his bits and pieces flop about under the sweat-dampening wool of his costume. We giggle to see it, though our mother would tut us.

'Penis and testicles, girls,' she'd say, 'penis and testicles. The latter within the scrotum. Nothing to chuckle at. Half the world has them.'

We mirror our father, arms up and back, legs jump and bend and spring.

'Feel how strong your young bodies are! Like iron! Like steel! The strength and grace of Mon-sewer Eiffel's tower! Magnificent ratbag youth! Feel that steel spring in your step!'

We feel it even without our father's insistence. We feel our strength, the whole length and breadth and height of our bodies, and beyond them, where our power spreads like light, like air, as we stretch and fold and jump and bow and run and shout and fill and empty our lungs on this grand beach, on this bright morning, in this our eighth year on this wonderful Earth.

We have the beach to ourselves, most mornings. Sometimes Mrs R—on her daily ramble, collecting seaweed for the garden, or just taking the air—joins us, huffing and puffing as much as our father. But Mrs R never lasts long, giving us a wink, wiggling her jacket down and hitching her trousers up, taking a moment to roll and light a cigarette before she heads back up the beach towards the house in Karaka Bay that she shares with her very dear friend Jane Deere the Cameleer.

Sometimes Hermit Louis is there, fishing from the rocks at the far end of the beach, collecting bottles from the high tide's line, or selling his catch, a few pennies a fish. Our father is always kind to him and buys fish from him every week. We are kind to him, too, though he smells of fish and tobacco and the privy. Our mother speaks with him in language words we cannot understand, and we think this is the Lady's language, too. We always say *hallooo!* to Hermit Louis, and our father tells him *bone-jaw*, and Hermit Louis nods his head and scratches his big moustache in reply.

But today there's no Hermit Louis, no Mrs R, no Jane Deere. We have the beach to ourselves. When we're done stretching and bending and reaching and twisting, our father shouts *bathe!* and we strip off our kit—we three, and our father—and run quickly to the water. We dip quickly in, then dip out, winter-style (when the water warms, we linger longer). Then home we go, teeth chattering, cold to the bone, salt-water dripping from our noses and fingers and toes, singing our names in chorus to the sky

oona oona oona

ada ada ada

hanna hanna hanna

and our father sings *Charlie! Charlie! Charlie!* in his beautiful bass, like the ocean rolling under us, carrying our voices, lifting us, supporting us. We slam in through the front door and run down the hallway, our father holding his finger to his mouth—*Shhh! Shhh! Don't wake Her Nibs!*—as we go.

In the kitchen, we wriggle out of sopping salty vests and knickers, slip into the robes our mother has warmed by the fire, and slide onto the bench seat, plop plop plop. Our mother places bowls of porridge on the table, and we eat and eat and are silent but for our eating, like three tiny monks in our hooded blue robes.

Our father thunders out to the privy, then returns hoisting his braces over his shirt sleeves and shoulders, dressing himself as he walks. He sits in his accustomed chair at the head of the table, a Charlie-sized bowl of porridge in front of him. He lifts the lid of the honey crock, sticks his porridge-y spoon straight in, ignoring our mother—*Oh, Charlie!*—and then, with the spoon-shaped stump of his left-hand-half-a-ring-finger, he pushes the great gob of gleaming honey off the spoon and onto his porridge. Our mother says again *Oh, Charlie!* in the way she always does, and shakes her head as she sprinkles salt on her porridge and eats it neatly.

We are seated at our father's left hand, closest to his half-missing finger. We don't know for certain how he lost it. He has told us so many stories that we don't know what's the truth. Ada reaches out with her right pinky finger, touches the tip of it to our father's stump of a ring finger, and sings a line of song, then we all join in

where is ring man?

                                                where is ring man?

                    here I am

                                                there you are!

how are you

                                                this morning?

                    very well, I thank you

run away

                    run away

and we sit forward, in anticipation of today's story of loss. It's one we've heard before, involving a ship, some rope, a shark on a line, a moment of inattention, much blood, and the terrible fingery contents of a plate of fish and chips. But our father's distracted, and he tells it in a hurry, without flourish, so we almost wish we hadn't asked.

He wipes his chin with the back of his hand and pushes his chair back from the table with a screech.

'Right. I've things to do, your mother needs her sleep, and our visitor needs peace and quiet. Finish up and head outside, quick sticks, ratbags. I don't want to see you again till tea-time.'

He claps his hands, kisses the top of our mother's head, then turns and walks out the door.

Our mother wipes her hands on a tea towel as she watches him leave, then echoes him, 'Finish up, darlings, and off you go.'

We slurp the last of our porridge and carry our bowls to the washtub.

After breakfast, we have jobs to do, taking them in turns. One of us washes the porridge pot and all the bowls and spoons and cups, and one of us puts the dishes away and puts the porridge on to soak for the next day, and one of us sweeps the floor. There is a job the three of us share, though, always together. From the corner of the kitchen, we take the bucket of fruit and vegetable and porridge scraps and carry it out the back and around the side of our house to the field where lives our dear friend and companion, Ernest Rutherford the Horse. She nickers when she sees us, as she always does (and we snicker at nickers, which sounds like our drawers). We hang the bucket on the big nail on the fencepost, and Ernest Rutherford slips her big whiskery horseface into the bucket and starts making the magnificent grinding noise that horses make when they eat. (The Whittaker boy at school does a good job of approximating it, so we call him Nickers Whittaker, and whinny whenever we see him.)

We stroke Ernest Rutherford's neck while she eats. She looks uncannily like the Famous Gentleman and Scientist (and our mother's very dearest old friend) Ernest Rutherford, which is how she earned her name. Ernest Rutherford the Horse has Ernest Rutherford the Scientist's moustache, the very same, and the very same lock of gold hair falls over their kind old eyes, horse and man. The Gentleman Scientist lives far away across the world, though he met us one time when he came home to visit. We were only wee, so we barely remember, but we know from his letters to our mother that he is funny and kind. He always remembers us in those letters—and remembers our father, Charlie, too, so we don't know why that makes our father harumph and roll his eyes and shake his head at his mention. We hope to one day meet the Gentleman Scientist again, to thank him for sharing his name with our dear old horse.

Ernest Rutherford the Horse is these days only rarely ridden—and never driven in harness. Her job is to eat our kitchen scraps and turn them to manure. The Scrapper and Crapper, our father calls her. Our father shovels her leavings—*lovely horse doovahs!*—and piles them onto the garden, keeping us in lettuces and cucumbers and potatoes. *Scraps to Ernest, crap to spuds, amen*, our father says. Once upon a time, Ernest Rutherford worked at Wonderland, earning her keep by driving our father there each day in a little cart he kept for that purpose. But Ernest Rutherford hurt her leg, and our father bought a bicycle instead, and that was very nearly that for poor old Ernest Rutherford the Horse. Our father says he should've put a bullet in the old Scrapper and Crapper when he had the chance, but we know he doesn't mean it, and we know he never will. We're sometimes allowed to ride her (she can manage the slight weight of the three of us, together we're barely half a grownup), though just around the paddock, or slowly down the beach.

The smell of Ernest Rutherford is on our hands, the smell of stiff hair and dust, and great hot piles of leavings. There is somehow the heavy smell of saddle leather too, though Ernest Rutherford has not worn a saddle since we were tiny babies. Her smell stays there all day if we are not made to wash it off. We push our hands under each other's noses, and we savour her smell, keep it to ourselves. Then we bid Ernest good day and run to our bedroom to retrieve Queen Cuttle from under the bed, where she lives in a wooden beer box with our other doll friends.

Queen Cuttle is our latest doll, the queen of Worser Bay. We made her body from cuttlebone, her face from shell. The smell of her is sweet and salt, somewhere in between socks and mothballs and the sea. Her arms are sticks stuck into the cuttle, her legs two stems of seaweed skeleton, brittle and white as bone. Her hair is fine red seaweed lace. Like us, the queen's front has no bosom. We love her proud smooth chest, its gentle curve, its whiteness and chalk. We love her shellac back. Her crown is a simple loop of shell, worn smooth by the sea, white lined with grey. On her sweetly smelly seaweed feet are scraps of brocade shot with silver thread, wound and bound to make slippers. All the queen lacks is a gown, rich and bright, but we have a plan for that.

We love to make dolls, as our mother does, too. She learned the making from her own mother, long ago when our mother was little, like us (imagine!).

Our mother made our first dolls, a baby-shaped wool-stuffed linen bundle for each of us. She dressed them in our colours, violet, white, green (though years of constant spit and dragging faded all three to uniform uncoloured grey). We loved those dolls to pieces before we could speak, so they never did get names. We knew them by their smell. We knew them by their always being with us. We have them still, the scraps of them, the pale ghosts of them.

We've had paper dolls and rag dolls, china dolls and flax, and dolls made of nothing but the shadows of our fingers on a lamplit wall. We love them all. We've had good dolls and bad dolls, kind dolls and mean dolls, dirty dolls and clean dolls and dolls that can't be seen.

Now our mother has little time, day or night, for doll-making, living her busy topsy-turvy life, sleeping in the day, going off to work at night, when we are all asleep. But she still makes doll repairs, replacing an eye that will not blink, an arm that has been lost, hair that's fallen out in handfuls.

Our mother keeps her doll parts in a Cabinet of Wonders. Jars of glass eyes, ranged in colour and size, a tangle of arms (hands for waving), a muddle of legs (feet for tickling). The eggshell curves of china heads wrapped in tissue paper, and hanks of human hair, brown and black and golden and white, each colour in its own glassine paper bag. There are threads and needles and pins and scissors, and fabrics in folds and little rolls and scraps. There are awls (we call them owls) and picks and tiny hammers, a metal scoop on a wooden handle (for easing glass eyeballs in and out of sockets, though we once saw our mother use it on a rockmelon).

Oh, we love our mother's Cabinet of Wonders and all it holds!

Our mother and father told us we must play outside, stay away, give the Lady peace and quiet. But we can be quiet as three little mice

we need bits

for the queen

from the cabinet

snippets of silk

a dress

for queen cuttle

a robe

a gown

but the cabinet is in the room

lady radium's room

maybe she's asleep?

maybe we can creep?

let's see

let's try

so with Queen Cuttle tucked down Oona's vest, we all creep down the hall (step over that creaking floorboard, and this one) to the Lady's room. The door is open just a crack. Lady Radium sits in the almost-dark, on a chair pulled up to the desk of the Cabinet of Wonders. A lamp shines on her hands, her notebook, her fingers tight on the scratching pen. Her head is bent close to the page as she writes. Even from here, we can see ink on her fingers, deep blue, as if she's forgotten to breathe.

The Lady looks up, sees us at the door. She frowns, for a moment, then the frown turns almost to a smile. But we run, anyway, down the hall and through the kitchen and out through the back door and around the side of the house and past Ernest Rutherford

hallooo ernest!

can't stop!

dear old ernest!

and across the road to the beach, and we throw ourselves down into a hollow in the sand, breathing excitement and wonder and fright

that lady

could we make her?

a doll like her

with inky fingers

we could make her

make her better

make the lady

to make her well

We fall asleep to the soothing wash of voices, our mother and father, Matti and Charlie, words we cannot quite hear. On nights like tonight, when our mother does not have to pack her bag and oil her bicycle and fasten her ankle clips and ride into Newtown to work at the baby hospital, she sits by the stove, a sock to darn, a button to replace, a hem to lower and restitch. Perhaps, a broken doll in hand, she attaches an eye, or stitches an arm to a body, or threads hair into fine nets to patch a balding scalp. There's always mending needed.

Tonight, and every night we can remember, lately, while our mother makes things better, our father sits at the kitchen table and mutters over the Wonderland accounts (we love the red ink best, though we know it makes our father sigh).

When sleep is slow to come to us, we hear them. Sometimes we watch them, through the slit of the just-open door. Our father closes the red-ink-filled book, rubs his eyes, yawns with arms stretched high above his head. Then he goes to our mother, kneels by her and takes her hands, stills them from their hem-raising or arm-stitching or eye-painting or hair-plugging or body-stuffing. He holds her hands, and they look into each other's eyes, and—ah, we always seem to fall asleep, no matter how restless the night, so we can only imagine the words that Charlie says to Matti, and Matti says to Charlie, as they tuck each other into bed at night, kiss kiss kiss.

We imagine the Lady, too, imagine her tinctured and tucked in, all alone in the front room, imagine sleep making her well.

And the three of us tuck our own selves in, Ada curved around Oona's back, Oona's arm drawing Hanna close, Hanna stretching her arm across to link us all together, and we drift to sleep, to the gentle rock and tug and rhythm of the wind on the timber and tin of our house. We dream of doll-making and hand-taking, of ink on fingers, of healing sleep, and light underlining a closed door.

CURE
Matti

Once the children are in bed and her patient is medicated and settled for the night, Matti joins Charlie in the kitchen, picks up her mending basket. Each time he sighs over the accounts, or mutters numbers aloud, Matti tries not to look up, she tries not to flinch. *Ach, Charlie, Charlie, love.* She stitches in time, she mends, instead, making good whatever is at hand, while she waits for him to slap the book closed, and to come to her, as he always comes to her, each night they share at home. She waits for him to lift his hand to her face, to cup her cheek in the pool of light-within-dark in which her hands work, her eyes watch. And when he comes to her, as he always comes to her, she leans outside the pool of light, into the surrounding darkness, into Charlie, and they kiss, sweet, sweet. Tonight he does not lumber alone to their room, to sleep, and she does not settle back to her making and stitching. Tonight she stands, keeps hold of Charlie's hands, and they go to their room together. And Charlie does not lumber, no, not tonight. Charlie does not lumber, but neither do they hurry, the two of them. They take all the time in the world. Matti tucks herself into his side, under his big wing, and his big arm folds around her, holds her close. She reaches around his waist, as far as her thin, strong bones can reach. They sing loud with love as their bodies strike and match, at the heart of the house that sleeps around them.

~ ~ ~

In the kitchen, in the weekday quiet of afternoon, Matti is marking time. Looking up from the notebook in which she records medication notes for her patient, she lowers her glasses and watches the clock on the mantel. When the minute hand shifts Matti stands, moves to the stove, lifts the parts of the syringe—plunger and barrel and needle—from the pan of boiling water and lays them on a clean cloth on the kitchen table to dry. She wipes her hands down the side of her dress, wipes the back of her hand across her forehead and sits again, closes her notebook, caps her pen. The children will be home soon. Tea needs making.

There is always something that needs making, or doing, or cleaning, or mending. Matti loves her work at the hospital, and the escape into the world that it brings. And yet, and yet. While she is at home, her work at the hospital is managed, covered by Agnes Bennett, or a locum brought in. When she is away at work, though, everything waits for her at home, undone unless she does it. Everything revolves around her, everyone relies upon her—her daughters, her husband. Even the horse expects her attention.

And, now, there is the woman.

You may call me Marie, the woman has said to her, but Matti finds herself avoiding anything other than formal address. The woman speaks her own first name as if rolling it around her mouth, like a marble, or a pebble, as if it doesn't fit, or doesn't belong, or surprises her by its presence. Perhaps her reluctance to call the woman by name is a nod to Ern's letters; he always calls her Madame C. Perhaps, perhaps, perhaps it's to preserve her anonymity, as Ern has emphasised is imperative. *She's not coming across the globe to give a lecture tour, you understand. She'll be incognito. She'll travel under a nom de guerre while she's hors de combat, if that's not mangling my francophonic references too baldly.* Just so, the woman arrived under the name of Skłodowska—*my maiden name; it exists on my travel documents*—and this is the name under which Matti records the woman's sickness and health, the timing and doses of medications administered, and the woman's response to treatment. Matti carefully reproduces the little slanted cross, unfamiliar, on the third letter of the woman's name. She hears the crossed *l* as a swallowed *w* when the woman speaks it, the written *w* spoken as a soft *v*, so *Skwodovska* is what Matti hears. *Marya Skwodovska*.

Perhaps Matti's avoidance of addressing—or even thinking of—the woman by name is a way of forgetting who she is, this great woman of science, this *discoverer of elements* for goodness' sake, this very hero of hers. Not-naming is a way of pretending she's what Charlie calls *a punter*, one of her everyday patients, no more or less important or interesting or special than Mrs Lucy popping out a baby every year, or Mrs Wilkinson's wasting disease, or Miss Hawkes and her unfortunate situation, now resolved.

The woman—*Marya Skwodovska*—always says to her, *You are so kind, too kind*. But it's not kindness, Matti thinks. It's work. Her healing, curing work. And—she can't deny it—she's motivated to a degree by the frisson of curiosity.

Ern has been discreet, in his letters, about the scandal surrounding their visitor in the weeks and months before her departure from Europe, and that surrounds her still. He's indicated nothing but support and sympathy for the woman, defending her against insult and calumny, while acknowledging the apparent truth of the widely reported liaison. *I cannot help,* he wrote, *feeling a sort of fellowship with her as a stranger in a strange land, she from Poland, I from New Zealand, neither of us quite belonging, having always to watch our pees and queues.* Ern knows the married man—the colleague—with whom their visitor has shared the scandal. *An old chum, from Cambridge days,* he had written, *our rooms were next to one another. He was the one true foreigner there, other than me. A good chap, through and through. It was via his invitation that, visiting Paris with Mrs R, I first met your visitor and her husband, before the latter's tragic and untimely demise. He did me a great kindness—her late husband—a stronger radium source, for my research. I have always liked and admired her, though others find her prickly. She always works much too hard, and this latest business, on top of ill health, has proven too much even for her.* That dear Ern has steered discreetly clear of details of the scandal does not surprise her. His curiosity has, she thinks, never been truly boundless; it's been limited, applied to affairs of physics, of chemistry, rather than those of biology, or of the heart.

Matti reaches for the tin in her pocket, and the box of matches. She lights a cigarette, drawing in sweet, sweet, haloing herself with blue-grey smoke, relaxing her shoulders, her neck, her every part and limb. Boundless curiosity has landed Matti in good times and bad, though, on the whole, she'd have to say it's been to her benefit. Their daughters have inherited her curious nature, it's clear even at this early age, and she has encouraged them in it, schooled them, fed their enquiring minds. She has introduced biological concepts to them: how the mammalian body works, how plants respire. The basics of reproduction, of course—how could she not, in her line of work? She has taught them the value and beauty of names, whether of plant or marine species, or body parts. Naming is knowing, she tells them. Names connect us, describe relationships. She aims, most of all, not to quash their curiosity, but to foster it, reward it; to teach them to delight in it, and to follow it wherever it may lead. Good or bad.

Good, bad; who's to say? Curious, curiouser. She does not judge or begrudge the woman—their visitor—her recent affair. She knows the woman's history—how could she not, she reads the newspapers—the celebrated scientific coupling, husband and wife both prized, adored, elevated; the tragic accident that left the woman widowed, her daughters fatherless. Matti tries to imagine how that would feel. She tries to imagine the loss—the great emptiness—left by the husband's death. She imagines the desire to fill that forsaken space, if only for a moment, as a kind of forgetting, or for comfort. Or perhaps plain and simple lust. Biology, or the heart.

The schoolday is done. The girls will soon be home. She draws hard on her cigarette, the paper crackling. The long, straight ash column of burnt cannabis and tobacco holds its form, until she presses it into the saucer, killing it. She stands, brushes ash from the front of her dress. She will check on the woman—her patient—before she starts making their tea. Corned beef, carrots, potatoes. Mustard sauce, thinned with the beef's salty broth. Something green, whatever Charlie can raise from the garden. Then tomorrow it starts all over again.

There, there, her daughters are home, and they come to her now, breathless with excitement, with a plan that seems fresh-hatched, perhaps formulated on their walk down the hill. It is mostly Ada's plan, she is sure, though Oona speaks it into existence.

'Mother,' Oona says to her, 'might Wonderland cure the Lady?'

'Even though it's closed now for winter,' says Hanna.

'And Father only sighs,' says Ada, 'when we ask him if there'll be a Winter Gala this year.'

Hanna shows an old postcard, palmed from her pocket, WONDERLAND CURES ALL ILLS.

'We thought it might cure all the Lady's ills,' Ada says.

'But we're not sure that's how it works.' Hanna's brow creases as she speaks.

'So, Mother, Mother,' Oona says, 'we want to take the Lady to Wonderland.'

Matti tells her daughters that their visitor is too sick, still. 'Too tired. You mustn't bother her,' she tells them. 'You know that. My good girls, I know you know.'

Oona steps forward again, speaking for the three of them,

asks what their visitor does all day, and all night, in the front room, and why is she so sickly.

'And might we catch it?' Hanna asks, as if calculating distance and modes of transmission.

Matti gathers them to her—Oona on her knee, Hanna in her left arm, Ada her right—and kisses their beautiful foreheads, kiss kiss kiss. She tells her daughters about their visitor, that she has a sickness in her belly—her abdomen—and it is internal—on the inside. 'Her kidneys,' she presses her own belly to show them where, 'have a disease, though it is not contagious. You cannot catch it, and nor can I.' Their visitor needs medicine, and rest, and sleep, and quiet, most of all; their famous visitor needs to not be famous while she's here.

And as for Wonderland, and the Winter Gala—well, we shall see, Matti tells them, we shall see. 'If anyone can open Wonderland again, and make the Winter Gala happen, your father's the man. Just give him time, eh? Don't pester him. Give him time.'

The children nod, sage and serious, as if they can understand time.

'Though perhaps our visitor may be in such fine health by then, by Winter Gala time, that she will have returned to her own home, to her own two daughters! Wouldn't that be wonderful for her?'

She huddles the children in her arms, jollies them, lifts her voice so it's light as a feather, and they mirror her smile back at her, lean their heads onto her shoulder, relax into each other.

Who knows, Matti thinks but does not say, whether her patient will survive until then, or ever be fit to sail, and why ever did the woman come here, why ever did she come, why ever did Ernest send her to them, whatever was he thinking, and whenever will she leave, oh when will she leave?

NARWHAL AMY
Triplets

We know the terrible poem that others say to get to sleep, about the dreadful sleeping creature named Narwhal Amy, and keeping souls, and dying before you wake, and—worst of all—being taken in that dark, dead sleep before morning. *Narwhal Amy, down to sleep, we pray the Lord our souls to keep.* It scares the willies out of us.

So at night we sing a different sleeping song, that we have made. Our song starts soft and counts stars. It sounds light and turns dark. Our song measures breaths and keeps them rising and falling until morning.

Our mother has taught us about breathing and blood. She's drawn hearts and veins and lungs for us, on sheets of white paper, for colouring in. Once, when we found three dead kittens under the house, we split their tight little bellies with a knife from the kitchen and scissors from our mother's sewing basket, curious to see what we could see. Their insides looked different from our mother's drawings, though all their bits were there.

When we were done, we made a tiny raft of driftwood, tied together with seaweed stems, and sent the dead kittens out to sea. We sang a sailing song, a kitten song, a breathing song, a goodbye song, but not a dead song, for we do not mourn the dead. Death is the end-point of life, our mother says, and you can't have life without it. We know this to be true. Though when we told it to Minna Hofmann, after her mother died while popping out the tenth and very final baby Hofmann, she cried and told Miss Grimshaw and our mother had to come to school (again) and we had to apologise to Minna Hofmann (again). We said our sorries, and we each had to kiss Minna Hofmann on the cheek. We did as we were told, Ada first, then Oona, then Hanna, though we crossed our hidden fingers in our pockets as we did so (and Oona gave Minna's pigtail a pull, for good measure).

Soon, soon, we will knock on the Lady's door. We'll show her the postcard, tell her about Wonderland and its miraculous curing. It won't matter, we'll tell her, if she's tired, and she's sick. We'll help her. We are our mother's eyes and ears and helping hands, after all.

For now, though, we tiptoe past her closed door and leave her be.

BEGIN AGAIN

The Lady

Footsteps   fleeting   pass my door, not the
mother-doctor-wife, but her little daughters   three
girls, one voice.
   Is it day? It cannot be day.
   Is it night? Star light, star bright.

The mother-doctor-wife comes with her drink me prick me
sleep me tonic   and I succumb, and utter thanks.
   You are so kind, I tell her, so kind   so kind.
   There is ease in the space and light that her tonic brings.
In that ease I rest, I breathe. I sleep, I wake. I take a little
food and drink. I walk across the room, though slowly.
   Perhaps tomorrow I will walk, in the   sunlight,
this strange   suddenly southerly   autumn light.
Perhaps, tomorrow, I will brace   against the wind.
   And perhaps the light and the wind will start to cure me.

I thought   today   to stay awake, but I did not.
Instead, I slept, in fits   of pain   and dreamt of
my girls, of my lost husband, of home, of work I have not
strength to do.

She comes to me again, before the house retires,
administering care and tonic and   prick me
ease me   medicine, and the pain slips away once more.

~ ~ ~

I have slept the day away again. But here in the night, now, I pull my notebook to my knee. Stiff, inky fingers press my pen to the page. I cannot think well enough to work, though perhaps my thoughts can form a letter.

My sweet Little One, I begin.
My darling Big Girl, I begin again.
My dearest sister.

But how can I disguise the tremble in my hands? How can I not write this pain? How can they not see it in the ink, this blue?

And yet I try. I begin again.

Beloved sister,

I know you will forgive my spidered marks upon the page. My thoughts are nearly impossible to collect, to keep together. Forgive me if these words unstick themselves. Words, thoughts, all fly apart.

As I, too, flew apart, flew away, though in my haste it seems I got my seasons all in a muddle—or perhaps I thought of this place as the balmy south seas, not the subantarctic outpost it has proven to be.

It is night here, now, and day where you are, so very far from here. Yes, here, night, now. The rest of the household sleeps. The pain, my pain, is managed well, though it is worse at night. Or perhaps it is worse when I do not sleep. Or am tired. I cannot tell the difference.

Ah, there it is   that   tiredness.
I am unstuck.
Forgive me, sister dear.
Forgive me.

I could write my pain in letters to my beloved, my lost husband. Surely the dead can understand the pain of the living?

But I cannot. I cannot. To write to him would make him feel further from me, not closer; it would make him feel *more dead*, if that were possible. (It is not.)

He is with me in my notebook, where I write my thoughts as if I am speaking to him, with him. It is as if he is in the room with me.

There is the sound of a door closing itself in the wind, creaking, slamming. The wind in this place is inescapable, even inside the house.

Imagine walking outside, into this wild wild wind. How it would tease my hair from its neat bun; how it would press the cloth of my dress against my body, press cloth against leg, against shin, against thigh. How it would make me feel immodest, and perhaps a certain shame.

And I am so tired of being made to feel shame.

So tired. So very tired.

I wake from unexpected, welcome, delicious sleep. There is the bass boom, the father's call to action—*allez, allez, allez!*—then footsteps thundering, the bang of the front door, scrunching shell, a shout. Voices become distant, faint.

It is only just light. The day's arrival once again surprises me, time upended, strange.

Today would appear to be a good day, by which I mean this moment is a good moment. The pain is dull, yet. I draw my nightdress close at my neck, slide my legs from under the covers, step into thin slippers. I stand, carefully, slowly. My head is light. I can feel my blood, hear it. I take up the stick that rests, ready, by the bed. The mother-doctor-wife brought it to me, in kindness.

I wait a moment, make sure of my balance. I walk slowly down the hallway, concentrating on each three-legged step. She stirs a pot on the stove with a wooden spoon, so there is no clang, just the dull tap of wood on iron. A kettle mutters on its way to the boil. Her coat hangs on the shoulders of a chair. It sits with a back as straight as hers. The medical bag that she brings to tend me, each night, each day, is on the side table, gloves flat beside it, empty. In her bag is the medication she will give me   soon   soon   away with the pain.

I rest the stick against the table and grip the back of the chair so I do not waver or fall as I answer her first question, the same first question she asks each day: yes, the pain is tolerable, I tell her, lying out of habit, the lying, the dissembling somehow easier in her tongue, this other tongue, in this other place. I take the tea she offers, decline the breakfast, and she fixes me with a doctor's stare over her glasses, down her nose, mouth in a moue, eyebrows drawn together. She tells me with respect, Madame, that I must eat. And I know this. I do. But the smell of the gruel in the pan on the stove makes my stomach turn. In the moment, I think of good Parisian bread, warm still, crackling crust, slathered with butter, a pot of good sour plum preserves; I think of coffee, dark and bitter and sweet all at once; I think of a pear on a plate, beside my bone-handled fruit knife with the carved bee upon its spring.

I think of my dear husband at the table across from me, buttering bread, smiling.

I think of my girls, quiet at their breakfast, as they are quiet in all things.

I think of the four of us in our old house in Boulevard Kellermann: the four of us—my husband, my Big Girl, my Little One, myself—four-squared, like the corners of a room, or its walls, each in place, each touching each, each supporting and supported.

I think: it is six years since the death of my beloved husband. Six years. Most of the lifetime of my Little One, so young, a year old when her father died. My dear Little One; she is the same age as this woman's daughters.

~ ~ ~

The woman's lips move, but she has slipped once more back to her mother tongue, and I find I cannot muster the effort to understand what she says. I focus on her mouth, the shapes it makes, the sounds. I translate them from language to language to language and—ah!—there is sense: the children will return soon, she hopes they do not bother me; she will bring a tray to my room, if I promise to eat; she'll prepare my medications, and bring them to me.

Yes, I tell her, as I feel the pain approaching.

Yes, yes, yes.

She is kind, and efficient. She nods at me, calls me *Madame Professor*, addresses me in the formal sense, though I bid her call me by my given name. I nod, I turn, take up the walking stick, and return to the room. I am ready, lying on the bed, when she comes to me to lift my pain.

Here is the woman-wife-mother-doctor   her
head at the door   offering solace   offering
solution   bringing relief in a bottle
drink this   this fluid   this spoon   take
this   this syringe   this medicine
this lightness   lifting me above   the pain.

I am already drifting   lifting   close to sleep when I hear the front door fling open and the children and their father whisper loudly past. Their mother hushes them, bids them quiet. Like little mice, she says. I hear her clearly now, and the brightness of these three   these girls   sharpens my senses   as oxygen, when tripled, becomes sharp, cleansing. The smell of the sea, like air after lightning, pricks my nostrils. Every tiny hair stands on end, at attention. Sea blue   sky blue   pale blue, like ozone gas. Imagine it condensed, the blue

darker   and darker, until liquid, until solid. Three
phases, all different, all the same. Imagine: as alike as ice
and water and steam. Not alike, yet completely alike.
These three are ice and water and steam. Sublime.

Carry me up in this   sublime
and the sigh of the sound of it all
and the steam
and the feel of it now

the feel of it.

PAIN

Matti

Ah ah ah, shush shush, quiet now, Matti tells the girls as they clatter through the front door, bringing salt-bright beach air and thoroughly exercised attitude with them. Can you be like little mice, uh, as quiet as that? Charlie is as bad as the girls, she thinks, noisier, encouraging them. Go, there is breakfast, she tells them all, as she closes the door on their visitor. The girls run ahead. Charlie brushes a whiskery kiss against the soft skin of her neck, and she frizzles at his touch, her nerve endings primed, oversensitive with tiredness.

'How is she?' Charlie inclines his head at the door. 'Lady Muck?'

'Ach, Charlie, don't,' Matti says. 'She's no worse, at least. Let us say she is stable.'

He lowers his voice, widens his eyes. 'And how much longer will it be, do you think? That she's here?'

'Until she is ready. Until she is well.'

He shakes his head and rolls his eyes, and Matti sighs—tired, so tired—as she kisses his worried face, and nods him away—'Go on, love!'—to follow the girls to the kitchen. She opens the door to the woman's room again, just a sliver, and peers into the curtained dark, notes settled, sleeping breath—good, good—and quietly clicks the door closed.

The woman reports that her pain is managed, though Matti sees her wince, and knows this is not true. Matti can read pain as another might read words on a page. Pain, the course of her illness, is written on the woman's body, and in her sometimes-staccato voice, the catching of her breath, the way she moves in and out of lucidity, though the woman may not realise it. Matti medicates her accordingly. If only, she thinks, the woman would succumb to the pain, rather than resist it. So much energy is expended in resisting, withstanding it. As if withstanding is heroic, worthy of a prize.

The woman barely eats, which does not help. Matti wants to bring her dainties, morsels she might crave or miss, but she is a martyr, will not tell Matti what she desires. It is as if she lives on air, Matti thinks. And so, the woman gets thinner and thinner. This morning Matti brought her honey, scented with thyme, on a silver teaspoon. There was something animal about the way she ate it, the tip of her tongue flicking from her mouth to snuffle the intense savoury-sweetness of it.

There, there, from the kitchen voices rise, a pan lid clatters, a spoon rings against cast-iron stovetop trivets. Matti pushes off from the enclosing door of the sick room, and moves towards the sound of her family, their rude health.

She drinks tea while she watches her girls hungrily shovelling food. As they eat, the three girls watch their father. Oona is tapping Charlie on the knuckle with her spoon. Charlie responds by opening the tapped fist to reveal what was concealed, an unburnt match, red tip bright against the pale palm of his hand, at which Oona shouts *Bloodnut!* Hanna reaches across the table and taps his other fist. Charlie uncurls it, shows a match burnt just at the tip, and Ada and Hanna and Oona and Charlie all shout *Blackhead!* in unison. Some mad game the four of them have invented, Matti thinks, wondering what the rules are, knowing there's no point asking.

'Father, when will we go to Wonderland?'
   'And can we take the Lady?'
   'Wonderland cures all ills, you always say.'

'And her ill is a big ill to cure, we see.'
'So can we, can we—'
'—and when oh when can we—'
'—please can we go to Wonderland soon?'

Matti has a direct line of sight to Charlie over their daughters' heads, and just for a moment his face falls, shadowing with grief, or shame, or sadness, expressions she's not used to seeing on the face of her optimistic husband. He recovers, paints a Charlie grin on his dial, and takes the box of matches from the table, rattles it, opens it. He lights one match.

'Wonderland, wonderful Wonderland.'

They all watch the match flare and burn. He shakes the flame out before it moves past the tip, spits on his finger and thumb, then presses them to the dark tip of the match and drops it onto the table next to the bloodnut, the blackhead. Another match, the hissing scratch of the lighting strike, shake, spit, hiss, drop.

'The Mecca of Merry Souls, phosphorescent, fabulous, can you imagine it—'

Matti feels herself mesmerised by the flame, by Charlie's versing voice, his misdirection, his sleight of hand. She can see the girls are the same, all thought of going to Wonderland forgotten, even though Charlie speaks only (but spell-like, incantatory) of Wonderland.

Charlie lights another match, '—the Pride of Miramar, fantastical fireworks from Professor Bickerton, anything can happen!' then drops the spent match, and another, and another, until there are five blackheads and a single bloodnut on the kitchen table, and the burnt phosphor smell hangs in the air above them.

And in that moment, magicked, they all and each hold their breath.

Charlie arranges the matches in a regiment, each next to the other, all six of them standing to attention, and he names them, pointing with his finger, 'Now, this is your mother, Matti. And this is Ada, and this Oona, and here's Hanna. And here am I, at your service.' He lifts the Charlie match, bows it at each of them in turn, replaces it on the table. Having ticked off all the blackheads, he points to the redhead, the bloodnut that is left. 'And here's our visitor, Lady bloody Radium.' The girls all titter. 'Or I should I say Madame Professor Lady bloody Radium. Here we all are! And so, I leave you with a puzzle, daughters mine—'

The girls leap from their chairs, mesmeric spell broken, clamouring at their father, tugging his sleeves.

'Ah, ah, calm yourselves, wee beasties.' He waits for quiet. 'The challenge is this. How can the six of us—blackheads and bloodnut all together—build a house? And, before you ask, without anyone breaking, mind.' He pushes his chair back from the table, rises to his feet, pats each girl on the top of her head. 'I leave you to it. Farewell and good day, ratbags. You too,' he kisses Matti as he passes, rests his hand for a moment on her cheek, 'Matilda mine.'

Matti leaves her daughters puzzling, heads bent over the matches, fingers prodding, trying solutions, their hands darting over and under each other on the table so it's hard to know where one girl ends and the next begins. She opens the door to the bedroom she shares with Charlie. He sits on the far side of the bed, his elbows on his knees, his bowed back to her, his shoulders shaking almost imperceptibly. In the long half-minute she waits at the door, she cannot hear a sound from him. She closes the door, quietly, carefully, and leaves him be.

DAUGHTER ELEMENTS
The Lady

I am not myself here on this other side of the Earth. I know its physics, I understand it. But I feel myself upended. Tipped up, tipped over, ungrounded, overturned. It is not just the drugs. It is not just the pain. It is not just the constant effort of language. Everything is—this is a word I have learned from these girls—topsy-turvy. That summer is winter. That north is the sunny aspect of the house. That everything and everyone I know and love is so far away, so very very far away, the whole of the world away from me.

What on Earth was I thinking, to come here?

What I was thinking, in fact and indeed, was escape.

I could not escape the clamour at home. The everyday of it, the newspapers, the constant sound of it like the twitter of little birds that are everywhere though you cannot see them. I have always found fame impossible—painful—to weather, wishing only to be left at peace, to my studies, my research, my science.

Who am I?

Who in the world am I?

Eggs were thrown, and insults, and accusations. Duels were fought, lawsuits brought. I escaped it all, escaped scandal, escaped ignominy, not with glory, not with my head held high, but here   in pain   in silence   incognito. Surviving, but denying.

~ ~ ~

If I had the energy, I would write to the friends who helped achieve the plan that sent me here, who understand the gravity of the situation, and my need for escape.

My dear friend, Hertha, I would write.

I am sorry to burden you with this secret. With this fuss. You have been so kind: to offer me sanctuary in England, and—kindest of all—to indulge my whim to escape here, instead. I could not have achieved that escape without your enthusiastic embrace of the plans of our mutual friend, Ernest, and your willingness to ... let us not say *deceive* or even *dissemble*; let us say, instead, *make believe*.

There, I find it is easy to write a letter like this, holding the pen in my mind, while the words form in the air like smoke, or like a conversation in a dark room lit by fire, or by radium in a phial.

Do you take the newspapers from Paris, I would ask Hertha in smoke words.

Are they still convinced I'm with you? Do they even care? I imagine what they say: *This unnatural woman, past her prime. This foreigner. This once-great widow of one of France's greatest sons. How could she break another woman's marriage? A Frenchwoman's marriage! Did she bewitch the man? What alien wiles did she employ? She's never been one of us, we always thought so. Foreign! Unforgivable!*

I—widowed, still and forever grieving—never expected to find myself in this position. I cannot believe or understand that in my middle years, as I so plainly am, I could be in the midst of this affair of the heart. Though to be blunt, my dear Hertha, it was not so much the heart but a different part of the body that was involved. He is a good man, a good keen man, with a keen mind—though not as keen as my dear dead husband's mind, no, never that keen, and never that dear—and a good intellect. He and I, we fitted together—you know, don't you,

Hertha? You know what it is to want? To act on what you want? We have spoken, you and I, in a way that is strangely straightforward. As soon as I met you—was it in London, in '03?—I felt a connection extending beyond our shared heritage, our lives of science. We talk, you and I, in a way that feels new, modern. But I have a suspicion, dear Hertha, that women may have talked this way, together, forever.

Smoke words, deepest night words, vaporise in the dark.

I could write—had I energy to write—to my friend of these three little girls. She would appreciate their curiosity, their freedom.

There are three daughters in this family, I would tell Hertha. Identical triplets, peas in a pod; uncanny to see their likeness. They are intelligent and, though they are yet very young, have clearly been taught well by their mother. She is a good woman—doctor, teacher, wife and all—intelligent, good-natured, kind. She is blunt and plain and practical. She speaks French after a fashion, not as well as you, dear friend, but—thankfully! easily!—better than her fellow countryman, our good friend Mr Rutherford. She has the grace to leave me be when she is not doctoring me. The daughters go away each day to school, though I expect they would learn more at home from their mother. These girls—these bright girls—take regular gymnastic exercise, their father sees to that. I watch them, each morning, on the beach; I watch them through the window. I feel myself breathe deep with them, that salt air, that brisk sweetness fills my lungs. How I miss the wild, the sweet outside. How good it will be to walk, to run, to bicycle once more. To lose myself in a wood, or on some wild shore.

Ah, these girls, I would tell Hertha in my letter, if I could wake enough to write it.

These girls are like a strange sideshow mirror that reflects, not once, but twice. They hide in my room, the three of them, behind the heavy curtain. I hear them breathing, rustling, moving. Sometimes they appear to communicate by touch, hand to hand, hand to arm, hand to face to shoulder to head, fingers fluttering in patterns I cannot read.

They are intriguing, I would write to Hertha, if I could focus on the page, the pen, the ink. Of course, I can understand the *biology*, but their very existence seems to me a mystery.

There   there   there is the pain   back again
big again   I reach for the bottle   again
a tonic   perfect
drink it   drink me   drink it.

Was I wrong to run here, to the other side of the world from all that I faced? As sick as I was, I was not in my right mind. Nor was I in my right body. It takes strength—physical and mental both—to withstand constant attacks. Not even to fight back. Just to withstand.

They cannot forgive me what they see as sin. There is already the sense that I am unnatural—a woman scientist is like a pig that talks, or a house that flies. It was my beloved husband that let them tolerate me. And my girls, of course. That I could be a French wife, a French mother, that let them accept me—even love me—as scientist. And they *did* love me. They loved *us*. But they could not forgive adultery, or even its suggestion. Once I had slipped—or was even thought to have slipped—I was tainted. I was once more foreign, *La Polonaise*, no longer French. I was other, alien, unnatural. I was not like them. I was not of them.

I dream again   in dreams lit blue   that science is
outlawed   and magic reigns   alchemical.

~ ~ ~

The sounds of the household tumble me from sleep. A floorboard creaks. Three faces peek. There: three little hands on the edge of the just-open door. Voices titter. I lift my head from the pillow, lift my hand to my forehead, push my hair back from my face, find my own voice.

'Good morning,' I say, wondering if it is, in fact, morning. I cannot tell; the blind is closed, the heavy curtain drawn over it.

'But it's afternoon,' one brave voice offers.

'We're home from school,' says another.

'We had breadandbutterandjam for tea.'

'Well,' I say, 'thank you. For telling me the time. Very kind.'

Three faces smile broadly, six shoulders lift in pride, all framed by the door and its jamb.

'You may come in. If you wish.'

Six feet shuffle, move a few steps into the room. I wrestle my shoulders free of the bedclothes, haul myself to sitting. Pain shoots through my lower abdomen. I wince, blink it away, smile a smile that I hope is not a wolfish grimace.

'Ah, ah, come, come!'

They slip towards me, closer, and the three of them align themselves at the foot of the bed.

'But I can barely see you! If we are to converse, surely we should admit light? Perhaps one of you could—'

I wave my hand towards the window, and all three leap there, moving together, two of them dragging the heavy curtain aside, one of them untugging the cord that secures the blind, three of them hauling to lift the blind. Light streams in, almost painful. I blink, as my eyesight adjusts.

'Ah, now,' I say, patting the bedclothes, 'I am glad you are here, so you can help me. With a puzzle.'

They crowd closer, and clamour.

'We are experts at puzzles!'

'And riddles and such!'

'What is your puzzle? What can it be?'

'Well,' I say, 'I feel very foolish, but—'

'Yes, yes, tell us!'

'There is no such thing as a foolish question—'

'—so our mother always tells us.'

'Your mother is correct. My foolishness is this: I do not know your names.'

'But we've told you!'

'We are Hanna, who is really Johanna—'

'—and Oona, and there's Ada!'

'Yes, yes, I know your names, the three of you together, Hanna and Ada and Oona. Of course. I told you it is foolish. But the puzzle is that I'm afraid I cannot tell you apart.' I lift my empty hands, palms to the air.

The three of them laugh, leaning on each other's shoulders, crowding towards the bed.

'Don't be afraid!'

One of them—is she Oona?—pats my arm, the lightest touch.

'No one can—'

'—tell us apart!'

'Even our mother and father have trouble.'

'And Mrs R—Mrs Reddy, that is to say—has no hope, none at all.'

'Though her very dear friend Jane Deere usually gets it right—'

'—but she's used to camels—'

'—which all look the same to us—'

'—so we know she's especially good at Telling Apart.'

They step away from the bed, all three in unison.

'But we can tell you the trick,' one of them—is she Hanna? No, Ada?—says.

'The trick for Telling Apart.'

'The trick of who we are.'

They form a line, hands out to the side, the three of them joined: image, mirror image, and image mirrored again.

'Ahem—'

'The three of us are one, but three.'
'Our differences are plain.'
'As plain as the almost identical noses on our faces.'
'Look: Ada's nose has a tiny turn at its tip—'
'—facing left.'
'Oona's nose has a freckle on the right—'
'—just near the nostril.'
'And Hanna, well, her nose doesn't have a turn—'
'—and doesn't have a freckle—'
'—so it is what it is, the nose without—'
'—and that's the three of us.'
'Ta-daaah!'

They throw their arms in the air, then—hands still held—they each drop into curtsey, low, low, low, then they tumble to the floor in a laughing heap, and I laugh, too, the feel of it light, and lovely, the first laugh I have laughed, I think, since I cannot begin to know when.

A knock on the door, then the knock comes again. The door opens just a crack, through which crack sounds the voice of the girls' father in a loud stage whisper—*Ratbags! You bloody pardon-my-French ratbags! Out of there right now!*—and I say to the door, 'They are no trouble, Mr Loverock, I assure you.' He apologises again, and insists.

'Leave you in peace. Come on now you three, quick-smart.'

The three of them whoop and leap across the room and climb their father as if he is a piece of gymnasium equipment. He laughs, hugs them to him, and I see him kiss the top of each of their heads in turn before he closes the door, returning me to solitary silence.

My daughters were never like this.

No such noise erupts from my girls.

And of course, no such father.

No more.

My own dearest girls. I close my eyes, and they are with me.

~ ~ ~

Tonight I will write to my daughters.

    Dearest Little, I will write, and My dear Big Girl. One page for each of them. I can manage that much, my pen sharp when my mind is not.

    I am here, I will tell them, and here, there are three little girls, three daughters, and they are dear things, good girls, but I wish only that these three could be you two.

I close my eyes and see   as if on the inside of my eyelids
radium's three lines on a flame spectrum   those
spectral lines   two faint   one stronger
all three required   all three together
instrumental   characteristic   elemental.

No, not tonight, but tomorrow. Tomorrow I will write to my daughters, when I am not so tired. When I can hold the pen, and my thoughts, in place for more than an instant.

    I will say to them   to each of them

    I kiss you   with all my heart   on your beautiful tired forehead.

    A thousand kisses from your dear Mé.

PLAY
Matti

Matti hears her daughters at play, their voices low together, in their own company, as they so often are. *I was like them, when I was young*, she thinks, though as a singleton, an only child to ageing parents, her time had often been solitary. She had provided good company for herself, comfortable in her skin and in her own mind. Her three, though, *our three, our girls*, she thinks, have each other. They are never alone. Sometimes, when they are quiet together, she wonders if they can read each other's minds, though rational thought tells her that they cannot. And yet. And yet. She'd hoped that once at school, they would make friends more readily than they have. Charlie and Matti had sent them to Worser Bay School for that very reason: to play. They had been learning well, and fast, at home under her tutelage, but she could not play with them as another child might, with that innocence and inventiveness, with naivety and joy. Charlie fulfils that role—dear Charlie, there is such joy in him; will he ever grow up?

Matti knows, though, that other children are sometimes—perhaps often—cruel to her daughters. Just weeks ago she had watched, bewildered, as a group of loitering schoolboys filled their mouths with dry rice, then spat the rice, slagged into a slurry, through bamboo pipes, ambushing the triplets as they passed. Matti, furious, had rushed from the house and cursed the backs of the running boys, while spreading her arms to encircle her girls. She'd ushered them into the kitchen, cleaned the grainy spittle from their eyes and hair and the necks of their shirts. They'd picked rice grains from each other like little grooming animals, calm, quiet. Matti wonders how often the girls have suffered such indignities. Just boys, she'd told them that day, I'm afraid it's in their nature.

Nature, nurture, which takes dominion? However well Matti and Charlie have nurtured them—and they have nurtured them well, of this Matti is sure—and however evenly, their daughters' natures are clearly distinct. Similar but distinct. It's in their nature (as well as their nurture) to be similar. A stranger might look at them, expecting them to be identical in their thoughts and dreams and wants. And maybe they are, to a point. But each of them has nuanced skills, interests, and these are apparent already. What did the Jesuits claim, or was it Aristotle? *Give me the child till seven, and I will make what no one will unmake.* Her seven-year-old daughters' strengths and weaknesses are, it's true, already apparent, though it's unclear to her to what extent she and Charlie have made—or indeed unmade—them. They seem inherent.

Hanna's joy in numbers, and in science, she inherits—Matti surmises—from her, though Hanna shows prowess and predilection Matti lacked at the same age. No, Matti thinks, Ada is my echo, their leader, in control. Where Hanna seeks the why and how, Ada asks the what—straight to the substance, straight to the point, straight to the heart of the matter, no nonsense. Ada, like Matti, is a fixer, of course. And Oona belongs to Charlie, forever in the middle as dear Charlie, too, is forever in the middle, torn this way and that trying to please everyone and be everything to everyone—but also bridging, connecting. Oona asks not how or why or what, but *who*. And Oona's great gift is her voice, not just sweet—as all their voices are sweet, and true—but strong and sure, like Charlie. Oona gives voice. Together, their voices are astonishing.

Their visitor's younger daughter—Ern has told her in his letters—is the same age as Hanna and Oona and Ada. Matti knows the girl is with her older sister, and that they are with family, they are safe; they are, she is certain, loved. Matti knows how much their visitor, as sick as she is, seeks only the best for her daughters. But her youngest daughter is seven years old. Could I leave my children here, Matti wonders, and travel to the other side of the world? She lets the question drift, unanswered.

The clock on the mantel strikes the hour. She can hear the girls, still at play. Matti draws deep on her smoke, stubs it into the enamel plate. Time to make a start on tea before she checks, once more, on their visitor.

DREAMS LIT BLUE
The Lady

When we go to Wonderland! When we go to Wonderland! I hear the three little girls say it over and over, a chant, an incantation, a spell.

When we go to Wonderland, they say.

When we go to Wonderland, you'll see, they say to me.

But how would I have the energy to go to Wonderland when some days, still, I cannot get out of bed?

I have barely left this house since the journey here. Ten days ago or seven days. Seven weeks. Seven hours. I do not know.

The mother-doctor-wife comes to me, touches my brow and talks to me now of hospital, but I cannot leave this bed this house the sanctuary of this place so she sits with me in my delirium.

I dream in dreams lit blue by soft moonlight the soft blue light of radium, of my darling husband, my truest and deepest loss, the loss I feel forever in my heart and my mind and throughout my whole body and being. When I am too tired to write, when I am too tired to think, when I am too tired to keep my eyes open, I close my eyes and speak to my dead husband.

I see the way these three girls are. Their one-ness. Their singleness. Like one organism with three magnificent parts. Look at them   the three of them. The stability of the shape of them. The one-two-three of them. Forever joined, each forever stabilising each.

He and I, we were like that: two parts, each stabilising each. Two magnificent parts, forming an even more magnificent whole. In the space between my worrying hands, he is here.

That I am here without him   is what I find so very hard to bear. In the night I lie in the dark and tell him so. I speak to him in whispers that only he can hear. I hold his invisible   unholdable   hand, and he holds me.

Think of a man on a Paris street   leaving a luncheon meeting, walking to his publisher, distracted   perhaps by a thought   tiny   invisible   or by an idea. Or thinking of the proofs he is on his way to correct.

And in that precise   moment   of the man's distraction, a horse is worried by another tiny thing: the rainbow of light on a puddle; a bright scarf or an umbrella; or the sudden movement of an absent-minded man; or a piece of paper that has wrapped bread, a tranche of cheese, a bouquet of flowers.

That tiny thing   that flutter on the street, caught in the deepest corner of vision, not properly seen but half-seen and, because only half-seen, mis-seen startling. In that moment the paper   or umbrella or scarf   or man, that fragment, that flare in the edge of the horse's vision, is moved by air currents, or flickers in the half-light of the city in rain.

And so the horse mis-steps.

The man thinks   of his lunch   and his proofs and the scrawl on the blackboard in the laboratory, and how the scrawl on the blackboard is a representation of complexity, of this atom   and that particle   and every thing around us; and he thinks of his wife and how he

will describe to her the feeling of this complexity
and she will understand what he means, and she will find
words to describe it more clearly than he can.

    In that moment, lost in thinking, the man steps into the
road. The man and the horse do not touch

    the man
               falls
                       that eddy of air
                                 that slippery pavement
                                           that fluttering paperwhite

The horse steps over the man, leaving not a mark, so fast that
no one can see, so remarkable that newspapers will mention
it for days and weeks to come

    and   we   hold   our   breath
    and the world slows
    and we grasp this   moment   when the man,
    the good man, the great man,
    is still whole and unbroken,
    his darling face, his beautiful fingers,
    his beloved little beard

Then   slow   slow   slow   the
horse continues, and the carriage it hauls moves,
inevitable, unstoppable, down the road, and the front
wheels   pass him   without the lightest whisper
of a touch.

    It's a miracle!

    See his face, his darling face, smiling now, beaming. As the
carriage's front wheels pass he opens his eyes and sees wheels
and horse legs and the uneven road and human legs spaced
and clustered and a fluttering something.

    The horse continues. The carriage moves.

They say three's a charm, but this third time is unlucky. The
rear wheels strike him full force, poor man. Unrecoverable.
   A mortal blow   the newspapers will say.

I see   all this   in my mind   every day.

My pain   is nothing   except imagining his pain.
Though the hardest is not to imagine his pain, but his relief
in the moment before it. *The horse has passed me by.
The wheels have passed me by. Death has passed me by*
   Who in the world am I   to imagine that?
   To live   when my beloved does not?

When he was alive   when he was with me   we
would write in the same notebooks, add to each other's
notes. His hand was my hand; mine, his. He inscribed his
initial on the front cover of one notebook, a clear claim.
I overwrote it, in counterclaim. The overwriting was not
obliteration, but more an intertwining, a joining, a hint or
riddle on the notebook's stiff card cover: his P, the plump
ball of it, the straight shaft of it, engulfed by my cleft M.
Our joke, our private code, an answer to who am I there
for anyone to see.

After he was gone, my days and nights—my life—
closed around me, defined by his absence, the gap
the space   where he should have been, but
was not.
   He was not in the laboratory. He was not at the
table in our apartment   eating too much bread
or forgetting to eat. He was not in our bed   to
turn to in the night   and at the break of day.
He was   still   everywhere
but he was not there. There was only   instead
the space of him   the gap of him   the lack of him.

~ ~ ~

And here I am in the dark, on the other side of the world. I am without my daughters, though they are safe with their dear aunt and their nurse, I know. I am without my work, though my work is always with me unless and until I lose my mind. I am without my radium, though I dream of it, blue, beautiful, terrible. I am without my lost beloved, though he, too, is always with me

    I close my hand around the air
    and the air is him
    and we are there
    and here
    together   still

BREATH
Matti

In a chair by the bed, beyond sleep herself but resting her body, at least, Matti watches the woman's chest rise and fall. The power in that simple movement is everything, she thinks. Breath is everything.

The woman had been so well, her health improving over several days in a way that was obvious to Matti, measurable, observable. She had been up and about, talking with the children. She had seemed, quite simply, well. Then a day ago—or has it been longer?—she suffered a sudden, dramatic tumble into fever, the precise cause of which Matti could not and cannot determine.

All Matti's instincts, all her professional knowledge and medical expertise, impelled her at that point to move the woman to hospital, to seek help, advice, support from her peers. But the woman had consciousness enough to protest the move, to plead for her privacy, to insist on staying. Matti knew that the woman was—even in her fevered delirium—right, that a move to hospital would end the anonymity and secrecy she has travelled half the world to maintain.

And so Matti has sat by the woman's side, vigilant, observant, ready to make the call to shift her to hospital, even against her patient's insistence. Wilma Reddy—thank Saint Katie Sheppard for discreet, dependable Wilma—has helped keep the house running, while Matti has continued to read what is written on the sick woman's body, on her breath, in the tremors of her hands, the flighty flutter of her pulse, the blood in her water, the stink of it. Matti must trust her own judgement, as she knows her old friend Ern trusts it; as she knows the woman has come to trust it, too. She does not wish to breach that trust. And so she sits with the woman and watches her breathe, and her own breath slows and shallows to match it.

In the night, at the peak of her fever, the woman speaks of her husband. And when Matti dozes, at a point, she wakes to find the woman grasping her hand, tight as a rein, whispering *Who am I to live?* over and over, in and out of knowing, *Who in the world am I to live?*

In a moment of seeming lucidity, the woman in the bed reaches out and takes Matti's warm hands in her own chill hold. *Two parts, each stabilising each,* the woman says, her eyes meeting Matti's, holding them, her breath sweet as a child's.

In the early hours that make or break a sickness—the early hours that so often give life and just as often take it—the woman stills, and settles, and shifts from fevered unrest to sleep, deep and curative.

INVISIBILITIES
The Lady

I dream   no, not a dream   a memory of a time and place. On the table by my side a glass phial gleams, neither dark nor light, and yet both at the same time. A tiny fairy glow—stopped with glass, sealed with wax—as delicate as life itself, its luminous blue my companion, my guide, my hope, my love: radium, my radium. My touchstone, my focus, my familiar, my amulet.

If this exists, then why not magic?

What other invisibilities are there in the world to discover?

I wake and hear breathing that is not my own. I open my eyes and see, in the almost-dark of dawn, the shape of the mother-doctor-wife, sleeping in the chair by my bedside. My fingers, barnacled and worn by the invisible touch of radium, my radium, tremble on the bedcover, and then the trembling stops.

I lose myself to untroubled, untremor'd sleep.

NOT EVERYWHERE IS LIKE THIS

Triplets

We three are tucked up tight in bed, breathing dragonsbreath into the cold of the room, ready for a story. Our mother has been with the Lady, in her room, all day long and all the night before, bustling from kitchen to sickroom, whispering with Mrs R, shushing us. We hear our mother in the kitchen, now, a pan clashing on the stove, a smothered cry, and our father, in the chair by our bed, hears it too. He flicks through the pages of the book on his lap, stops at the red ribbon that marks our place, and asks, 'Now, where in the world are we up to, ratbags, in this wonderful *Wonderland* book?'

Our father reads to us, of the hookah-smoking caterpillar asking 'Who are *you*?', of Alice stretched on tiptoe, nibbling a giant mushroom, and of the Antipathies ('Please, Ma'am, is this New Zealand or Australia?').

How we love this other Wonderland! When we were littler, before our mother started teaching us our letters, we recognised just one word on the front of this grand and special book, and it matched the word we knew the best and loved the best and saw the most

WONDERLAND

our beloved other home.

We have spun through the empty spaces of our own Wonderland, spinning fast as fast can be, but also spinning slowly, like Alice falling down the rabbit-hole. We remember time moving differently, and the three of us moving differently, and we know how grand and strange and wonderful it is, and we cannot describe it, but we know that this feeling is something we never want to lose.

We ask our father, when will we go to Wonderland?

'Every night in your dreams, my baby girls,' he tells us. His smile looks upside down as he kisses each of us on our foreheads, kiss kiss kiss, and pulls the covers up tight. The room goes dark when he leaves.

We love the storybook story of the girl called Alice in her Wonderland, but if the truth be told, our favourite stories of all are the unwritten stories of us, and the beginnings of Wonderland, our Wonderland. Our father, Charlie, tells them. The very beginning of us is the story of our mother and father, Matti and Charlie, meeting and courting and marrying. We remember the story to ourselves in the dark

> *she was looking for a sideshow*
> *   for her baby hospital*
> *not looking for a husband*
> *   though he had eyes only for her*
> *   he swept her off her feet*
> *   come a-waltzing Matilda, my darling*
> *and he waltzed her, and she was smitten*
> *   and here we all are*

and in our sleep we drift and dream around the dancefloor on the satin-slippered toes of our mother-to-be and the Radium-bright boots of our father-to-be, all of us together before we began (what a muddle time can be!).

This morning, we are ready (calisthenicked, breakfasted, faces washed, chores completed) bright and early. On our way to school we have a deposit to make—three fresh tail hairs from dear old Ernest Rutherford, picked up (glinting silver in the muck) from the yard this morning, popped into Oona's pinny pocket for safekeeping. They'll make a fine addition to our Reliquary.

We discovered the word *Reliquary* from Minna Hofmann, at school. She told us that it's a word for a special box for holy relics, and she crossed herself as she said it (it's a wonder she doesn't wear a track across the front of her dress, and another one up and down, from all that crossing).

Our own Reliquary of Lost Things Found started with an empty Grimault's Indian Cigarettes tin, still smelling of our mother's lovely cigarettes. In the tin we keep a tiny white feather from a parson bird's bow, the little fluff of it, barely there, gone in a breath if you huff too hard. We call this The Lost Breath of Doctor Matti Loverock.

We have a blunt pencil stub that fell off Miss Grimshaw's desk at school one day and straight into Hanna's pocket. We call it The Lost Words of Miss Grimshaw.

There's a brand-new doll's arm we found on our mother's desk. This is The Lost Arm of the Doll Who Never Was.

There's a hanky Minna Hofmann dropped in Girls Playground, that she'd used to stem one of her many bloody noses (The Lost and Holy Relic of Not-So-Saintly Minna Bloody Hofmann).

The shaft of a knife, a misplaced thimble, the broken body of a doll.

Our old fingernail tips, trimmed by our mother, rattle in a matchbox (The Lost Moons of Us).

We have a moa bone, we're sure (though it might just be from a big chicken). This is The Lost Thigh Bone of the Last Great Moa of Miramar.

There's a smooth green beauty that we picked from the beach, green as the greenstone Mrs R wears on a cord around her neck (though ours might be from an old bottle, we cannot be sure). This is The Lost Greenstone of the Sea.

We have a brown bottle with a tiny glass stopper, that once held medicine and still holds its smell if we stick our noses right to the mouth and imagine hard. This is The Lost Pain of Jane Deere the Cameleer.

There's a scabby crust in a fold of glassine paper, that we found in the secret drawer in our mother's desk. This is The Lost Cord of the Lost Baby Whose Name We Do Not Know.

There is a cuttlebone, carved by the sea.

There is a pale stone, dotted dark, that looks like a currant bun from Mrs Tracy's shop in Seatoun.

There is a bone that's the size of a finger, that we found in the sand at the side of the house one day when we were digging to make mud cakes for our morning tea. And though we cannot be sure, we call it The Lost Fingerbone of Carnival Charlie Loverock.

We pick up our lunches (cheese sandwiches with a smear of jam for sweetness, and a carrot for afters), whisper-shout goodbye to our parents (careful not to disturb you-know-who), then we're out the front door and off to school.

The switchback track up the hill behind our house leads to Worser Bay School, up on the ridge. The track tickles its way under scrub, tricking its way up the hill, not the quickest way, but the most interesting. We've added our own trail markers, signposts. Here's a tiny red bow on a branch. Here's a ribbon faded to palest blue. Here's the skull of a bird that we found on the beach, picked chalk-white, glass-clean, smooth. It's lodged in a fork in a tree (like a warning, though we do not mean it to be).

It takes just a few stolen minutes to detour off the school track to our secret cubbyhole, a space just big enough for three, hidden by gorse and flax and mirror-bush. We crawl into the gap, uncover the tin box that serves as our Reliquary, and—taking from Oona's pocket Ernest's three long silver hairs, coarse as broom straws—we untie the ribbon and add them to the sheaf of The Lost Tail of Ernest Rutherford, tucking everything carefully inside.

We hear First Bell ring out from up the hill. We close the tin box, return it to its hidey-hole where no one will find it, and scramble up the track, slipping through the gap in the fence just as Second Bell rings.

At the end of Morning Play, the wind hits—a southerly buster—and it lifts and lifts, becomes wilder and wilder, whistling through the roof, shuddering the building on its stumps. We would not be surprised, as we look out the rattling windows of the classroom, to see anything, no matter how large—even a cow! or Ernest Rutherford, our dear old horse! or a great whale! imagine!—borne past on this great wind.

Our father was expecting it. He's going to Wonderland today while we are at school, to batten down the hatches in anticipation of a decent bloody blow, he told us this morning. We imagine the Wonderland Water Chute picked up, flying across the harbour to Town. We imagine the Tea Kiosk ripped from its pilings, flying away to Japan, leaving the round floorboards like a wooden pie ready for serving. We imagine the Katzenjammer Castle lifted, upended, falling down, down, down.

We've heard that not everywhere is like this, that not everywhere has wind that can lift you up and set you back down again, just like that, or knock you off your feet. But we are glad to live in this place, where the wind smells of nothing and everything, of ocean and faraway and the bay outside our door. The wind tastes of sky and salt, and it sings its way into all our dreams, howling in our heads and under our bed and through the cracks in the window frame and up and under the curtain, and into everything, right where it belongs.

STILL
Matti

In the afternoon, the back door slams, open then closed, fierce and jolting. Matti goes to check it, to latch it shut, but it was not just the door slamming in the wind. It was Charlie, returning from Wonderland. He sits, his head on the kitchen table, his hands rubbing over his head. He turns to her, and she sees a look on his face that she has almost never seen. He is utterly abject in the moment. The look is there when he turns, and in the instant in which he sees her, focuses, the look is gone, the darkness lifts, and her Charlie returns to her. *Charlie, oh Charlie.*

'What is it, my love?'

He jumps to his feet, grabs her around the waist, whirls her around the kitchen.

'Come, come a-waltzing, Matilda my darling, ah ah it's nothing, Matilda my love. Nothing to worry about, all is under control. I was worried about the wind, that is all. But there was no damage, no damage at all, at Wonderland. All shipshape and Bristol fashion. Aye aye.'

He holds her close, kisses her, tucks her head under his chin as they sway in the dimlit kitchen. Matti feels her body shape to the shape of him, each of them softening, lowering their guard.

Her thoughts flash unbidden to the look she caught, just a moment before. She has not seen such bald pain in Charlie's face since the baby boy slipped from her womb.

~ ~ ~

The child never drew breath. She carried him, lifeless, inside her for days, until he slipped from her, slick as you like, as life had slipped from him, poor wee one, poor lost boy.

Wilma Reddy delivered her of him, and Wilma did not whisk him away unseen, as another midwife might have done. Wilma cooed to the baby, though he could not hear, as she wrapped him into the blanket dear Jane Deere had knitted, called him *dear one*, and *tamaiti*, and *baby boy*. She placed him carefully, reverently, in Matti's arms, arms that had not warmth enough to wake him. Matti sang to him then, soft. There was screaming keening deep in her, a wailing pain, a howling, but she silenced it, stilled it, kept it close inside. There there, my quiet one, she sang. There there. There there. She pressed his cold cheek to her lips.

They'd buried him in a box of Charlie's making, and planted rosemary over him, and rue. The triplets, toddling, three years old, had helped their father pat down soil around the plants above their unknown brother.

Matti kept his cord, dried to a nut, wrapped it in a sleeve of glassine paper, pressed with a stem of his rosemary. She tucked it out of sight, safe, in the back of a drawer of the cabinet in the room where the sick woman now lies.

They call such a baby *stillborn*; they call such a birth *still birth*. The birth did not feel still, though. It felt like a shipwreck, breaking and foundering, felt like ruin and loss. As well blame the weather, or the tides, or the moon. As well blame something monstrous beneath the waves.

Not every birth is like this.

Three children survive from her three pregnancies. The ordinariness of that statistic—that average, that mean, one and one and one makes three—obscures the enduring pain of two losses: the baby carried to term, then lost (her tamaiti, her stillborn boy); and the miscarriage she thinks of as her comet child. That fleeting thing. Conceived under the flarelit skies of the comet's first pass, their son (she always imagines him so) failed to lodge. She carried him for only six weeks. He failed to quicken. *Quicken*, she thinks. An old-fashioned term. His quickening stilled, never started. She lost him as the Earth passed through the tail of the comet. The bright flare, the high drama, faces turned upward, uplit, in wonder. Two years ago, this month just gone, she lost their comet child. Charlie never knew. This loss is hers alone. She feels it still.

Charlie waltzes her to a chair, sits her down, places a hand on each side of her face, raises her face to his, and kisses her, slow, warm. She feels her own response; her pulse races. *Quickens*. Then he breaks away, groans, rubs his hands together, stalks to the pantry, finds flour, places it on the table.

'The ratbags will be home soon. Are you hungry? What about Lady Muck?' He inclines his head to the front room. 'I'll make damper for tea. Or scones.' His face shines. All the darkness she glimpsed—*the trouble with Wonderland*—is gone, or buried, or pushed aside.

The back door blows off the latch, slams open, makes them both jump. Wind blasts into the room, chill, urgent, disruptive. Flour puffs from the table as Charlie kneads and messes, and Matti gets up to secure the door. Her daughters—their daughters—will be home, soon. They will all be here, around the table. All of them together, in this place, their home. What a wonder.

REFLECTION
The Lady

I wake as if from a fever dream that eased to calming, balming sleep, the deepest sleep imaginable, despite—perhaps because of—the raging wind that rocks the house.

Today is a good day.

Finally, a good day.

Sleep becomes me. When the mother-doctor-wife comes with medications, she and I agree that the dosages can drop. Easing. Easing.

And now, I sit at the little table, pulled up before the window, where there is light. I write in my notebook. My hand—the mark of my pen on the page—is strong, almost as it was before. Before this sickness. Before I fled. Before it all.

I concentrate, while I can. I write.

A knock on my door.

'Yes, come,' I say.

It is one of the three sisters. As if the tricking mirrors have been veiled, she is alone, unreflected.

'Ah! Already school has finished for the day! But your sisters are not with you?' I stall, unsure which of them she is. This one, separate from the other two, remains alike, indistinguishable.

'Ada and Oona,' she says, identifying herself by omission, 'have gone to the beach. I came here. On my own. To the house. For something. We forgot.'

Her hands shift behind her.

'And did you find it?'

'Find what?'

'The something you forgot.'

Her hands shift again, and I hear sand grind under her feet as she shuffles her canvas slippers.

'Not a something. Or forgetting. But an asking. A question. A puzzle.'

'Oho,' I say, 'and you are all so good at puzzles and riddles, I know.'

'We are.'

'And so? The puzzle?'

'The asking. The question. Perhaps it's two questions. We wonder …'

'Yes, yes?'

'We wonder, are you better? Are you cured?'

'Ah, perhaps not entirely cured,' I say. 'But certainly better. I do feel better, every day that I am here.'

She nods her head, as though the answer I have given is pleasing, or correct.

'And the second question? You said there were two.'

'Well, it's that we wonder if it's true, as we have heard, that you are a famous lady scientist, as famous as our mother's friend Ernest Rutherford?'

Fame, that astonishing mirror. So often distorting. Impossible to bear. Like the convex glasses of an amusement park sideshow, shifting the reflection beyond recognition. Beyond identity.

Who am I? Who in the world am I? That is the question.

'Me? Famous? Yes, Hanna. Yes. I suppose I am.'

She seems to hold the fact and hug it to her like a prize. As she turns to leave, I say her name.

'Hanna.'

'Yes, Lady?'

'Perhaps fame can be our secret, just for now.'

Miramar

Winter 1912

WHO'S IN THE HILLS?
Triplets

As each day dawns later, our morning regime has become as brisk as the air, so cold it turns our breath smoke-white. These winter mornings we're up, out and exercised as quick as we can, then back into the kitchen's warmth to eat. This morning, all the while, our father's been muttering about Wonderland, and the possibility of opening for a winter holiday season, as well as the Winter Gala we've been hoping for. He has his big blue counting book open in front of him on the kitchen table and we watch him run his finger down the columns and across the lines of red numbers dancing down the page.

When can we go to Wonderland? We ask him over and over, and we ask him again as he closes the counting book with a sigh.

'Nothing's settled yet,' he tells us when we leap about at the thought of it, 'so settle down.' He stands, stretches, takes his watch from his top pocket and holds it out in front of him as far as his hand can reach.

'But I *am* going to meet Mr Bickerton today about some fireworks—'

(Swoon!)

'—then I'm off to see a wise man about a dog. But all in good time. All in good time. Speaking of which,' he taps his watch, 'your mother will be late tonight. She's gone to a meeting in Town with some of her cronies, so it's just us for tea. You can keep yourselves busy until then, eh, ratbags?'

We can, of course we can.

'Now,' he puts his watch back safe in its pocket and pulls out a clutch of pennies. 'Hands.' He drops a big coin into each of three outstretched palms.

'Keep yourselves quiet.' He rolls his eyes and inclines his head towards the front room. 'And don't be a nuisance to you-know-who.'

We know who. We do.

'Right, off outside. And listen for the whistle!'

Oh, we will, we will!

'And stay this side of the tunnel!'

We nod our intention. We will!

We scramble over the rocks and along the beach towards Seatoun Wharf, then cross at the tearooms and walk up Wharf Street to Mrs Tracy's cake shop, where we swap one big coin for three iced buns. We take our buns outside, to talk to Mrs Tracy's parrot, his big metal cage shifted from its usual spot inside the door to bask in the sun.

Unable to urge anything more than *hallooo!* from Mrs Tracy's parrot, we lick the pink from our sticky fingers, look across the water at the hills in shadow on the far side of the harbour, and play the looking game we invented, that we call Who's in the Hills.

We squint, squeezing our cheeks so our eyes almost close. It makes the looked-at thing become strange, not quite itself. It helps us see in a different way. We see what we can see, in the shadows and light and trees of the hills, and we conjure characters that might or might not be there.

In the hills on other days, we've seen the face of Miss Nella Jonassen the Famous Aerial Queen (swoon!), and we've seen the shape of her Bound to Rise balloon. We've seen a great beast without a name, and a teapot without a lid, and a fish without water. We've seen the Egyptian mummy from the museum in Town, and we've seen a leg of roast lamb. Once we even saw the face of Ernest Rutherford the Gentleman Scientist in the hills!

Today in the hills we think we see a cat, her eyes turned up to the sky, as if she's watching birds. Mrs Tracy's parrot squawks loudly (perhaps she sees the cat in the hills, too) and says a word that sounds like *gingerbread*. When we've stopped laughing, we wipe our sticky fingers on our trousers, say goodbye to Mrs Tracy's parrot, and set off up the shallow slope of the road that leads to the Seatoun tunnel.

We skip along the tramline up the middle of the road. There's no need to keep an eye out for trams. None have run here all this year, not since the earthquake last summer, when the ground cracked and heaved, and the tramlines buckled and broke by the Rongotai Knob, and then—hot on the earthquake's heels—the tram strike struck. They still haven't fixed the tramlines, and we wonder if they ever will. Our father regularly curses the heaving cleaving Earth (though he never curses the striking tramworkers, fair play to them, he says).

When we reach the tunnel's mouth, and stand on its silent tramlines, we feel the pull of the darkness within, and of the light at its other end. This—this tunnel—marks our boundary.

'Stay this side of the tunnel,' our father always insists.

As curious as we are to venture beyond, we will do as our father says. Our father knows best, after all.

Standing just inside the bright curve of the tunnel's mouth, we turn to look again to the hills across the harbour, and the snowdusted mountains beyond. We see the loafing cat in the hills, clearly now, see the whole of it there in the shape of the land, the fat of the dark green of the lower slopes. The black valleys make the folds of the cat's legs. The paler green tops form its cat-loaf back and the curving switch of its tail. And then, as plain as it was there in that instant, in another it is gone. Like the cat in the big book of Wonderland, there's just the flickering shade of it. Just its eyes, and the flash of its sharp-toothed smile. Then it's gone.

We step out of the mouth of the tunnel and emerge into sunshine, and march back down Wharf Street and across the road to the beach.

The three of us proceed like ducks in mud, tails up, heads down, sifting the tideline's litter for treasure. As we puddle further along, we see a pale bent figure at the other end of the beach, a blue-grey shape tideline-shuffling as we are. Hermit Louis is out early today.

As we walk towards him, being careful not to run (our father has told us that not everyone loves three running jumping girls, though we find it hard to believe), we keep ourselves small and quiet, until Hermit Louis himself looks up, and then we *hallooo!* him and *bone-jaw* him, our shouts carrying in the still morning air. He nods at us, and we stop a polite distance away and *hallooo!* him again, but quietly, with our inside voices, and he nods again, and wags his finger, and we think we see him smile, and he *hallooos!* us back but with a sound like *aloe*, which we know is the big plant in Mrs R and Jane Deere's garden.

We ask if he's found any treasure today, and he brushes his hand over his walrus moustache and looks at the sky, then the sand, then the sea, without answering. He reaches into the hessian sack tied at his waist and draws out a pāua shell, the great flat snail of the sea, that our father calls abalone. He turns the shell over in his palm, and though we know what to expect (we've collected pāua shells before, of course we have, and we've watched our father carve the flesh from fresh shells to make fritters for tea, hot and crisp), we have never seen colour like the colour of this shell.

'This blue,' he tells us, but when he says it, it sounds like *blur*, 'is like the heavens.' He tells us we are good girls, *jontea, tray jontea,* and he bows, holding the shell towards us in both his hands. We do not know what *jontea* is, but we like the buzzing sound of it, and we smile back at him. Hanna takes the shell from Hermit Louis, and passes it to Ada, who passes it to Oona, who nods and puts it carefully in her pocket with the day's lesser treasures. And we bow and *bone-jaw* and *tray jontea* and *mare-sea* him, and wave, and he raises his tobacco-y finger to the sky and hoists his fishy hessian bag up high on his waist and walks off, towards the Seatoun end of the beach, to the wharf.

Up through the scrub we go, turning off at Red-Bow Branch, past Ribbon Blue and Birdskull Tree. We dive into our cubbyhole nest in the flax and the gorse and the mirror-bush, and Oona fishes in her pocket and pulls out the shell. Its blue seems even brighter than it did on the beach, and we see within it, at its centre, a shape of darkest deepest blue, outlined black (like our kohl-rimmed eyes in costume), made up, beautiful, all-seeing.

We name this beauty The All-Seeing Eye of Hermit Louis.

We uncover our tin box and prise off the lid. To make a place for The All-Seeing Eye we must rearrange the relics already in our box. We turn upwards The Lost Arm of the Doll Who Never Was, to reach for the sky. We rest The Lost Fingerbone of Carnival Charlie Loverock inside a silver thimble, to protect it, and we nest The Lost Cord of the Lost Baby next to that. Hanna lifts out the brown bottle with the glass stopper that is The Lost Pain of Jane Deere the Cameleer and holds it up to the sky. We watch the sky turn orange behind it.

We've kept ourselves to ourselves all day, kept ourselves busy and stayed away. It must be afternoon by now, nearly time for tea. We can tell by the beach having slipped into shade, and by our bellies grumbling.

Now we lie on our fronts in the low sandy dunes, propping ourselves on our elbows. Our bodies are aligned in a star, a collapsed triangle, our dark heads defining a space at the centre, three girl-sized burnt matches (blackheads!) arranged on the sand for a match puzzle that needs solving. Queen Cuttle is with us, hauled from under our bed. So is Mother Brown, another of our doll friends, who we made from clay mixed with straw and a little of Ernest Rutherford's sweet leavings, her horse doovahs. We're making a new doll today. Hanna fusses with a tiny blue glass bottle, Oona ties a scrap of fabric around the bottle's middle as a dress, Ada jams a bristly sea-twig down the neck of the bottle to make a head with flyaway hair.

There, we've made the Lady.

We name her Lady Bluebottle and make our introductions
lady, pleased to meet you
meet queen cuttle
and mother brown
bone-jaw
tray jontea

our big heads looming over the three dolls. We are giants next to them, even as we are our normal size, girl-sized (though we know from the Alice book that girl-sized is a tricky thing and does not stay the same). We place them—the Lady, the Mother, the Queen—together, back-to-back, in between the three of us in the space we make, the three of them together, but each their own, distinct.

There is the family whistle, four unmistakeable notes, the first low and long, then three quick notes dancing and tripping above it. The Loverock Whistle, our father calling us home. We stand and brush the sand from our clothes, shoving poor old Mother Brown and Queen Cuttle and Lady Bluebottle into Oona's pockets as we run whistlewards.

We burst into the house, creep down the hallway (being quiet for you-know-who), and arrive in the kitchen to see our father and Hermit Louis together at the back door, shaking hands with a theatrical flourish, as if they have just performed a magic trick. We call *bone-jaw* and *mare-sea* and *jontea blur* to him, and Hermit Louis raises his finger in salute as he turns away, heading off into the darkening afternoon.

A great fat fish rests on a plate on the kitchen table, shining silver and blue, still wet and smelling of the sea.

'Fresh fish for tea, ratbags! You're just in time to make yourselves useful.'

We get to work, curling potato peels into the scrap bucket, hungry for our fishy tea, and determined to stay awake—no matter how late—for our mother's return (perhaps she will bring her Cronies, swoon!).

The sounds of our mother and her Cronies (yes!) wake us. We hear them stumbling—or perhaps they're dancing, they sound so merry—on the verandah and run to meet them. They push through the door on a blast of cold night air and salty ferry breath. Our mother whisks Hanna up in her arms, Ada leaps towards Mrs R's rosetted bosom (Votes for Women!), and Jane Deere the Cameleer hoists Oona up onto her hip, while our mother's friend Doctor B (B for Bennett and B for Baby) from the Baby Hospital watches and laughs, smoke surrounding her, as usual, from the neck up.

While the Cronies make themselves at home, and our father makes them all tea, we make ourselves little and quiet, tucking under the daybed in the hope that we won't be noticed and sent to bed. But our father is onto us.

'Three little ratbag mousekins, off to bloody bed right bloody now! Tea's made, ladies, so I'll retire. And I'll retire these three ratbags too.'

Jane Deere says, 'Let me.' She lifts Ada onto her shoulders, tucks Oona on her hip, and picks Hanna up and places Hanna's feet on the top of her own feet in their big leather boots. She walks us all to our bed and tucks us up tight, kisses us goodnight. And when she goes, she leaves the door open a crack.

We lie in bed and watch the light and the smoke and listen to the Cronies talk and laugh and clink and dance, lulling us to sleep.

DANCE
Matti

Jane Deere twirls Matti Loverock in the space between the kitchen table and the daybed, *waltzing Matilda, Matilda my darling,* then Jane dips Matti backwards, kisses her cheek, and they fall to the floor in a heap, to the cheers of Agnes Bennett, standing, clapping, cigarette clamped in the corner of her mouth. Wilma Reddy reaches an arm to Matti, hauls her to her feet. Wilma does the same to Jane, pulls her to her feet, then into her arms, and they kiss, hard, as Agnes cheers once more.

'Shhh, shhh, shhh,' Matti hisses loudly, pouring drinks.

There they sit at the Loverocks' kitchen table, smoking like chimneys, billowing clouds above their heads, ashing into a yellow enamel pie dish, dropping the cigarette ends to hiss into near-empty bottles. There is a brown bottle on the table, and a green one, and one that has no colour. There are glasses, some empty, others full of pale yellow and pale amber and full of the colour of nothing. There are papers and pamphlets on the table in front of them, brought from the evening's lecture in Town. Agnes reaches across and scoops them towards her, flicks through them, lifts one, waves it in the air.

'Truby, the booby! Such bloody twaddle. But people listen to him. Good lord,' she reads, '*the stresses of higher education impair the health of the nation's future mothers,* is that so? Oh, the silly old bastard!'

She throws the pamphlet across the table. It skids off the edge and lands on the floor by Matti's foot.

'And his dreadful wife is just as bad.'

'Or worse.'

'She's worse.'

'They do good, though. In other ways. It cannot be denied.'

'The good does not cancel the harm.'

'Will you speak against them, Ag? As you have done in the past?'

'I will. I cannot keep silent.'

'I'll drink to that.'

'You'll drink to anything.'

They lift their glasses, clink them.

'Cheers!'

'Your good health, sisters!'

As they clink and drink, the door from the hallway opens. They all turn as the Loverocks' visitor stands in the doorway, the dark of the hallway behind her dark clothes so it's almost impossible to see where she starts and where she stops and where the darkness begins. There is just her pale face, her piled hair, her tired eyes.

Matti stands, moves unsteadily towards her. 'I'm so sorry, Madame Sko—Madame Sklo—Madame Skwodovlov—Chère madame! We've woken you!'

'No, I was—'

'Won't you join us?'

'I should not—'

'Plenty of room for one more.'

'Perhaps for a moment—'

'And a drink.'

'No, I must not—'

'It'll settle you.'

'Well, perhaps I—'

Wilma Reddy stands and pulls her chair closer, and the woman nods in thanks, and sits. Agnes reaches her hand across the table. 'Good to meet you, I'm Agnes Bennett, Matti and I work together at the hospital.'

The woman touches the tips of her fingers to Agnes's fingers, briefly, then withdraws them to her lap, as Matti mutters an introduction, *a very dear friend of my friend Ernest's, all the way from Paris*, and something about convalescing. Agnes strikes a match and lights another cigarette, breathes in hard, breathes out blue, as she says to the woman, 'Ah, but aren't you—? No, I'm sure—'

The woman stands and moves to the door, 'I really must, I'm so sorry.'

Matti has not been strictly truthful with Agnes about their visitor, her identity. Now is the moment, she thinks, unless it is too late. She watches Agnes, waiting for comprehension to dawn—but it does not. The woman's face, in its closed blankness, shows something almost like fear.

Matti stands then, and she stumbles. 'Oh you must be tired, we've disturbed you, off to bed.' She takes the woman's arm—*that's better, no stumbling*—and they turn to leave the room. Matti turns back to Agnes and Wilma and Jane, makes a shushing shape with her mouth. As she closes the door behind them, to disappear them into the darkness of the hallway, Matti hears Agnes say, 'But wasn't that—I'd've sworn she was—'

'Top up, Ag?' she hears Wilma deflect.

'I wouldn't say no. Go on then.'

When Matti returns from putting her patient to bed, Agnes and Wilma and Jane Deere cheer, their cheers hushing to whispers and celebratory arms in the air when Matti shushes them again. She sits, raises her glass to toast them, slips back into the conversation around the table, thinking no more—for the moment, at least—about the woman, the patient, her visitor.

~ ~ ~

When they've drunk all there is to drink, smoked all there is to smoke, and ripped the offending pamphlets to pieces literally and figuratively, they all call it a night. Matti waves Wilma Reddy and Jane Deere off down the road and closes the door on the cold outside. She returns to the kitchen with a bundle of bedding fresh from the linen press. Agnes is already asleep on the daybed, flat on her back, snoring louder than gunfire. Matti's head spins, her stomach roils, acid erupts in her throat. She leans on the doorframe, clutching the bundled quilt tightly to her, swallows the sickness away. *Your good health, sisters*. Steadied, now, she lets one end of the bundled quilt drop, and she shakes the folds from it. It smells of dried lavender, and soap. She places the quilt carefully over Agnes on the daybed, tucking her in like a child. She kisses her on the forehead.

'G'night, Ag.'

Agnes inhales noisily, her breathing stalls for a long moment, then she snorts with a start, and rolls onto her side. Matti laughs, and snorts, too, and turns around, and sways down the dark hallway to tumble fully clothed into bed next to Charlie.

SCATTERING
Triplets

We half-wake as chairs scrape, plates clatter, glass breaks. Words are murmured, goodnights uttered, the front door opens and closes. We creep out of bed, peep through our door at Doctor B asleep in the dark on the daybed in the kitchen, snoring like a train. We imagine Mrs R and Jane Deere the Cameleer rolling like sailors down the middle of the road, their arms around each other's waist, all the way home to their own little cottage just around the shore in Karaka Bay.

In the morning the kitchen table is rich with empty bottles, dirty glasses, papers and ripped-up pamphlets, an empty Grimault's tin next to an overflowing dish of cigarette ends, matches and ash. Our father turns from the stove, picks up one of the bottles from the table, swings its emptiness from side to side.

'I fear Doctor B and your mother will be spending the day in Katzenjammer Castle,' he stage-whispers.

Oho! We've felt the feel of sickness in Katzenjammer Castle at Wonderland, the tip of its floor, the stumble of Drunkards' Walk, the clambering clatter that rattles the very insides of your brain! Our poor mother! Poor Doctor B!

Doctor B murmurs, clutches the blanket, pulls it over her head and rolls to face the wall.

~ ~ ~

After breakfast and washing and sweeping and scraps-to-Ernest, we hold our own mad tea-party on the beach, with a bottle of ginger beer from under the wash-house (our father bottled a new batch last week, and none of the bottles have exploded yet). We pour the murky fizz into three cracked teacups that we rescued from the rubbish pile behind the Kiosk at Wonderland and keep in the box under our bed. We lift our cups and clink them together, the way the Cronies did last night, shout

cheers!

here's cheers!

your good health, sisters!

and we talk in smoky groggy voices, low and croaky, then bright and shouting, the way the Cronies' voices go. We lean close to imagined matches, and hold each other's hand with our hand, to steady them as we light imagined cigarettes. We breathe in deep, then lift our chins to the side and blow out, sending imagined blue-grey smoke up into the grey-blue sky. We sit **Queen Cuttle** and **Mother Brown** in the sand between us, pour them ginger beer in shells for cups, and give each of them a tiny twig to smoke. We clink our teacups again and drink and smoke our invisible smokes in silence, for a time, as the Cronies did last night, and often do.

Oona brings **Lady Bluebottle** from her pocket, and flies her gently down through the air, swooping to settle in the sand between Oona and Ada. Queen Cuttle asks, in Oona's voice (that sounds like Doctor B's voice), whether she'll join them, whether she'd like a drink. We all take turns with all the voices

won't you join us?

won't you will you

will you

won't you

come and join the dance

always room

                                        for one more

perhaps for a moment

                                       and a drink

yes a drink

                 mustn't really

should not

                 would not

                                    could not

                 oh please do!

                                   and by the way

who in the world

                    are you?

We hear voices from across the road. We pop up—like curious rabbits—from our hiding place in the sand dunes, to see Doctor B and our mother standing on the verandah, their heads inclined towards one another in farewell. Doctor B waves at us and we *hallooo!* her as she strides along the road towards the ferry wharf, back to Town. Our father appears from around the back of our house, a tin plate and a tea towel in his hand, muttering to himself about a promised feed of abalone, and finding our French friend (pāua fritters for tea, hurrah!). And walking down the steps of our house, across the road towards us—barefoot, lifting her skirt so it grazes her knees—is our mother, and we see that over her dress she wears our father's fishing jersey. Then the Lady appears on the verandah, standing with her hands on the railing, steady, still, watching us, or our father, or our mother, or the sea.

And the three of us burst from the sand dunes, and we scatter like particles in Mr Rutherford's gold leaf experiment that the Lady has tried to explain to the three of us, but only Hanna understands.

~ ~ ~

Hanna skips across the road towards the Lady
>*and I skip up the steps*
>*and onto the verandah,*
>*lady bluebottle in my hand,*
>*to show her to the lady*

Ada runs down the beach towards our mother
and I stand with her in the cold
shushing water of the shallows,
as see-through sea-silver fish skim
our ankles and toes,
the tops of our feet

And Oona takes two steps towards our father
>*and I see him stand—still holding the tin plate*
>*and the tea towel—on the sand, looking*
>*out at the bay, at the hills,*
>*at the faces in the hills, and*
>*at all that is beyond, and I stand*
>*next to him, and take his big hand in mine,*
>*and I, too, look out at it all*

WHO IN THE WORLD AM I?
The Lady

I stumble awake to the sound of the wretched front door, and the sound of the mother-doctor-wife, and the other doctor, her friend, who questioned me last night, quizzed me, and looked at me in that way.
    Who am I? Who in the world am I?
    Perhaps it was just curiosity. To ask, after all, is normal.
    So why does it unsettle me so?

The two women stand outside the house, on the balcony that they do not call a balcony, but that sounds instead like a woman's name; I hear it as *Miranda*. They talk, outside my window. I can see them through the gap in the curtain, inclined towards each other as they speak. I cannot hear their words, though, just their murmur.
    And birds, I hear the birds. That joyous noise, like gargling, or laughter. I have come to recognise these parson birds, their dark iridescence, and the white at their throats, as if they have swallowed a tiny white mouse and coughed up its tufted balls to wear for decoration.
    The women on the Miranda embrace and the quizzing doctor descends the steps and raises her hand as she walks away.

I could have replied to the quizzing doctor: I am mother, doctor, wife.

No, not wife.

I am widow.

I could have said: I am patient; I am sister and daughter; I am lover.

And I am scientist.

You may call me Madame Skłodowska, my mother's name, the name I travel by.

But who in the world am I?

I wrap myself in a blanket, slip out to the Miranda. The mother-doctor-wife is on the beach, now, too, up to her ankles in water that must, surely, be like ice. I clutch the blanket more tightly around me, shivering to think of it. I watch the children, her three little girls, on the beach, moving like birds in the air, unconscious of themselves.

One of the girls runs to the Miranda, to me.

'Hanna,' she tells me, pointing to her chest, 'I'm Hanna.'

I nod at her, smile, as she uncurls her hand to show me a blue-glass bottle swathed in silver, a pretty little thing.

'You,' she says, 'she's just like you. We made her just like you.'

STARLIGHT
Matti

Oona calls to Ada. Matti feels the warmth of Ada's hand slip from her own cold fingers as she leaves Matti's side to run down the beach to her sister and their father, to examine some seaweed or shell or other sea wonder.

Matti hugs Charlie's too-big jersey close around her, runs her hands over the greasy-wool glide of it, lanolin-smooth, the familiar fat bumps of its twisting triple cables, the pattern her mother taught her long ago. She suddenly feels the cold, feels exposed on the beach, feels the folly of standing in the freezing water, even if only ankle deep. She feels, too, the throb of her head, the acid roil of her guts, smells stale smoke in her hair as she pushes it back from her forehead.

She turns, walks from the water. Her feet are white, bloodless. Down the beach, the girls are kneeling in front of Charlie, who is bent at the waist, looking at whatever Oona and Ada are showing him. Charlie straightens as Matti turns. He lifts his hand, palm forward, not quite a wave. Matti lifts her own hand in response, and smiles, though he will not see her smile from this distance. Her stomach churns again, and she belches, raises her hand to her mouth, swallows the sourness of the night before.

Charlie watches Matti—she feels her husband's gaze, though she cannot see it—as she walks up the beach, into the dunes. She stops to brush her feet over dune grass and pigface, but the sand sticks to her skin as if with glue or paste, or as if embedded, not on the skin, but just under its surface, subdermal.

As she crosses the road, she shakes her head to clear the fuzz of last night's drink, but the shaking feels as if her brain is bouncing off the inside of her skull. She holds the stair rail to steady herself as she climbs the three steps to their house.

On the verandah, Hanna holds a little glass poppet towards their visitor.

'It is—a clever construction,' the woman says, addressing Hanna, with the slight hesitation or awkwardness Matti always notices when she hears her speak in English.

Matti rests her hand upon her daughter's head. 'They are always making things, inventing stories.' Hanna leans into Matti's side, and nods at her mother's words, while all the while her eyes remain fixed on their visitor.

'Always making and inventing is an admirable way to be. I applaud you and your sisters. May you always continue thus.'

Matti watches her daughter blossom under the praise. Hanna shimmies her shoulders, lifts her chin, smiling wide with pride, then the pride shifts thought to query, her mouth chewing a question, tasting it before she spits it out.

Would the Lady come with her, Hanna asks, to the beach, then she says something—about showing her a shell, an eye, a bird—that doesn't quite make sense. Matti interrupts, 'Hanna, heavens, leave Madame be!'

The other woman demurs, but Matti gently insists, 'Off you go, go on,' and Hanna shrugs her shoulders and skips down the steps, away.

'She is no bother,' the woman assures Matti. 'A bright young thing, it's clear.'

'Bright as starlight, and as impossible to bottle.' Matti shuffles her feet, switches to French, searching for words. 'Speaking of bottles, I am sorry for our ... rowdiness last night. My friends and I—'

'Ah, not at all, it is I who must apologise. I hope your

friend—all your friends—did not find me rude. To appear like that, in your midst, and then to leave abruptly. Not to converse, or introduce—'

'Not at all—'

'I find it difficult, you know—'

'Of course, of course. She was curious—my blunt friend—that is all.'

'Curiosity, I understand. To ask, to wonder, is normal.'

'We need speak no more of it.'

They have both turned to face the bay, both rest their hands on the rail of the verandah, both lean on the rail for support. The woman breaks the silence.

'Well, nonetheless, I thank you. For your discretion. Last night, and at all times.'

Matti hears her own stomach turn again, and she raises the back of her hand to her mouth to cover it, to quell the acid stink of herself, cursing her indulgence, her overindulgence, her failure of will. She should know better. She wonders if this is how the woman feels about the scandal that she has fled. If it is shame—at her indulgence, her failure of will—that has sent her across the world, into hiding. She thinks that, perhaps, it's not the case. That the woman retires and retreats as much from fame and recognition of the positive kind as she does from infamy and scandal. That she protects her self, her own self, and holds it close.

When Matti focuses again, the woman seems to be talking about ... flowers. Can that be right? Is Matti mistranslating the words, or is she imagining it? Is it her katzenjammered brain, making false connections? She concentrates, with difficulty, on the woman's words, even as the woman—perhaps seeing Matti's lack of comprehension—switches, mid-sentence, to English.

'—and I find I miss them, so very much. In the streets where I live, they are always for sale, at all times of the year, at markets and so on. We always have flowers at home, bunches of them. The simple, constant pleasure of flowers, so much missed, I find. I know it is winter. But perhaps, here— as at home, even in the dark of winter—there might be early violets. Or some such delight. For colour, and perhaps for scent. And to bring the wild outside into the home.'

Before Matti can answer, Hanna leaps from under the stairs, shouting—*hi, Lady!*—that she will pick them, she and Oona and Ada will pick them, that they know where there are flowers that bloom—*tra la!*—spiky but golden, smelling of cake.

'Hanna!' Matti cautions, but kindly and with good nature, as the girl races away, to the beach, to her sisters.

'Starlight in a bottle, as I said.' Matti sighs. *So tired.*

'No matter, no mind. It is a delight to see her energy. A reminder of what I have to regain.'

'Well, indeed.' Matti turns to the other woman, places her hands together in what she realises is a semblance of prayer, though she means it to indicate determination and professional focus. 'Might we speak on that, for a moment, as doctor and patient?'

'But of course.'

'Your health is much improved.'

'I feel it, I do.'

'The medications are gentler, now, lower in strength, and they seem to manage your pain.'

The woman hesitates before she answers, 'Yes, yes, I find it so,' and her hand waves vaguely into the air, a kind of misdirection, Matti thinks. 'I sleep in the night, now; indeed, not just sleep, but all my numbers are better—you know I keep a chronicle, each day, of my temperature, my inputs and outputs—'

'Yes, yes, you have shown me your notes. And so ... the pain?' Matti asks, again.

'No pain.' She waves her hand again. 'Essentially, no pain.

I breathe more easily. I walk, I dress, I sleep, I wake. Indeed, there is such delight in doing these simple things that I could not manage so recently.' She smiles. 'I even eat, as you have observed.'

'Indeed. I am glad. You are stronger.'

'I am.' She draws herself up, straightens her back.

'It is good to see you returning towards good health.'

'I feel it. And I am grateful. But I should ... I should leave you soon. With my health recovered, I should plan my departure.'

Matti is silent, for a moment, considering what has been said. 'That is your decision. I would say ... that is, my professional opinion is that, while you are better than you were, you are far from fully recovered.'

'But I must leave, I should. I have burdened you for too long already. Such an imposition—'

'Ah, please, it's no burden at all. I insist! It is an honour, and a pleasure, to have you here.'

'You are kind. Our friend Mr Rutherford said so, and now I know it to be true.' She hesitates, then says, softly, quietly, quickly, 'I do not know how much Mr Rutherford told you, or you know, of my affairs. My non-medical affairs, I mean. That is to say, of the scandal concerning my colleague, my friend. There have been stories in the journals and newspapers. It has clouded my life. It has clouded my every decision. But to be here, so very far away. The clouds have lifted. Not just the cloud of my illness, which has lifted thanks to your exemplary care. The clouds of scandal, one might say, feel to have lifted and cleared with this distance. As if all is antipodal, shaken upside down, reversed.'

The woman catches her breath, and raises her index finger to her lips, as if to silence herself, or to silence reply. Then she lifts the finger into the air, for emphasis, to make her point.

'But now I feel it is time. To return to my work. To my daughters. To home.'

'Of course. I understand. But, please, take your time. Your

journey home is long. We must be sure—thoroughly sure—you are well before you embark on it.'

'Yes, yes. Very sensible. And thank you.'

Matti shakes her head, shrugs off the thanks, fixes her eyes on those of the other woman. 'For as long as you wish, you are welcome here. So very, very welcome.'

And then her stomach roils again, and she excuses herself and hurries inside, through the house, and out to the backyard privy, where she kneels and empties herself in heaving, wrenching waves.

UNDARK
The Lady

The mother-doctor-wife left me, rather precipitately. I remain alone with my thoughts on the Miranda. It is true that, as I told her, the pain is for the most part—and in most of my parts—less, but it has not entirely abandoned me. Still, at times, it spikes, surprising me, stopping me in my tracks. I felt the need to minimise the pain in my report to her. I walk, I dress, I told her blithely, as if I do these things with ease. In truth, some days I can only just bear to dress; I can stand, I can bend a little, I can walk across the room. I can, with care, lift my leg to ease my stockings on. I can sit on the chair and, raising my foot carefully, slowly, onto the low woodbox by the fireplace, I can lace my shoe. But I can make myself *seem* well, even on those days when I am not.

Voices flitter from the beach, now, in not-quite-words I cannot catch, high-pitched, darting quickly. Upon three little dark heads that appear from behind the low sand dunes, I see green and white and purple, feathery flowers and dark glossy leaves wound in coronets to crown them. The three of them leap, and then they link hands, form a circle, and whirl down the beach towards where—I see now—their father stands looking out to sea.

I wore a crown of flowers on my wedding day. A simple crown, for a simple service, after which Pierre and I mounted our bright new wedding-present bicycles—our only nuptial extravagance—and off we cycled, bright-eyed, from his dear father's house. That night, the two of us together in that strange bed, I placed the crown of flowers upon my husband, my Pierre.

We lay together in a meadow of buttercups, of periwinkles—how whimsical the English names are!—and I picked sweet violets to thread in his little beard. I cannot think of violets, even now, without the smell of them recalling the smell of him, on our first married day.

And I cannot think of buttercups without recoiling from the memory of the flowers we picked, years later, on another meadow day—one of our last days together, though we did not, could not know it—that remained in the glass on his desk in our home on the Boulevard Kellermann, the flowers still alive, days later, when my beloved was no longer.

A biting cold arrives with the afternoon—as the sea-watching father had, on his return to the house, announced it would—driving everyone off the beach, indoors. Rain threatens, but hangs off in the distance, though the air feels thick with its promise. The household is quiet for the rest of the day, as if making up for last night's revels. The father makes a pot of soup. There is cheese, and bread. There is fruit on the table. There is tea to drink. By the time the rain clouds break, everyone in the house has retired.

In the night, I wake to the spit of gentle rain on the roof, unsure of the hour, aware only of the press of my bladder. I do not like to use the pot in my room, now that I can help it. I wrap a blanket around my shoulders and pass through the dark house en route to the backyard facilities.

When I return minutes later, relieved, the kitchen is lit, though dimly, the overhead light scarcely brighter than a thin candle. One of the three girls is in the kitchen. She sits on the low chaise longue, that they call *daybed*, her slippered feet poking from under the hem of her nightdress, her dark hair pillow-rucked at one side. She looks up at me, her eyes soft with sleep.

'Ah! What do we have here? A little midnight owl chick.'

'Heard something,' she says, yawning wide, screwing her fists into her eyes to rub them awake. 'Heard you. Woke up.'

'I'm sorry I woke you. All is well. All is well. I just …' I wave my hand in the direction of the WC. 'As you are awake now, should you—take a visit yourself? Outside? Before you return to bed?'

'Yes,' she says, and looks at me, and grins. 'The privy. Yes.'

She eases off the daybed on the edge of which she's been perched, tucks her arms across her sparrow-thin chest, shivers. I ease the blanket from around my shoulders. It is spotted with wet from the rain, the quick dash outside.

'You will need this. For the rain and the cold.'

I drape the blanket around her, and it drags to the floor, trailing a metre behind. She looks over her shoulder, takes a slow processional step forward.

'A train. Like a queen,' she says, looking up at me with wide eyes, 'or a bride.'

'Oh, dear, a train! When all you need is an overcoat! Here, let me—'

I fold the blanket in three and drape it again across her tiny shoulders. I take a wooden clothes peg from the line near the stove and peg the blanket-cape closed across her chest.

'There. That should—'

'Dolly,' she says, her fingers on the wooden peg at her breast.

'Do you want—I could—come with you—to the—'

'Oh, no thank you, Lady, I mean *Madame*. No need.' She nods at me, turns, opens the door, then turns her head and looks up through the fringe of her hair. 'But could you—'

'Yes?'

'Would you—'

'Yes, yes?'

'Would you wait? Please? Just while—'

She inclines her head towards the outside door.

'Of course. Of course. Go quickly now. Before the rain worsens. I will wait for you. I will wait right here.'

The little girl—'Hanna. Can't you tell? But we told you the Telling Apart trick! Hanna. Johanna. I am Johanna!'—sits across from me at the table, the two of us in a soft circle of light from overhead. I sip tea; she, warm milk sweetened with honey. We talk in low voices. She speaks, as if in an excited dream, of their Wonderland, of dragons and castles, merry souls and miniature trains, donkeys and camels and parrots and monkeys, a castle, a kiosk, a chute.

'We have a tower,' she tells me. 'It's enormous! Our father says it's just like Mon-sewer Eiffel's tower in Paree!'

'I am certain it is grand.'

'Just wait until you see it!' She tells me of a great spectacle—the Winter Gala, she calls it—and the many performers assembled. When she speaks of singing and dancing and posing, her eyes shine. I cannot tell if her talk of the Wonderland Gala is a dream, a memory, or in anticipation.

'And fireworks! Of course! The great grand finale. Mr Bickerton's a bloody genius, our father says. The best in all the country. The best in all the world, probably! Our father says Mr Bickerton's not just a pirate parrot pieman pyro—' she takes a big breath, 'py-ro-tech-nician, he's a real scientist!' She smiles at me, sideways, slywise, as she speaks. 'A magician of chemistry!'

'Well,' I say, 'a magician, a scientist *and* a genius. Mr Bickerton must be, indeed, remarkable.'

Hanna tips her head back to drain the milk from her teacup—that pale throat, the sweet softness of this child, so like my girls, my sweet girls, when they have woken in the night—then wipes her mouth with her hand, wipes her hand down her nightdress.

'We heard our mother say,' she says, looking me in the eye, 'that you are a magician of chemistry too. Like Mr Bickerton, but without the fireworks, is what our mother's friend Ernest says.'

I laugh, without thinking of laughing, and it feels like honey in my throat, sweet, nourishing.

'Yes, yes, it is true, my work is in chemistry, which is sometimes like magic, and sometimes like fireworks, but mostly plain hard work, in truth.'

'Oh,' she nods, looking serious, as though looking serious is called for at the mention of hard work.

'But, yes, there is magic in my work. The most astonishing, the most beautiful.' I close my eyes, and all glows blue.

I rest my closed fist on the table, lay it there, fingertips facing upwards.

'Imagine there is a light, a faint glow lining the tracks where my fingers meet.'

I unfurl my fingers, slow, slow.

'And imagine: there in the palm of my hand is a little glass bottle, a phial, glass-stoppered, wax-sealed, fairy-sized, and in it a grain that glows like moonlight's palest silvered blue. Imagine,' I tell her, 'the glow of it, of the air around it.'

Her eyes are wide, watching me. Her face seems to glow in reflection.

'Radium,' I tell her. 'This wondrous light. It is radium.'

'Oho! Radium shines like sunshine!' She butterflies her fingers apart to frame her face with a beaming smile, looking as if she's solved a particularly tricky riddle. 'Our father always says so, whenever he shines his boots! But how do you get it in the little bottle?'

Ignoring that which makes no sense—her riddle of sunshine and boots, whatever can it mean?—I talk to her of the wonder of radioactivity, the infant science—this beautiful science—that I have raised with all my strength. I talk of the strange and cruel families that the radio elements form, each daughter born from her mother substance, transformed. I tell her of invisible forces, bones revealed, of the showing of shapes of things inside things. I talk of my dear husband, how he would illuminate learned gatherings and informal parties, lectures and events, with a phial of radium—that precious grain, that fairylight, spiritlight, homelight—that he would draw from his pocket and hold in his hand, a little lamp lighting the way. And I think—but do not tell her so—of my beloved husband and of nights, long past, when we two would walk the night-lit streets from our house on Boulevard Kellermann to our laboratory, and once inside that dear old miserable old cold shed we would not light the lamps, but would stare, instead, at our own wonderland lit blue, the moonlight glow from the shed's many glass bottles and phials quite bright enough to read by, or to love; the showing of shapes. Our great joy, always new to us.

'It must be beautiful! A darling light!'

'It is. It is.'

'Like a little lamp!'

I want to tell her more, feed her luminous curiosity. I tell her of the finest of fine three-hair brushes licked and sipped to a point to paint dials and numbers on watches and instruments, to illuminate, with the special radium paint, called Undark.

'Undark! Undark! What a wonder!'

It is made, I tell her, in America, where money is no object.

'*Ahhh-MEH-Di-Kah!*' she shouts, her little fist punching the air. 'Where our mother learned all about babies!'

'Shh shh! We mustn't wake your family!'

'Yes, yes, quiet, yes.' She leans towards me, across the table, speaking in a whisper I can only just hear. 'But just imagine! A room painted with AhhhMEHdikan Undark! It would be one of the Wonders of the World. Our father would love to have such a room at Wonderland.'

For a moment we are both quiet, lost in the thought of a

room, a whole room, lit with Undark, lit with radium.

'But it is very costly,' I tell her, 'for even a tiny amount. Radium. So rare, it is not possible. Just a dream.'

'Well. Perhaps, perhaps, a pretending of Undark. A room painted blue. The darling blue of radium.'

'Perhaps. Perhaps.'

We sit, still, in the strange light of our reverie.

She yawns, a great wide yawn, and I realise the time, and the circumstances.

'Well now,' I say. 'It's late, and I am tired, and you must go back to bed without waking your sisters.'

'Of course! Of course!' She backs towards her room, a hushing finger lifted to her lips.

I raise my own finger, whisper across the room to her.

'Goodnight, Hanna.'

'Goodnight, Lady,' she whispers in reply.

The rain has stopped, though wind still pushes against the walls and windows of the house. I wrap my blanket around my shoulders, clench it warm across my chest. I take up the walking stick that the mother-doctor-wife has lent me, walk from my room and turn into the hallway, and—gently, quietly—open the front door. I step into the night-time outside, into the smell of it, the wet feel of it.

I take four steps down from the front door to the ground below, the path of shells and stones gathered from the beach. Shell grit presses through the thin slippers into the underneath of my feet, as if to test whether I am still alive. I feel the prick and cut of tiny edges, little glittering sharpnesses in the night. The clouds scud across the sky, pushed by wind that must blow strong and cold all the way from southern ice. I pull the blanket close at my throat, but the wind still cuts through. I feel it on my neck, like fingers, or rope, or a too-tight scarf.

Across the water a light blinks, far away, on the other side of the harbour entrance. There, it blinks again. I wait and yes, it blinks again, and as if one-two-three-hypnotised I recall my daughters, my husband—my family—our summer in Normandy, the detail of it. I recall a lighthouse scanning and sweeping the water, light streaming into the window of our rented house. Our daughters on the beach, brown limbs and red swimsuits rolled in silver sand. Walking the sandy causeway to Le Mont Saint-Michel, on the day of the solar eclipse. My darling, magicking the eclipse through special lenses, for the children, for himself, for me.

The lighthouse blinks again, undarking the winter night. I cherish the cold seeping into my bones. I cherish the prick of these shells, these stones, in the soles of my feet. That I can feel their local pain, now, tells me that the big pain, the always pain, the chronic pain has dulled, that I am getting better. I can start to feel the world around me. Feel pain, and the absence of pain. I can start to return to the world, my work, my life, and to my daughters.

A lighthouse warns sailors: do not approach. Danger lies here.

Or, to look at it another way: here is the path to safety.

Here, traveller, let me light your way home.

MIRANDA
Matti

Autumn's crisp tail, sliding swift towards winter, marked their visitor's arrival; now, solstice fast approaches. Just when winter's drawing in, the weather slips—as it is wont to do in this place—all out of season, upside down. Days dawn fine, warm, and dry, and stay that way until dusk, as early as it falls, brings cold nights that match the season and the days' short length. Matti feels the lift this weather brings to everybody's mood, and to their circumstances, as if the year has gifted a reprieve, every weight become light, every darkness turned light. Charlie brings unexpected news, of backers and buyers, punters and players, fireworks and finessing finances. He taps his finger against the side of his nose, waltzes Matti around the kitchen table, and confirms that the Winter Gala will proceed, a grand splash to launch the Wonderland Winter Season.

Their daughters, always bright and beautiful, are fired incandescent with this news, burning with delight and determination to perform again at Wonderland, as if the Gala's success depends upon it; Charlie rarks them up, spins their expectations skywards. They rope Matti in, describe their costumes to her, stars and colours and shine, and Matti finds the wherewithal—from fabric and pennies and time she has stashed—to start cutting and stitching and fitting and trimming, day by day, trouser by trouser, stitch by loving stitch. Even Matti's work at the hospital goes unseasonably, unreasonably, unusually well: every birthing mother healthy, every birth an easy one, each baby slipping bonny, bawling and bold into life as if they were, well, born to it.

'The whole week's been like a fairy tale,' Matti says to Wilma Reddy at the end of their night shift as she and the midwife change out of their soiled work clothes and into their clothes for home.

'Almost too good to be true,' Wilma Reddy lifts her eyebrows and widens her eyes at Matti, before she's engulfed by the woolly black jersey she pulls on over her head.

The woman, their visitor, her patient at home, has developed the habit, just this past week, of walking on the beach, her health much improved. They walk each day, now, together, while the weather holds.

'To gain stamina,' Madame says, 'and for the marvellous air.' She breathes in deep; they both do. Salt and ozone, the sulphur burn and mineral tang of decaying treasures on the tide. 'I have always loved the ocean, the beach. It smells of holidays, yes? No, of course not for you, living here. This is not holiday, but life, for you, here in your Worser Bay.'

'Quotidian life, indeed.'

'Worser Bay.' She rolls the words on her tongue, carefully enunciating—almost whistling—the leading W. 'Worser. An odd name, no?'

'Named for a man of the sea, they say.'

The woman blows air through her lips, smiles. 'I would call it Better Bay. Much Better Bay. Or Good Health Bay.' Matti has rarely seen her smile or heard her pun. It adds to her body of evidence, her observations of the woman's return to good health.

Matti's motivation in accompanying their visitor on her rambles had been, initially, one of duty and caution. *The woman is in my care.* Should she stumble, should she fall, should she fail, Matti would be by her side—*should* be by her side, *must* be by her side—for support. But as, each day, her patient proves the rudeness of her health, as she starts to outstride Matti on the hard-to-walk sand, as she walks without puffing or pausing for breath, Matti realises: the woman is well. *Soon she will no longer need me.* She is becoming quite well.

As they walk on the beach, they talk, make connections. The woman seems more free in her speech when she is outdoors and, indeed, talks much to Matti about her love of what she calls *the wild*.

'We left the city whenever we could, often by bicycle. I love—I love very much—to bare my feet. To feel the sand.'

'You can do that now.'

'It seems strange in another land, somehow. So far from home. Shall I? Should I?'

'You should. We shall.'

They both sit on the sand and loosen their laces. Matti kneels at the woman's feet and helps her ease her boots off. They each sling their boots, tied at the laces, over their shoulders—one to the front, one hanging down their back—and resume their tramp along the fine line of the morning's high tide, feeling shells scratch under their feet and the cut-glass squeak of wet sand, the feather of fine tidecast seaweed.

The woman says, 'Your daughter, Hanna, was telling me yesterday, on the Miranda, that—'

'—Miranda?'

'Yes, the front of your house, the—how would I call it?—balcony, the covered entranceway, the pavilion. Miranda, I have heard you call it.'

'"Admired Miranda!"' says Matti. 'Oh, Madame, I must learn to enunciate! Not *Miranda*, as in *The Tempest*, but *verandah*. With a V.'

'Verandah? Verandah! Oh, I do not know this word.'

'A word from the Indies, perhaps, much used in Australia where my husband grew up, and he has brought the word here. Admired verandah!'

'Ah, verandah, just so. I thought *Miranda* from your Monsieur Shakespeare, for shipwreck, for being on the pavilion so close to the sea is like being on the deck of a ship. Or *Miranda* from the Latin, for wonder, perhaps.'

'"Worth what's dearest to the world!"'

'The very opposite of Worser, in fact.'

'An apposite opposite. I think I'll call the verandah *Miranda* forever more.' Matti steps in front of the woman, walks backwards in front of her, bows a big stage bow as she walks. 'Thank you for mishearing, madame le professeur. Merci pour *Miranda*, malentendu.'

'De rien, madame.'

Matti looks sidewise at her, smiles, slips her arm between the woman's arm and her waist, so their elbows link, warm, companionable, and their strides fall into an easy matching rhythm. They walk in step, in time with one another.

LUMINOUS
The Lady

Another glorious day dawns, crisp and bright, to match my bright new mood. In my room I read, I write (marvelling that I can sit, and read, and write; marvelling that I can marvel). As the morning progresses, the house around me empties—the children to school, the father to his Wonderland, the mother-doctor-wife to do errands, she says—until, once more, all is quiet again, as quiet as night.

I stand at the window, filled with wonder that I can stand, at the window.

I feel well.

After so long, and so much pain, this week I feel quite well, entirely well.

The return to my body of some semblance of health feels miraculous.

I dress in a dark wool dress, thick stockings underneath. I button my winter coat, pull on gloves, push my hat down low on my head, lift the collar of my coat, and walk out the front door, across the Miranda, down the steps, and—can it really be, for the first time without accompaniment?—I cross the road, onto this beach.

The air is delicious on my face. I open my mouth, and taste the day on my tongue, feel its chill sweeten my teeth. There is no one on the beach, not up, not down, no boats on the water: there is no one. I lower myself to sit on the sand, the low dunes rising behind me. The sand is fine, dry, the colour of bone. I lie back in the sand and dune grass, and look at the sky, and remember other skies. I remember, again, I remember: meadow flowers in the basket on the handlebars of my bicycle, and in my straw hat, and pinned at my breast. Our honeymoon—not that we had time to waste on fripperies, on nonsense—and yet we did, we did, we bicycled, we picnicked, we walked, we loved. We lay in the grass and looked at the sky, then.

The sand now is soft-hard-soft under me. I sift my fingers through it, feel it stick and slip. Silicon, calcium carbonate, the bones and shells of tiny sea creatures, the crumblings of great cliffs, and of the Earth, and of islands. All reduced to this. This dry softness. The dune grass pillows me, and I lean into it. I close my eyes, to dream of other beaches, other skies, other bones, other softness, other horizontality.

I open my eyes to the ripe smell of fish, and human. A face is upside down above me. I blink, take a moment to observe this interesting face. The life that has been lived shows in its lines and furrows and, yes, even in its smell.

Interesting eyes blink once at me, then the face withdraws, and I see that the face is attached to the man I have observed—but only from a distance—from my window, looking out over the bay. He is the man from whom the husband-father buys fish from a wet sack, shaking hands to seal the deal.

'Good morning,' I say. 'Do not be alarmed. I am not dead, merely resting.' I prop myself on my elbows, then lift myself to sit on the sand.

He replies—surprising me—in that beloved tongue, and I brighten at the sound. I answer him in the same language, extending my hand, and he bends to take it. We shake hands and introduce ourselves. He lowers himself to sit by my side, and we sit on the sand and talk.

It is good to converse again with fluency in the language of my daughters, my husband, this murmuring tongue. I have missed it. The doctor-mother-wife speaks a little, but—she admits—at the level of a child. She only has words of the surface, lacking depth, nuance; she shifts always to English when she speaks of medical matters. My mouth makes different shapes when I speak this language, and I feel it in my chest, deeper than when I speak English, though not as low and deep and heartfelt as when I speak my mother's tongue, my father's tongue, my sisters' tongue, my own.

I have heard the little girls call this man Louis, but his name, he informs me, is Léopold. His accent is formal, older, from last century. His voice is slow, as if he is unaccustomed to using it. It lilts, oceanic, wave-like, salted. He smells of fish and seaweed, urine and tobacco, a heady mix, and not altogether unpleasant. He dresses in *bleu de travail*, moleskin worn smooth as velvet, blue faded to the colour of the sky. He seems unimaginably old, though his voice—sweet, high, clear—makes him seem to me uncannily young, or perhaps I mean ageless.

We speak in that language, back and forth. I learn that he has always lived by the sea, or sailed or worked upon it, and that he has lived here, in this southern land, for decades, now, he says. Down the way. Karaka Bay. There's a place, he tells me, where he stays, a little cave. Those girls, he says, those three, and his fingers twitch a cross at his breast, good girls, kind. The mother, the father, good people, fine people. He rolls up the leg of his trousers and points to a neat, long scar on his shin. A fish, a hook, a knife, and pain. The mother is a seamstress, a surgeon, a saint. Good people, kind people.

He comes from the north of the old country, and I tell him I know that coast. I know the light as it falls across the land. I know its plants, its flowers, its rocks and birds. The castle on the water, the causeway that leads to it, and that does not, and that does once more when the tide falls. I tell him a story, of my daughters on that beach, and my sister. And my husband.

He looks to the south, nods. He tells of change, of rain, of going now, and of shelter. He stands, smacks his palms together, then offers me his hand and I take it in my own and rise to his gentle lift, until I am standing beside him. I smack my own hands free of sand, then wipe them on the sides of my skirt. I put forward my right hand once more, and we shake hands in farewell and acknowledgement of a fellow traveller well met, and in anticipation of meeting again. *Au revoir. Au revoir.*

I watch him walk down the beach, away, then I turn back to the house, as the air chills, the sky darkens, and the weather turns, suddenly southerly. I reach the Miranda, and shelter, just as the rain starts sheeting.

The weather is relentless. All week, rain angles at the house, wind swirling so the rain seems to come from everywhere at once. I miss my wild beach walks with the mother-doctor-wife, on which we have formed an easy companionship, walking side by side—often arm in arm—into the bracing wind. I shiver at the weather's sound, though the fire I have lit is warming the room.

The front door bangs, footsteps shudder past my room. Tiny voices sharp with cold siren through the house, and I cannot help but follow them.

A trail of wet clothes leads down the hallway and into the kitchen, where the little girls stand naked by the stove, shivering pink as three newborn mice. They pass a linen towel between them and hop up and down, switching and turning to roast themselves warm. They are not shy, or shamed, nor should they be.

They got caught in the rain on the way home from school, they tell me as they hop and dry and warm themselves. The rain washed them wee wee wee wee all the way home, like the little piggy from the market.

'So I see,' I say.

Squealing like that very same little piggy, the three of them pass me, padding by naked to their room. There is no sign of their mother to quell their squealing—she worked a shift at the hospital last night, and she must still be sleeping—and their father has gone to Wonderland, it seems. So I hush them gently, and busy myself boiling water and finding cups, mothering as I have not for so long.

They return with arms full of bright clothes that they drop on the floor by the stove. They slither into bloomers and vests, shirts and warm woollens, toe their feet into canvas slippers. I place three cups of sweet milky tea on the table, and pour a fourth cup, black, for myself.

They sit at the table, their hands clasped to warm around the teacups and ask me if I feel better now.

'Ah,' I say, 'I think, yes, I am much better now. Your mother is a fine doctor.'

They clap their hands and tell me she's the best doctor in the whole country, and possibly the whole world, and that they are almost never sick. They blow on the tea, sip loudly. Their feet swing under the table. They seem to be constantly in motion.

One of them—the curious one, Hanna—asks, if I am better, will I come with them?

I find Hanna's unwavering gaze unsettling. Perhaps it reflects my own manner, which—I am told—some find overly intense.

'Come where?' I ask, though I think I know the answer.

'To Wonderland!' they shout in unison. They leap from the bench and crowd around me, speaking at once, of their father's plans for the Winter Gala, and that I must must must come with them, that Wonderland cures all ills.

'Well, perhaps,' I say. 'Perhaps I could—'

They tell me I must; that they'll sing, and dance. They talk of fireworks and sideshows, camels and cream buns.

'Perhaps I will—'

The three of them perch on the bench, still for the moment it takes them to drain their tea, noisily sucking as if they are straining tea leaves through their teeth. Then they leap up again and begin to hoot once more.

'Hush hush,' I tell them. 'Your mother is sleeping—'

But it's hard, they try and fail to whisper, to keep excitement quiet. They hop around the kitchen like little rabbits, their fingers to their mouths to signal quiet. They have work to do, they say, a song, a dance, to rehearse for the Gala.

'Well perhaps,' I say, 'your bedroom is the place? For quiet, and for rehearsals?'

Tra-la! Of course! they say, and the three of them bow, and thank me for the tea, then they run through the door that leads into their bedroom. They slam it closed and all I can hear is laughter, a sound like the song of parson birds, or water rippling over rocks in a stream.

They are strange little things. I have heard it said that all children are beautiful. But these three are not. I cannot be certain what it is that brings me to this observation. I think it is something to do with the uncanny, with mirroring, and its unsettling effect on the brain.

I waltz three kitchen chairs—one chair at a time, nodding as I change partners—across the room, so they circle the stove as if ready to watch a performance. I dress the chairs in the triplets' wet clothes, that I pick up—stooping and straightening carefully, slowly—from the floor. I imagine: making my stiff arms and tight shoulders work and shift to lift my own dress over my head, unbuttoning my chemise and combinations, unlacing shoes, rolling off stockings, leaving them all in a pile by the stove. I imagine: running out into the rain, running over the road and across the sand and leaping, naked, into the cold water of the bay. I imagine: my arms pushing through water luminous with microscopic creatures.

~ ~ ~

I do not—of course I do not—strip, nor swim. The kitchen is warm. I stoke the fire and settle by the stove, losing track of time as I lose myself in letters. I write first to my dear sister—signalling my intention to begin plans to return, soon, soon, though swearing her to secrecy for the moment, until plans progress—and then to each of my daughters. I write to the tattoo of six little feet drumming, three voices counting time, singing rhyme, in the next room. Dah dee dum, dah dee DUM, dah dee DUM di-dee DUM di-dee DUM. Floorboards thud, my teacup rattles on its saucer.

I finish the letter to my Little One, sign off in the usual way—your sweet Mé, dear Mé, sending you kisses—and fold it, write her name across the face of the paper. Dah dee DUM. I bundle all three letters together, address them in my sister's name, ready to catch the next day's post. I cap my pen, align it with the spine of my notebook. Dah dee dum, dah dee DUM. My finger taps in triplet time on the tabletop, my foot taps on the floor. Dah dee DUM di-dee DUM di-dee DUM DUM DUM. Though I sent them to their room to rehearse, I find that I am curious, after all, to see what these little ones are up to.

I stand, smooth my skirt, tuck my hair behind my ear. Dah dee DUM. I cross the kitchen, rest my hand on the doorhandle. Di-dee DUM. I make a throat-clearing noise and open the door into the triplets' bedroom.

Three little bodies freeze in tableau, as if captured photographically, in light and dark and grains of silver salt. Three faces lift, smile wide at me in welcome, and delight. They are dressed in woollen jerseys, over roomy bloomers for ease of movement. Set up on the bed, in semblance of an audience, a motley crew of dolls and figurines watches the performance.

The little girls aha! in welcome and ask if they can show me their dance.

'Of course! I hoped you might,' I say.

Hanna steps towards me, takes my hand, while the other two—Ada and Oona, though I cannot tell who is whom—

clear a space for me to sit on their bed among the strange dolls, the stick figures.

They will show me the start of their winter dance, their midwinter song, they tell me, and they ask me if I might count them in. Di-dee DUM di-dee DUM di-dee DUM DUM DUM.

They dance for me, and when they stop, all out of breath and heaving chests, they tell me it's a midwinter dance, especially for the Winter Gala, and they talk of stars in the sky, and midwinter deep, and the longest night of all.

And I remember, and I tell them, of the midwinter time just past, on the other side of the world—imagine!—when my sister and my Big Girl and I went to Sweden, where I had gone one time before, with my dear husband when he was still alive.

'A time of special rejoicing,' I say, 'held on the year's longest night. Imagine hundreds of women, each wearing a crown of lighted candles, heads held high and careful as they dance, the colours of their costumes vivid in the wavering candlelight, reflecting on the snow.'

The triplets marvel at the thought of snow. They have heard of it, they tell me, and think it must be like vanilla ice cream, delicious and for celebrating.

Then, 'Imagine,' I say, 'that shortest day, when the sun stays low and cold. Imagine that here, on the other side of the world, that shortest day is your longest day, the middle of your summer—'

'The world is a wonder,' Hanna interrupts, rapt.

'It is. A very wonder.'

They sigh and wish aloud for candled crowns, though they know, they say, without asking that their father would think it too dangerous. But fireworks are even better than candles, they tell me.

'I do not think crowns of fireworks sound sensible.'

No no, they say, fireworks are crowns in the sky, and they twirl again, dancing fireworks and candles and dark and light all at the same time, and the brightest one—Hanna—takes my hand, and Oona and Ada take my hands, too, and we dance, all four of us, out of their bedroom and into the kitchen, whirling dervish-like, wondrous.

WATCH
Matti

A rhythmic thumping rouses Matti from deepest sleep, and she stumbles, bleary-eyed and muddleheaded, from her bed. She has worked ten nights in a row at the hospital, taking as many shifts as she can. The extra money, though little, is welcome. She is tired, so tired, and the rain does not help.

There in the kitchen the three children and the visitor hold hands and dance ring-a-ring-a-rosy, pocketful-of-posy. Hanna holds the woman's hand and watches her intently, copies her moves. Matti follows her daughter's gaze and observes the woman too: her near-recovered patient, her treasured charge, her brisk-striding beach-walking companion, Madame Skwodovska, Mrs Miranda Malentendu.

In the dark of the hallway, Matti stands and watches them all, bathed in light and joy. Then Ada catches her eye, and she cheers and calls Matti's name, and all of them turn then, and cheer Matti—even their visitor cheers her, and calls her name—when she enters the kitchen. Ada comes to her and takes her hand, and all three of them curtsey.

'Will you won't you—'

'Please and thank you—'

'Come and join the dance!'

Matti joins the circle, and they all spin and spin and spin.

Wonderland

Cast off your dignity!

WONDERLAND! WINTER! WONDERLAND!
AT MIRAMAR!
WONDERLAND! WINTER! WONDERLAND!

THE MEGGA OF MERRY SOULS!

WONDERLAND by night
is an exquisitely beautiful sight!
Extending high in the dark night sky
myriad sparkling lights!

EVERYTHING IN FULL WORKING ORDER
for
THE RETURN OF WONDERLAND
THIS GALA WINTER SEASON

GHUTE THE GHUTE
and try the
EXHILARATION of the TOBOGGAN!
HELT THE SKELTER!

See yourself as you might have been in the
LAUGHING GALLERY!

Experience the WEIRD SENSATIONS of
the MAGIC SWING!
the ROOM OF ILLUSIONS!
the HOUSE OF TROUBLE!
and the KATZENJAMMER CASTLE!

See our very own EIFFEL TOWER!

CAMELS! CAMELS!
A touch of the East!

Lunches and Teas can be obtained at the
Japanese Tea Kiosk in the grounds.

WINTER GALA CONCERT!
FRIDAY! FRIDAY! FRIDAY!
FOR ONE NIGHT ONLY
AT 5 P.M.

Featuring
MIRAMAR'S TRIPLE STAR
THREE LITTLE MIRAMAR MAIDS
with
MUSIC! MUSIC! MUSIC!
from the WONDERLAND BAND

Followed by
FIREWORKS! FIREWORKS! FIREWORKS!
A GRAND PYROTECHNIC DISPLAY

Cast off your dignity,
jump off your base of solemnity.

Come and enjoy yourselves at
WONDERFUL WONDERLAND!
The Mecca of Merry Souls.

FERRY STEAMER
A ferry steamer will leave the Ferry Wharf for Miramar
at 12 p.m. and 2 p.m., returning from Miramar
at 4 p.m. and 8 p.m.

TODAY IS A WONDERLAND DAY
Triplets

We wake in the dark, when we can feel the sun beginning to rise. We leap from bed, and creep to the verandah to catch it.

Our blanket wraps the three of us, huddled tight together so just our faces show. We've brought Queen Cuttle and Mother Brown and Lady Bluebottle, and we hold them in the blanket, too, to keep them warm like us. We face to the east, across the harbour to the hills. And we watch now for the light to show itself above the hills and the water and the world.

We see just the glow of it, at first, just the lightening of the sky. Just the outline of the hills, now, out of the ink of night. And the lightening is and is and is, but we can't see it happening even though we're watching. We close our eyes and open them quickly, to try to sneak up on it. But there it is, and there it is, and there it goes and here it comes, yes, the day is coming up, and the sun, behind the hills. Ada waves her hand, commands the clouds that clot the sky. Oona hears the voice of the hills, and of the sun. Hanna sees ripples on the water, and knows the wind and how it changes.

And we all wonder how the world knows when the day begins.

We know the world turns (once every day, that's what the Lady told us), and we know the Earth spins round the sun (once a year, she said, though it makes no sense to think it, so we just believe). But where is the when of the time and the place in the world when one day changes to the next? When it's daytime today here in the Antipathies, it's yesterday in London, or night-time in Sweden, or tomorrow or next week or yesterday in our mother's diary. It's all very confusing, a riddle without an answer.

And just as we're pondering that riddle, at the moment when our minds have turned away from watching, the sun launches up over the hills, and it hits our faces and makes us glow, and Queen Cuttle and Mother Brown and Lady Bluebottle glow, too, and we close our eyes and we can still see the sun, that glow, that darling light, glowing our eyelids blood-red, sun-gold.

This day, finally, has begun.

Tonight is the Wonderland Winter Gala concert. We are as ready as ready can be. We have practised our new song-and-dance on our own until we know the sounds and steps in our sleep. We have even practised—just once, thought that's all we needed—with Mr Devenish Ruby and his Wonderland Band Piano, so we know all the cues. We have practised until our song-and-dance shines like the starry trousers our mother has made us, iridescent lizard-green for Ada, the brightest moonlight silver-white for Oona, and deepest ultraviolet for Hanna, stitched all over with ink-blue and rich gold stars. The World's Most Magnificent Trousers!

We'll show that we're still Miramar's Triple Star, like the fireworks that Mr Bickerton made for us in the summer of our birth. As stars blaze across the sky, so we three will blaze across the stage. The brightest stars that Miramar has seen! We are Miramar's Matariki (Mrs R's told us all about it), the starry sisters of Pleiades, rising now in the midwinter sky.

~ ~ ~

We creep home from the beach in the darling dawn, tuck our six icy feet back in bed and cuddle in under the quilt, before we're missed.

The World's Most Magnificent Trousers are clean and packed, and so are the horrible horsehair wigs and our old but serviceable kimonos, all folded into a basket at the foot of our bed, and ready to go.

Our song is as close to perfect as it will ever be.

Our hair is washed clean, our shoes are polished (with our father's tin of Radium boot polish, that shines like sunshine), our eyes are bright, our voices strong.

The sun is climbing above the hills.

Today is a Wonderland day.

GRAVE
Matti

Matti rolls over into the dip in the bed still warm from Charlie's presence. It's early still, barely light. Her body craves more sleep as an addict craves their drug. She hears her husband's footsteps in the kitchen, hears the kettle, hears the stove door clang. This is the sound of him filling space, killing time; this is the sound of Charlie's nerves. The day ahead means so much to him. The day, the gesture, the dream.

They had argued—she would even say *fought*—last night. Hissing voices whispered in the dark about folly and grand gestures, fireworks for heaven's sake. It all comes down to the usual thing, money, or—more precisely—its lack. Matti told Charlie this, and yet she did not tell him—though she had meant to—quite how tired she is, how tired of it all.

And yet, and yet. She has watched their girls practise their steps. How serious they are and how joyful, all at once. How much this means to them, how hard they've worked. How magnificent they are in their costumes, that Ada helped her stitch—she's good, careful, she has an eye for it, for mending and making, for what needs to be done—while Oona and Charlie worked on dance steps and staging, and Hanna hummed the music underneath it all. Her spirits lift to see them.

And so she will roll over again today, yes, she will roll over and pretend that nothing is wrong, and she will support Charlie's dreams—this Wonderland fever, his own unshakeable addiction—for as long as she can, and the girls will dance and sing and celebrate, and they will show their visitor—her patient, her charge, Madame Miranda—the whole damned spectacle, and Matti will smile and hold everything together. Of course she will. She always does.

Wonderland, Wonderland, when will it end? When will it ever end? When will he see that it must?

The bedroom door opens, closes. Matti hears him dress in the darkness, the slick glide of silk on linen, the rasp of stiff gilt braid. Last night he laid out his clothes with such care, with reverence. Now a low beam of light catches on a button, flashes brilliant in the dark room, then all is dark again. He whispers, so quiet she almost misses it, a low husk of voice, 'Tilda, Matilda mine,' but she does not answer him. He leans over her, traces the back of his finger down her cheek to her chin, then touches the tip of the finger to her lips and holds it there, light as magic. She lifts her hand to his face, feels it cold and smooth-shaven, but she does not speak. She murmurs, feigning sleep, and he turns from her and leaves the room.

In the hallway, Charlie talks with their visitor, their voices hushed so Matti hears only fragments. She rolls over, hugs the pillow against herself, the cool of it down her belly. She is not yet ready to think about the day. Wrangling the children; wrangling Mrs Miranda; mothering, smiling, hosting, doctoring. It will be easier if she—their visitor—comes to Wonderland today, so Matti doesn't have to worry about leaving her alone. She starts to mentally calculate medicines, doses and timing—but no, no, she has all morning to worry about that.

They are still talking, in the hallway. She hears Charlie, 'Wonderful Wonderland,' then something she misses, and then, 'Carnival Charlie Loverock!' as if he's announcing himself. Oh, Charlie. Charlie. Forever spruiking, performing. He never stops.

She hears the front door open, then close, voices on the verandah, footsteps on the stairs.

She pulls the bedclothes over her head, and in the muffled dark she hears her stomach roil, her blood pulse, she hears her own heart beat.

Today is a Wonderland day, heaven help us.

DARK GLASSES
The Lady

The day dawns, fine, sunny, cold. I hear the father-husband, early, before the rest of the household has risen. He passes me in the hallway, donning his hat, patting his chest, fishing fingers into coat pockets, holding a great ring of keys in one hand.

'I'm off now! Will I see you at Wonderland?'

'Perhaps. It is a fine day.'

'My little ratbags. My girls. They'll dance.'

'They have told me. I would like to see their performance.'

'It means so much to them,' he says, and I cannot read the meaning in the look upon his face.

'It is clear,' I say. 'Their enthusiasm is matched only by their talent.'

'Indeed, indeed.' A shadow passes his face, just briefly, then he shakes his head. 'Well, I must away. I hope you will come. You could see the Eiffel Tower, you know, just like home. It has the best view of the fireworks, though not for the faint of heart, nor feared of heights. Ah, never mind. Wonderful Wonderland, the Mecca of Merry Souls!' He sweeps off his hat, bows low, extending his arm to the side. 'Carnival Charlie Loverock, at your service, Madame. Mrs Doctor Loverock will show you where to find me. But now,' he fishes his watch from his waistcoat pocket, 'I'm late. I will see you,' he replaces his watch, 'at Wonderland.'

I smile, nod. I follow him out the door and onto the Miranda. I lean on the railing as I watch him leave.

The household is soon crackling and bustling, busting with noise and movement. I try to keep out of the way. I stay in my room, write two short letters. The sun is up above the hills. The landscape, familiar now, fills my window: the great dark mass of those hills, the curve of them across the water, the sun lighting them, carving sharp across the hill face.

And there, the little girls hurl themselves down the hallway once more. The energy of these children! If only it could be captured. Starlight in a bottle. Luminescence. Radiance. Imagine it harnessed, turned around. It could power a city. It could power their Wonderland.

A truck pulls up, right outside the house. Miss Deere descends from the cabin, walks up to the house, knocks on the door. The little girls race to let her in and rustle her down to the other end of the house. I feel compelled to follow their noise.

The kitchen is full of women and girls. The mother-doctor-wife is packing fabric, colourful, iridescing, from the table into a basket. One of the triplets helps her, mirrors her. The midwife, Mrs Reddy—oh, I think by now you can call me Wilma, she says, go on, do—sits smoking on the daybed. Miss Deere is on the floor on all fours, one triplet on her back, and one walking at her head, leading the pack of them around the kitchen. As they pass, the fabric-packing triplet leaves her mother's side and mounts Miss Deere, clasping her sister tight around the waist.

I stand at the doorway, watching them all, and I cannot help but smile, a smile that becomes a half-swallowed laugh.

The mother-doctor-wife turns to me. In the moment before she reflects my smile, I see how very tired she is. Perhaps I have been too caught in my own fatigue to notice hers before now. She covers it, smothers it, in an instant.

'Madame Professor! Welcome to the madhouse.'

The children shout that they are a sheik and a prince and a famous ballooniste, and Miss Deere shakes the two of them off her back and all three tumble on the floor, and then rise prettily to take a bow, and all we women applaud.

'Girls, get ready! Go on!' their mother tells them. Then she turns again to me. 'Will you come with us, Madame? Have you decided? It's such a beautiful day. Warm, fine. You may rest in my husband's office, if you need to. I had planned to be there the whole day. For the girls, of course, but also to enjoy it all.'

'I would be a nuisance—'

'No, no, not at all. Jane, Miss Deere, will drive us. There's plenty of room. Though of course, if you prefer to stay at home, I could stay with you, or come back to—'

The penny drops—as I have heard her husband say—and I realise I will be less bother to her if I attend with them. Of course I will come, I tell her, of course.

'Excellent! Now, perhaps, if I might suggest, before we go—'

And she leads me to my room and pours pale liquid into a glass, and I drink it down, drink all its thick familiar sweetness. I gather my coat, my scarf, settle my hat upon my head.

Ready now, while the house is still bustling, the thick liquid easing through me, I walk out onto the Miranda. Miss Deere is there, leaning on the rail, looking out towards the water. She turns, nods at me, blows smoke from the side of her mouth. I lift my hand to shade my squinting eyes.

'It's bright,' I say. 'Beautiful.'

She ferrets her hand in the top pocket of her long coat, holds out to me a pair of spectacles. The lenses are circles of dark green glass, the rims made of wire.

'Borrow them if you like.'

They feel heavier than I imagined. There are flaps of leather at the sides, as if to keep out dust. I lift them, fit them over my eyes, adjust them behind my ears. The light changes, darkens, greens. The world feels transformed, as if its medium has shifted from air to water; and yet it feels somehow safer, not drowning, but floating.

'Dark glasses. Good for hiding. From the sun, I mean. And so on.' She raises one eyebrow. 'Perhaps for disguise.'

'Ah,' I say. 'Yes. Well, thank you.'

Miss Deere nods at me, smiles. She puts thumb and finger to her lips, pulls away a tiny shred of tobacco, examines it, flicks it off in an arc. 'You know what they say,' she says, 'about Wonderland.' It's not a question. 'Anything can happen.' She frames the words in both her hands, in laconic approximation of Mr Loverock's enthusiastic carnival patter.

'Ah. Indeed. I look forward to—anything, then. And everything.'

She nods. She smokes. We stand and wait for the others to be ready.

A triplet runs out of the house at speed and grabs at the newel post as she passes, to stop herself. She stands, breathing heavily, exaggeratedly, one hand on her hip as if to cure a stitch in her side.

'Hello, Hanna,' I say. 'Are you ready for Wonderland?'

She looks at me, eyes wide. 'You know me,' she says. 'It's me—I'm me—and you know me from the others.'

'I do,' I say. 'I do indeed. You are Hanna.'

'I am. I'm Hanna.'

'Today is a Wonderland day,' I tell her. 'Anything can happen.'

WONDERLAND
Triplets

The morning passes in expectation and anticipation so intense we almost feel sick to our stomachs. Knowing our father has already left for Wonderland, early and without us, only makes the waiting worse. But wait we do, for the hands on the clock in the kitchen to meet, pointing straight up.

At midday we leave, as if in procession, following our mother, who walks with the Lady (looking mysterious and marvellous in Jane Deere's dark glasses) on her arm, the Lady's other hand resting on a stick. Our mother passes her up into the front seat next to Jane Deere the Cameleer, who waits in the driver's seat of her truck. We three leap up into the back seat next to Mrs R, and our mother steps up behind us. Jane Deere squeezes the bulb of the horn on the outside of the truck, parp parp parp, as she takes off with a jolt and we're off and around the corner and up the steep incline of Awa Road before we know it. We lurch into the switchback, and climb, climb, past our school on the crest of the hill before switchbacking down to the Miramar flats. Jane Deere turns, then straightens course, and we judder along at walking pace, dead ahead, parting the crowd that mills towards the entrance gates, that spills from ferry and horseback and cycle.

Today, finally, is a Wonderland day. Everything leads to this. Here we all are, right at the start of it.

~ ~ ~

We know that Jane Deere will drive through the side entrance, to drop our mother and the Lady at the office, but we pester our mother, can we go through the front gate? She agrees, Jane Deere pulls up, and the three of us leap down from the truck, wave them off and join the crowd on foot.

We happily bide our time in the queue, preening under the attention and nudges (*ooh, is it them, those Loverock girls?*), as we approach the magnificent Wonderland gate, the rays of the delicate ironwork sun rising above the wondrous word we know so well. We look up, as we always do, and marvel at how it changes as we pass underneath, how the word of WONDERLAND becomes just bars and curves of iron, how the name forms itself, then reforms itself in reverse, once we're through

ᗡNAJЯƎbNOW

and if we stand and look backwards, through the nonsense-backwards-mirror-letters, we can still somehow read them. They make a mirror sense that still means

WONDERLAND

and we can hardly believe that we are here, and that this day has finally come.

We walk on through the crowd, hand in hand, Ada leading, Oona next, Hanna behind. We smell the smells of Wonderland, of carnival, hot oil and sugar, sausages, sweat and saddle leather, tobacco, toffee apples, perfume, pomade, petrol fumes and pony plops, kerosene, bootblack and beer. We smell the lake at the bottom of the Chute, too, something in between the smell of a dead thing washed up on the beach, and the smell of our WC in summer (pee-ugh!).

Despite the pong, we linger by the edge of the lake, watching the little boats crash into the water, the crank of them as the great metal chain hauls them up the ramp, the crack of them as they're released, and clang down the track of the ramp of the Chute, all to the screams and shouts of the punters in the boats and around the lake.

We walk on, past the Japanese Tea Kiosk (we're not sure the pink-iced finger buns, inch-thick slices of fruit cake, milky tea and cheese and pickle sandwiches sold there are very Japanese), past the queue for the Chute, until we come to the half-height door marked OFFICE MANAGER, CHAS. P.P. LOVEROCK. We knock and enter all at once, leaping through the little doorway. Our father's office is wedged under the great high ramp of the Chute, tucked hard against the edge of the lake. The roof line follows the angle of the Chute, so it's very very high at one end, and very very low at the other, so low that even we can't stand up there. We bluster into the office, making the already crowded room even crowded-er. Our father stands tall in the corner, our mother sits in the visitor's chair, and there's the Lady in our father's chair, a cup of tea in her hand, her hat still on her head, walking stick by her side.

'Ratbags! You've arrived! I was just telling our visitor about the Gala concert. We have artistes from far and wide, but none so special as these Three Little Ratbag Maids!'

Our father is wearing his Wonderland costume today (how we have missed it!). Bright wool jacket, scarlet red with shining brass buttons, over striped silk waistcoat, yellow and black like a wasp or a warning. He fishes fat fingers into his tiny waistcoat pocket and pulls out his watch, squints at it.

'Now, there's plenty of time before the show for you ratbags to take our visitor on a tour. See the sights. The Mecca of Merry Souls.'

We leap up, yes, yes, we can show her the sights!

The Lady puts her teacup on the desk. 'I should like that,' she says. 'If you do not mind, dear doctor?'

Our mother shakes her head. 'Of course, of course. Perhaps I might accompany you?'

'It is not necessary. Your daughters and I will have a little adventure, yes? Though perhaps I will not Chute the Chute.'

She nods at the Wonderland poster on the wall. 'Nor Helt the Skelter.'

At the very mention of the Chute, as if she has conjured it, the crash and clank of the boats sound from the ramp above the office, the grind of the chains, the dull roar of the crowd outside. Then the Lady stands, and our mother stands too, and reaches out to the Lady as if to steady her, but the Lady raises her hand, 'I am fine,' her voice soft but strong.

'Yes. Yes, of course.' Our mother claps her hands, says, 'Well, girls, I propose that you choose one marvellous thing to show Madame Professor.'

Just one! Surely it's not possible!

'Then come to the Kiosk for afternoon tea. In plenty of time before the concert. Yes?'

Yes! Yes! Yes!

'Good, good. Remember, the Japanese Tea Kiosk, three o'clock.' She turns to our father. 'Charlie, you'll join us there?'

'Ah, my love, I'm afraid not.' He twiddles his little finger stump. 'I have to see a wise man about a dog.' He makes a funny shape with his mouth that makes our mother sigh, which makes our father kiss the top of her head, as he says, 'Right, so, are you all ready to go?'

'Just so, just so,' the Lady says, retrieving Jane Deere's dark glasses from her pocket and looping them on to hide her eyes, and 'please, no,' as our mother fusses. 'I do not need the stick, though I thank you very much for your concern.'

Hanna steps forward and takes her left hand, and Oona takes the Lady's right hand, and Ada leads the way, and we step out into the cool air and pale sunlight and wondrous smells and pushing crowd and swelling noise of Wonderland.

Wonderland!

We see the catalogue of marvels that Wonderland provides in our minds' eyes, as if on a poster, or an advertisement in the newspaper.

The MAGIC SWING!
The ROOM OF ILLUSIONS!
The HOUSE OF TROUBLE!
The KATZENJAMMER CASTLE!

Our mother has set us an impossible task. How can we choose just one marvellous thing?

But we think we know it. The most marvellous thing. We will take the Lady to the place where the three of us began. Though it is different, now, than it was at our beginning, still it holds our first memories in its walls. We will show her the marvel that was once Wonderland's Wonderful Infant Incubator, that is now the Fantastical Fernery (A Glimpse of Paradise! Lit by Electricity!).

The three of us and the Lady pass through the crowd, past the entrance to Sideshow Alley (where our father always says we mustn't linger), past the ticket box for the Chute, past the Helter Skelter (hear the screams!), past the Dancing Horse and the Japanese Tea Kiosk, Aladdin's Cave of Mysteries and the Tattoo'd Princess. We walk either side of the Lady, taking her hands in ours.

We pass a man who stares intently, then double-takes and doubles back to face us, taking off his hat and stammering to the Lady, 'Excuse me, but aren't you Madame Cu—'

'No, indeed,' she dismisses him with a grim smile and a wave of her hand. 'You must be mistaken. Good day.' She pushes the dark glasses with her forefinger, so they're firm on the bridge of her nose, and says to us, 'Shall we continue?'

We walk on, towards the great grey turrets of Katzenjammer Castle (we think the outline of stones painted on wood is very convincing, though we've never seen a proper castle ourselves), past Jane Deere's dear old camels roped to a rail, the four of them standing morose, fat lips lolling over great yellow teeth and big grey tongues. Their pelts are patchy, as if a naughty boy has sat on their humpy backs and plucked at them, here a pinch, there a handful, enough to knit our father a great big camel-y jersey (we imagine the smell, and our noses wrinkle with the good and bad of it). We wonder where Jane Deere the Cameleer is. We know she can't be far away from her camels.

At the front of Katzenjammer Castle we push past the punters (*Ah, it's those Loverock triplets. Awfully small, aren't they? I thought they'd be bigger. And isn't that Madame Whatsername the scientist? No, couldn't be, could it?*), tip a wink to Miss Hyde in the ticket box and hustle in under the castle's front arch. Once inside, we wait impatiently while the Lady removes her dark glasses. Then we take her hands and lead her past the wonky staircase to the Room of Illusions, up the sloping floor and along the curving wall of Drunkards' Walk, backwards through the Gallery of Mirrors, and on, to the heavy curtain at the gallery's opposite end. Hanna lifts the curtain, then Ada lifts it more, and Oona extends her arm with a ta-dah! to reveal the little secret door in the wall.

We three hold our breaths, relishing the moment of anticipation before opening that door, behind which lies one of our favourite Wonderland hideaways. Under the hum and glow of electricity, the Fantastical Fernery is a very wonder, as we recall it, beautiful, beautiful, its cool fountains (one high and mighty, another tiny, low and murmuring) with rocks placed between them as if by nature, though nature has never held the upper hand in the Wonderland glasshouse.

Ada turns the stiff door handle, Oona and Hanna take the Lady's hands, and we all pass through the secret service door, bracing ourselves for bright wet warmth, rich and green. Instead of lush ferns and watery murmur, though, there is the puff of musty mould, a damp sweet rise, as of something wet left to rot. As our eyes begin to see, the little light admitted through whitewashed windows shows the skeletons of ferns, everywhere. Some remain upright, like little withered ladders. Others are folded and fallen, splayed like pencil drawings of themselves over the surfaces of rocks that edge each garden bed. Water pools neglected in the fountains, and on paths. It is cold, so cold our breath forms smoke.

'Oh,' says the Lady. 'Ah.'

Ignoring our own disappointment (and the sick feeling it makes in our stomachs), thinking only of entertaining our visitor, we three encircle the Lady, and bid her close her eyes and imagine magnificence, as we, too, close our eyes, and remember. We tell her how we were born here. That we began here. That before now, this was the Fernery. And before then, this was the Infant Incubator.

'I beg your pardon?' she says, as if she cannot make sense of what we've said.

This very place, we tell her. Here. In this glasshouse. Before it was like this, it was the Fernery, and it was warm and wonderful (imagine!). And before that, it was where they showed the babies. And the babies were us. We were the babies. In the incubators. Like little sleeping beauties we were, the three of us under glass. It was the beginning of our biggening.

'But I don't ...' she says. 'Do you mean—?'

Yes, we tell her, each of us taking turns to explain, our words tripping over and under each other in our haste and excitement and remembering. It was when we were babies, tiny as any you've ever seen. Our mother brought the incubators from America (Amehdika is the way we say it, *Ahhh-MEH-Di-Kah!*). She set them up. This glasshouse had everything she needed, sunlight and water and electricity and lighting, warm as anything. So she said bugger the plants, we mean bother the plants, my babies are going in here. They used to pay to see us, we tell her. The Tiny Triplets! The Wonderful Wonderland Incubator Babies! We pulled the punters, our father always says. We were famous, we tell her, and everyone came to see, everyone pointing, our every moment and movement of interest, reported in the newspapers.

'Ah,' she says. 'I know the feeling.'

And then, we tell her, Doctor B at the Baby Hospital in

Newtown said our mother could take her incubators there, so the Wonderful Wonderland Infant Incubator was packed up, lock, stock and barrel when our mother went to work at the hospital. So our father turned the nursery back into the Fernery, in all its glory. Its former glory. We wanted to show you, we tell her, but we didn't know it was gone.

We three and the Lady stand at the whitewashed windows of the glasshouse. Through the smear of white we can see the punters passing, crowds of people. We imagine them looking in at us, when the windows were new and clean and clear, in the distant past when we were babies. We remember it. Don't we? Do we? The apple-box smell of it. The white-mask starch of it. The rubber-teat taste of it. The interruption of a knock on the glass, and another. The jump of it, the startle. The feeling of being on show. The touch of our mother's hands on our new foreheads, our tiny bottoms, our full bellies, our curled pink feet.

Do you think, we ask the Lady, is there something about a tiny thing, a thing that is smaller than it ought to be? Something uncanny about the miniature state of it? Of us?

Why would they watch us, we wonder aloud.

'Fame has its own peculiar logic,' she says.

We are almost running late by the time we leave the Formerly Fantastic Fernery, but it's just a short walk if you know the way (and we know all the ways at Wonderland) directly from the Fernery to the Japanese Tea Kiosk, and we arrive on the dot of the clock on the Eiffel Tower striking three. Our mother sits at a table with Jane Deere the Cameleer and Jane Deere's very good friend Mrs R, whose lap we three all pile onto. Mrs R hugs us to her, holds us close and gives us butterfly kisses, brushing her eyelashes on our cheeks.

Jane Deere stands up and offers the Lady her chair.

'I have to go. Must get to work. Punters will be waiting.'

Jane Deere huddles in close and surrounds the three of

us in her camel-smelling arms. She messes our hair with her hands, kisses Mrs R on the cheek, and bows with great flourish to the Lady and our mother. Then she turns on her heel, puts on her hat and adjusts the lapels of her camel-smelling coat, and hotfoots it back to the punters who will be waiting to climb up the stepladder and onto the backs of the roped-in-line camels, for Jane Deere to lead them around the dusty track, tuppence a time.

The Lady sits next to our mother, who asks her about tea, and tiredness, and pain, and other things of little consequence or interest. Before too long, though, a piled-high plate arrives, and so we get to work, scoffing tea and cakes and ignoring the grownups' chatter, until the clock on the Eiffel Tower strikes four and it's time to get ready for our performance. We bow to the Lady and Mrs R and our mother as we stuff the remaining cakes into our pockets and race off into the crowd, towards the Wonderland Theatrette.

We take the quick way, under the ramp of the Chute to skirt the edge of the lake, and as we pass, we see two very big men, and one little man in between them, exiting our father's office (it must be our father's meeting, though not a dog in sight which must be why he looks quite sad). Our father stands framed in the door of the office, watching the men get into their black car. We wave at him, but he does not see us. We're in a hurry, and we'll see him later, so we skedaddle, scooting quickly on through the crowd, past the theatre entrance and around to the back of the building, through the blue door marked NO ENTRY! PERFORMERS ONLY. In we go, past The Marvellous Zemphy curling his hair, and Miss Ida Berridge washing her paintbrushes and mixing paints, past Professore Giovanni and his Clever Cockatoos (all twelve of them!), past the Valdenes pumping their bicycle tyres, and Mr Harry St Jean (rhymes with engine!) in his underwear, sitting with those clever comedians Mr Morris and Mr Wilson, all of them gargling with whisky to strengthen their voices (so they say), past the tumblers Dunbar and Blake, also in their underwear, stretching and bending, past the Musical Cromes tuning violins and ukuleles, tooting horns and organising their sleigh bells in order, past Luella and Driscoll with their clown faces only half finished, so they're only half funny. We're running late, so there's no time for more than a hug and a bow and a handshake, a scratch under the neck of the closest cockatoo, as we run through the dressing room to our accustomed spot in the corner, behind a sheet strung up as a curtain, across the room from Miss Joan Devlin, who sits in front of a mirror propped on a cluttered table, straightening her wig and brightening her face. She blows waxy red kisses to us—*Hallooo, little ones!*—on smoky tobacco breath, and ashes her cigarette on a saucer on the table. We blow kisses back to her and duck under the curtain, into our own curtained dressing-room cubby. There is the basket we double-checked and repacked and triple-checked this morning, our kimonos, our horsey wigs, our fans, our dancing slippers. And underneath them, the World's Most Magnificent Trousers (lizard-green, moonlight-white, ultraviolet, fabulous).

Our mother will be here soon. Not long until our half-hour call.

Everything is in place.

Three little girls are we, together, here now at last.

Three Starry Little Matariki Maids we'll become again, Miramar's Maidens once more on the Wonderland stage, to open the Gala concert.

In our corner of the dressing room, our particular corner of the world, we make ourselves extraordinary. We put on our costumes, taking it in turns to wrap each other into our binding belts, broad and high on our little girl bellies, our flat chests. Our mother supervises as we slip into our wigs, great smelly black piles stuffed high with horsehair, smelling of old mattresses and Ernest Rutherford and mice. We tuck our own hair up under them. They make our necks nod with their weight. We slip into dancing slippers, slap on makeup. We become our other selves, though our own true selves remain. We hear the rise and fall of the other performers, on the other side of the curtain, across the dressing room, but we are apart from them, in our own place, our own world.

When we've done all we can do—checked the mirror, straightened wigs, hoisted trousers one last time—we emerge from behind our curtain and curtsey to Miss Devlin. She checks our makeup (kohl on our eyes, our faces white and matte with powder), and makes some final touches before nodding her approval, just as Mr Boyd strides up with our five-minute call.

Our mother kisses three fingers, then presses one and one and one kiss onto each of our foreheads in turn.

'Enjoy yourselves, my little loves. You look magnificent. I'll be in the front row.'

Then Mr Boyd bustles us off to wait in the wings.

We stand holding hands in the dark backstage. Even though we know our lines, our steps, every part of our performance, still we have dragon-sized butterflies doing somersaults in our bellies. We close our eyes to make the darkness darker while we listen for our cue. We wait in the dark and feel the hum beginning to rise.

Our father, Carnival Charlie Loverock himself, is there on the stage with his practised patter, welcoming everyone to the Wonderland Winter Gala Concert of Nineteen Hundred and Twelve.

'—surely a highlight of the calendar, Ladies and Gentlemen, and I thank you all for being here.'

We open our eyes to watch him from the side, the lovely shape of his belly pushing his wasp-y waistcoat out past his jacket. He flicks a giant hanky from his trouser pocket and dabs his face, bright and shining in the light, and there's a laugh from the audience.

'Ah, steady now, I'm not part of the show. There's better to come!'

More laughs.

'And to start, an act I know you've all been waiting for.'

Mr Boyd—the stage manager—rests his hands on our shoulders.

'Miramar's Triple Star!'

We grip hands tighter, close our eyes again, our stomachs dragon-butterflied with waiting. We have ears only for our cue.

'The Three—'

Now? No.

'—Little—'

Not now. Wait.

'—Miramar—'

Those dragon-butterflies take a tumble, breathe belly fire.

'—Maids!'

We open our eyes.

Now!

Go!

Mr Boyd holds the curtain aside and we burst onto the stage from behind it, the applause drawing us forward, forward still, into the brightness, a brightness so bright we can only see stars. We curtsey, and the applause is louder. We *are* the Three Little Miramar Maids—we've become them! they've become us!—and we hide behind our fans, lower our eyes, shuffle our slippered feet forward, until we stand right on the lip of the stage, where we can feel the heat of the lights on our ankles, under our costumes. The dragon-butterflies are gone, and it's as if they were never there. Three little girls with dragon-butterflies we were. Three Little Maids we've become, extraordinary once more, butterfly-free.

Mr Devenish Ruby of the Wonderland Band catches our

eye, Ada nods a tiny nod, and Mr Ruby flourishes a rolling chord right up the keyboard of the piano to the highest tinkling top notes. And in the ringing notes approaching silence at the chord's end, we snap our fans to open them, to hide our faces and smile our eyes over the top, and the crowd erupts to hoot and shout and clap and stamp. Three little maidens, all unwary. Three little maids are we. We grow tall with the music, the applause. Mr Ruby repeats the rolling trilling chord, to let the applause die down.

And then.

And then, we start to sing.

Our father is there, off in the wings at stage left, his arms folded across his waistcoat, his big mouth smiling at us, his big boot tapping out of time with the music, and our singing.

Three Miramar Maidens all unwary

Snap! snap! snap! with our fans, slippers shuffling, voices strong.

Tell us apart now, if you dare-y
Three Little Maids are we!

Snap! snap! snap! Kimono fabric swirls, we circle around the stage. Most in the audience are singing along.

Not an illusion, real or optical
Three matching ma-a-aids are we!

We circle, just as we practised at home in our bedroom, just as we imagined it, fanning our fans, shuffling our slipper-clad feet back into the limelight, then we snap our fans once more and Mr Ruby tumbles the music down then up and up and up through an octave, and when it hits the top note we throw our fans, toss our horsey wigs, strip off our kimonos, to reveal our starry sister-y selves and the World's Most Magnificent Lizard-Green Moonlight-White Ultraviolet Trousers.

Revealed, released, unhindered, unbound, we stand in star position, arms in the air, legs akimbo, heads thrown back and our chests pushed proudly forward. Miramar's Triple Star, her Matariki Maidens! We'd order fireworks at this point, if it was up to us, but sad to say it is not, so we'll have to make our own fireworks on stage, in our dancing and our voices. And it's just as it played in our imaginations, in our bedroom, in our minds. Unbound, revealed, star-powered, startling the audience to stand and roar, we tumble, we fall, we leap and become tall, we do it all with magnificence and poise. We stand front and centre and sing a starry song, a sister song, a winter song. We sing to the stars and the sky and the hills, and the sea and the rain and all the world. We sing and sing and sing, our voices raised above all the punters who cheer us on. We sing to Wonderland once more.

And it's not until we're standing breathless on the stage, the music stopped, our Magnificent Trousers bathed in sweat, and we are taking our bow, and another and another and yet one more, that we see, past the lights, our mother there in the front row, and the Lady beside her, both of them standing and clapping with delight. And there's Mrs R on the other side, blowing us kisses, and Jane Deere next to her, and Jane Deere puts two fingers to her lips and whistles the piercing three-note whistle that she whistles to her camels. And is that Hermit Louis in the shadows at the back of the crowd? And there, oh! there are Minna Hofmann and all the other Hofmanns, and even they are hooting and hollering! And there's our father, off in the wings, shouting and clapping over the top of them all. When we turn our smiles upon him from centre stage, we see him watching us with shining eyes.

We throw our arms in the air once more—Ada's left hand in Oona's right, Hanna's right hand in Oona's left—and we take our final starry starry bow, and turn and leave the stage.

We slip into the dark of backstage as if our feet don't touch the floor, as if we are flying on the wind of the applause, on the wind of Worser Bay, as if our Magnificent Trousers have wings. We hear our father on stage announcing the next act, '—the Fabulous Professore Giovanni, the Birdman himself, and his Tightly Trained Twelve, the Parrot Performers, yes, ladies and gentlemen, it's Professore Giovanni and his Clever Chorus of Cockatoos!'

We hug ourselves to ourselves to ourselves, all three of us in an iridescent vibrating huddle in the dark.

Mr Boyd moves us on with a gentle push and a whispered hiss and we scoot around past the stacked flats and unfathomable shapes and shadows, somehow nimble and untripping in the lacklight of backstage, and we find our way to the door at the side of the stage and out we pop, down four stairs, to the smoky hum of the seated audience, their beards and cigarettes and powder and spectacles, their handkerchiefs and toffee apple sticks and fuming pipes and waxed moustaches and fingers up noses and thumbs in mouths, their upturned faces glowing like hundreds of moons, all lit by the light from the stage.

We hunch and huddle and wriggle to the front row, and the three of us rest there, nesting in our mother's sturdy skirt, leaning on her wool-stockinged legs. She touches our shoulders with her fine fingers, smoothes our hair and tucks it behind our ears, leans down to kiss the tops of our heads, whispers, 'My talented, remarkable girls.'

We nest there while the whole of the Wonderland Winter Gala goes on. We are magicked, our whole selves overtaken by the high flight of our remarkable starry sisters performance, and the other acts all proceed without our attention, as if in a beautiful dream.

And in that dream, what do we hear?

What do we miss?

What do we misinterpret?

What does our father say, as he leads the applause at the end of the Gala concert? '—the last ever held at Wonderland, wonderful Wonderland—'

Why can we make no sense of the unfathomable words?

'—never again—'

And what can it mean?
'—our final night, a fond farewell to you all—'
What can it really mean?

It was light, hard light, when we entered the dressing room, but we walk out of the theatre into cold clear almost-dark. The three of us, still in our Magnificent Trousers, hold hands in a paper-doll line. Ada holds our mother's left hand. And Hanna holds the right hand of the Lady in her own left hand. And we all move together, as everyone in the crowd moves, towards the lake at the centre of Wonderland, where the fireworks will begin once the night has risen, once the dark has taken hold.

The crowd stands six deep, ten deep, twelve deep, uncountable, around the shores of the lake at the base of the Chute. Boys and men climb and clamber up up up, on the ramp of the Chute, the steep sides of the Eiffel Tower. All around us are candles clutched in hands, wax dripping into cardboard, tiny lights flickering. We are surrounded by skirts and trousers, wool and canvas muffling sound, all colours turned to grey in the dark, all smelling somehow of camels and smoke and tea. We look for our father in the crowd, but all we can see (as far as we can see) is a sea of serge, a forest of legs.

So we push our way past all the trousers, skirting this way and that until we come right to the front of the crowd, to the edge of the lake, where all opens up before us. In the lake's centre floats a barge laden with barrels and gadgets and we-can't-see-what-else in the dark, and the shapes of people and boats all around. At the edges, where the water is not busy, the ink-dark sky and the specks of stars reflect in the still of the lake. In the shapes around the barge there is movement, and its absence. There is a lantern, there is another, and then we cannot see them. There is a flame, in one of the boats, then it goes out. There is music, in the distance, then it stops.

(Or is the stopping in our own imaginations, or our memories?)

As the clock on the Eiffel Tower strikes to mark the hour, the crowd cheers and drowns the next six of the clock's seven strikes. And at that seventh strike, there comes a hiss across the water of the lake, and the hiss becomes a whine louder than any from Minna Hofmann, and the whine soars in the sky higher, higher, higher, and a great red flower explodes in the sky two moments before we hear the thumping crump of it, shaking the ground, breaking the surface of the water of the lake and pounding our ears as brightly as the red glow lights our upturned faces.

And Mr Bickerton's marvellous fireworks blow above us, grow above us, glow above us, and we all reflect their glow, turquoise and magenta, sun-yellow, bright orange, darling blue and brightest white, as the world around us explodes a hundred times, and a hundred times more. And we feel the explosions in our whole bodies, and in our minds.

STARRY NIGHT
The Lady

I did not expect the beautiful laboratory smell. Gunpowder, sulphur, perchlorates. Nor was I prepared for the chemistry of colours. Barium green, copper blue, sodium yellow, strontium red. This boundless laboratory is the sky above us, and all in the crowd bear witness to the great experiments above. All is illumined: the empty chute that ramps to the lake, the grey-white castle façade, the man-sized plywood tower in the shape of Mr Eiffel's. All the people in the crowd are colourless, yet brightly brilliant. They seem almost to phosphoresce, as if underwater, or to glow as if shone with ultraviolet, or the rays of light, of pure sunlight. All is radiant. There is nothing but radiance. I am mesmerised. The sky above swirls with light under the immoveable heft and mass of the broad hills that surround us, anchoring the brilliant sky to the Earth. The sky erupts once more, and again. I see the little girls, the stars on their costumes, the glow of the sky on their faces. I hold each burst of colour and chemicals and energy in my mind's eye, even when they dissipate, until my mind's sky is full of them all. There, a great red flower, strontium, lithium. There, a great orange-yellow sun, exploding cryolite, sodium, calcium. There, the swirling scroll, the rainbow wheels, moving through the middle of the sky, a wave, a crest, an energy pulse. There, a band of cream-white light, topping the hills like a thickening of snow. There, white forms an almost-skeleton, exposed in the sky as if by the action of the emanations of radium (my radium). There, iron or lampblack, made incandescent, forms a golden crown. There, the triple flower, the triple star, the triple energy of those three beautiful unbeautiful children: violet, from copper and strontium; white-hot magnesium, electric white against the sky; apple green, bright green, barium chloride green. There, a whole sky full of light, the sky massed and swirling with the upwards energy of it, all of it up, and when it is up, it is up, and when it comes down, down, down, it falls slowly, so slowly, as if gravity has given up the fight, and chemistry is king. Or queen.

FALL
Matti

And just for a moment, everything is still, and perfect, and beautiful, in the dark.

There is a sound that is the first hint. No, not a single sound, but a series of sounds. And also something beyond sound, or below it, something more like instinct, or dread, a prickling of the hairs on the back of her neck.

Charlie?

Then there is another sound, a cry. Then there is a light, and then it goes out. Then there is a crack, as of thunder, though she knows the sky is cloudless so that makes no sense. Then there is a shout, again, and the deep sound of men taking charge. There is running, and the animal sound of a shifting crowd. There is the smell, that is animal too, of fear, that is also the smell of excitement, or not-knowing, or curiosity. There is a hand on her shoulder, and she turns, and she walks, then she runs, towards the dark urgent huddle at the side of the lake.

Matti's instinct in a crisis is to switch to professional mode, ready to heal, but she does not, not now. Now, she folds to her knees in the shallows of the lake and presses herself against the ebbing still-warmth of Charlie's body.

THE LOOK OF DEATH
Triplets

There is a hand on our mother's shoulder, and there is her fallen face—just for a moment—before it takes its usual shape. There is the soft curve of Mrs R into which we fall as our mother moves away.

It is not by a sound, nor an action, that we know it. It is not by a word, not by a deed. It is by the look on our mother's face that we know it or start to know it. The look of death is in her eyes. Our father's death begins there, in her eyes.

Everything moves, in the dark. Candles are re-lit, like grounded stars flickering. The unnatural gunpowder smell of the fireworks fades, the black-blue sky still hazed with their burn. The big light on the tower is lit, and all at a sudden glows pale. The faces all around us (faces known and unknown) all turn in the same direction, all bright with watching, and with the light.

We turn, too, though the great enclosing arms of Mrs R still hold us together.

What we see is like a puzzle, or a riddle to be solved. Nothing makes sense. We look through gaps in the crowd that move and shift as the people move and shift. People change size, come close, move away, seem familiar, seem strange, all at the same time. We see as if we are ourselves moving through the crowd (though we are not, we are safe with Mrs R, held tight with love). We look back and see the three of us—we see ourselves!—and Mrs R, with the Lady by our side, all five of us with eyes wide, mouths wide, waiting. Yes, we move (without moving) through the crowd, past Minna and all the Hofmanns, past Professore Giovanni, past Miss Grimshaw from school, and Mrs Tracy from Seatoun, past Hermit Louis with his great moustache, until there we are, beside our mother and there is our father, oh! our father, Carnival Charlie Loverock, there in the water at the edge of the lake, with men all around him, heaving and huffing and hauling him, as if he can be saved, though somehow we know he cannot, and in that moment of knowing we are back across the lake, back in the arms of Mrs R.

A gap opens in the crowd. We see our mother in the light from the tower of the Chute, her hands reaching in front of her as if reaching in darkness, to find her way.

Miramar
Winter 1912

The Evening Post

ACCIDENTS AND FATALITIES
Death Mars Local Gala
"Carnival Charlie" Dies

By Telegraph—Press Association
Wellington, This Day

The body of a man named as Charles Loverock, aged 46, was removed from the lake at Wonderland in Miramar last night. Though hundreds were in attendance at the time of Mr Loverock's death, the circumstances surrounding the incident remain unclear. Mr Loverock, well known locally as "Carnival Charlie", has managed the formerly popular amusement park since its opening seven years ago. The Wonderland amusement park is closed again until further notice.

THE RADIANT EFFECT
The Lady

I know the radiant effect of an event   or an occurrence
of this event   and that   alone or combined
and I know how forces work in concert
and also   in opposition

for   every   action
there is an equal
and opposite
reaction

I watch
three girls   joyous
sing and dance on stage
in costumes stitched with stars

chemicals explode in the night sky
rain down   happiness   in colourful delight
everything falling   with control   where it should
except   the one distraction   the tiny invisible thing

                                        and
                          everything
                falls
        in

consequence

SHAPES OF OUR FATHER
Triplets

Our father is Mr Halley's comet, not falling but soaring in clear skies, most spectacular at perihelion (*perihelion*, like the name of a flower).

Our father is Mr Bickerton's fireworks, filling the ink-dark sky over Wonderland, reflected in the lake, a million stars, a million lights, a million candle flames, a million pinpricks, a million upturned faces, a million tiny explosions in a countless million colours.

Our father is a teardrop, tipped on its side, going nowhere.

These are the shapes of our father, as we saw him tonight, his last night on this Earth.

FAIL
Matti

What does it mean, to fall? Matti understands the physics, more or less. She understands this. She understands the biology, the effect that falling can have on a body (his body, his dear body). She understands this, too. But there was nothing she could do. She could not stop the falling. She could not stop the physics, the terrible collision. And she could not heal him, once fallen, once broken. Too broken to mend.

What does it mean, to fail? To have failed to save him. When he was down, he was down, and she could not get him up again, no matter how she tried.

She knows what it is to fail. To fail completely. To fail to act, to fail to heal, to fail to save, to fail to anticipate the unanticipatable. To fail to go to their daughters, when they need her. To fail—perhaps—to love enough; to fail—will she fail?—to survive this.

Matti forms a fist with her right hand and punches her left forearm numb, numb to the bone. She mutters and cries in argument—with herself, with Charlie—until the words turn to shapes that stick in the back of her throat, and she can barely swallow.

WHAT IT IS TO FALL

The Lady

I know what it is to fall
not under the force   of gravity
but   under other forces
and suspicion

I know what it is to comfort
a child beyond comforting
to hold   them
and their not understanding   and my own

I know what it is to hear
the woman in the next room
argue with her dead husband
as I have argued so often with mine

I know what it is to hold   my   breath
and for the world to slow
and to grasp   what it means
to live on

EMPTINESS
Matti

She has never known emptiness like this.

Charlie?

The world slows. Perhaps it even stops.

Matti holds her breath. She holds on.

WHAT A WONDER
Triplets

We do not know the order of things. We have lost the memory of it. Of what happened.

There were the fireworks. Our stars in the sky. And then they were gone.

And then there was a space of time, and it was filled with the shapes of our father (fireworks, comet, teardrop). And there was sound, and both light and darkness. There was shouting, we think, and silence, and light again. More light, before the darkness, again, and the shouting, again, and the sound of water and its movement.

There was our father, and then he was gone.

Our mother was there, beside us, and then she was gone.

Mrs R was there, and we were with her, and she held us close, until our mother called to her, and then she, too, was gone.

The Lady was there beside us, too, and she stayed and took our hands. She held us to her. 'Come, come,' she said, and 'there, there, there,' and we stayed with her as lanterns and candles and stars and tiny flames moved all around us.

We remember Jane Deere, dear Jane Deere, found us, and drove us home. The Lady held the three of us in the back seat of the truck. Her thin arms, the bones of them holding us together.

'There, there, there. Come, come. There, there, there.'

And nobody told us.
Nobody told us our father was dead.
Though we knew.

We remember the Lady heating milk. We remember the taste of honey in it, and another taste like bitter vanilla, or malt vinegar. We do not remember words. We remember sleep, and the darkness of our room, and the stove's low light from the kitchen, and the voices of Jane Deere and the Lady, low and warm and continuing, like the night.

We wake to the sound of the voice of our mother in the kitchen, and we blunder from bed and run to her, our eyes hardly open, and she takes us to her like little blind kittens, little blind mice, little unfathered things, and she holds us. And she tells us he is gone. Though we already know. (What a wonder!)

Our mother carries us back to our bed
narwhal amy
down to sleep
dee dum dee dum our souls to keep
and she lies with us, on into the night, and to the dark dead sleep before morning.

LOST
Matti

Her husband's dear body was taken away from Wonderland. They would not let him go with her, go home. They gave her his jacket, as if in consolation, handed it to her with solemnity and occasion. She thought to tear her hair and rent her clothes and scream, to make them give him to her, send him home with her. But she did not; she does not think she did. And they took him. He is gone.

The children are sleeping now. She lies with them for a time, nested in their bed, the four of them like sick animals, snot and touching skin, restless, writhing, unsettled. Matti can taste fermentation on her breath, as if she is rotting from the inside.

She leaves the children sleeping, and walks through the house, barefoot, blinded, moving by touch, feeling every wallpaper seam, every nub of hessian scrim below it, every tack in the timber sarking. She feels more aware than she has ever felt—synapses scream in her brain—yet at the same time she is numb, unresponsive.

In their room, his jacket lies on the bed, on the quilt that she stitched long ago for them to lie beneath. His beautiful jacket: scarlet, brass, braid, silk. She lifts it from the bed, eases her arms into it, the stiff wool yielding then weighing her down. It engulfs her. There is the stink of him, there inside the jacket, on its collar and under its arms. She sinks to the floor with him, under his weight.

~ ~ ~

Matti wakes on the floor, still wearing Charlie's jacket. She has pulled the quilt from the bed onto her, around her, in the night. The door opens a crack, and Ada slips in. Matti tries to speak, *Ada, my darling*, but no words issue. Ada shushes her mother as Matti has so often shushed her. She slips under the quilt with her, into her arms, and Matti curves her empty body around her daughter's tiny back. She breathes in the sweet slept smell of her. She weeps and weeps into the space between them, that is no space at all.

THE SOUND OF DEATH
Triplets

When we wake on the first morning after that terrible night, and on every morning of those first strange days, the sound of death is in the house. A non-sound of missing, of blankness and gaps. Mrs R makes tea in the kitchen. We hear the shape of her steps, the way she moves (and we hear that her ways of moving are not our father's). We hear our mother's voice from her room, low, low, then silent, then Mrs R, going to her, soughing. We hear steam hiss, the tea caddy's clat, the kettle replaced on the stove. Underneath and above and through it all, we hear the sound of death, the lack of him.

We utter soothing noises into necks and cheeks and elbow creases, into the tangle of our hair, into the tangle of our father's death. We keep our eyes closed, like newborn kittens. We listen for the day, and our new life, and the absence of our father.

And yet, we do not miss him, for he is everywhere, not gone. The shape of him is in the house, and the feel of him. The sound of him is in the house, and in us. We hear the echo of him. We hear him in the gaps where sound is not.

We hear him, even if that sound is the absence of him.

It is when we open our eyes that he disappears, almost as if our eye-opening is making it so.

So we keep our dry eyes closed, pull the blanket up, and nestle in the dark of before time, when everything is possible and nothing goes wrong and our father, Charlie, does not lie dead at the edge of the lake at Wonderland, surrounded by a crowd of cheering punters who think, for a moment, that it is part of the show.

All just part of the show.

The night before our father's funeral, we dream of a tiny raft of driftwood, kittens sent to sea. We dream of ink-blue fingertips, as if we've forgotten to breathe. We dream a sailing song, a kitten song, a goodbye song, a Carnival Charlie song, but not a dead song, for we do not mourn the dead.

We dream of Ernest Rutherford the Horse in harness once more, pulling a marvellous cart painted ink-blue, night-sky-dark, flecked with a million stars. On the cart lies our father, the great comet of him, as big in death as he was in life. We dream great perfumed piles of flowers to surround him, and salt-sweet seaweed from the ocean, and cream cakes from Godber's in Town and toffee apples from the Japanese Tea Kiosk. We dream the tin box of our Reliquary onto the cart, and around our father we place all our Reliquary's precious things (breath and moon and eye and tail, bird and cord and pain). Almost last of all, we dream of replacing The Lost Fingerbone of Carnival Charlie Loverock where it rightly belongs (but at a jaunty angle for a laugh, which our father would appreciate).

And we dream ourselves riding on the great bare back of Ernest Rutherford as she pulls the cart, stepping proudly down streets lined with punters three-deep, seven-deep, twelve-deep, all cheering, all waving, all saying goodbye. We clutch Ernest Rutherford's mane in our hands. We wear our Magnificent Trousers. We sing a Charlie song, a goodbye song, a fatherless song, full voice.

And Hanna sings for fatherless daughters
I sing to the sea
that brought the lady here

> *and I sing for her daughters*
> *far away*
> *who are fatherless, too,*
> *just like us,*
> *just like me*

And Ada sings to our mother
> *in the dark and the light*
> *I lie next to her and sing,*
> *and sometimes my song is a cooing sound,*
> *as a bird might make,*
> *or a mother*

And Oona sings for our father
> *I sing loudest and longest*
> *most like him,*
> *he, most like me,*
> *full voice, full heart,*
> *full no more*
> *I have never known emptiness like this*

And when our singing stops, Oona—loudest of all of us—falls silent, voiceless, lost.

TAPPED
Matti

All Matti knows is that Agnes (was it Agnes Bennett? or was it Wilma Reddy?) came to her this morning, after she had dressed, before they left the house. Wilma—or was it Agnes? and why was Agnes here?—snapped the neck of a glass ampoule, rolled up Matti's sleeve, slipped a tie tight on her arm, tapped to raise a vein, pricked Matti's skin, depressed the plunger of the syringe, and there was a rush that eased her, eased her, eased her. Just enough for this. This day.

She lifts her head, faces forward to where he lies, two yards from her, in the box at the front of the hall, so close she could almost reach out and touch him. Charlie lies under wood, under flowers (how can flowers and wood contain him?). Matti sits dressed in widow's weeds. Her hands are in her lap, her fingers tap, though she cannot feel them. Their daughters are dressed in their Gala costumes, silk trousers, starlit; they are gorgeous, glorious, and why ever not? Ada is at Matti's right hand. Oona and Hanna are at Matti's left. Their arms reach around each other, around their mother's back. Matti can feel them. *Their little hands*, she thinks. Their little fatherless hands.

RAFT
Triplets

Our father is buried, in the usual way of things. He is not carried to his funeral on a cart drawn by Ernest Rutherford, lined with flowers and seaweed and toffee apples. He rides in an ordinary box, on the back of an ordinary funeral car, with everyone dressed in ordinary black clothes, crying ordinary tears. Only we three and our mother are dry-eyed. We are allowed to wear our Magnificent Trousers (or nobody stops us wearing them, at least). We sit next to our mother in the front row of the hall in Worser Bay—no final church for Charlie, just a view of the sea and the hills across the harbour—and wait for the singing to send him away.

The hall is filled with people, all smoking, drinking, talking, clinking. We soon tire of the field of legs and skirts, the murmuring, the lowered voices. We tire of sad looks and pats on heads. We slink outside, around the side of the hall. Where the land slopes away there is just enough space for the three of us to slide underneath the building. Everyone walks above us, upon us, the scuff of their shoes, the tap of their boots, the thud of the tip of a walking stick, and another. And time passes. Tea pours. We lie on our bellies under the hall, on sand that still smells of the beach, facing the ocean that shows in a thin strip of light and bright between the ground and the boards of the steps at the front of the hall. We narrow our eyes, and the colour drains, and only the brightness and light are left. We let our eyelids flutter, and the scene flickers, and we watch it like a moving picture at the theatre in Town, like a rabbit down a rabbit-hole, a girl (three girls who are one girl, and one girl is all three) giving chase, down and down and down.

And we wonder why our father's left us, and are we three to blame?

Boots and trousers step up the steps to the hall. Shoes and a skirt step down and walk away. Above us, the sounds of shuffling and clinking and voices become louder, now, just a little, then they hush and fade again.

We crawl out from the space under the hall, wriggling on our bellies like three little crocodiles. We stand, brush the sand from ourselves, and run away from the silenced sound of the hall, towards the water. There is no one on the beach but us, and the gulls, and the clean slope of the tide-washed sand, and the wind and the light on the hills and the sea. We run along the beach, past the wharf and on towards the rocks, staying clear of the water. We stand at the rocks at the end of the beach and look to the hills across the harbour. There are no faces in the hills today. There is a shape, though. It's the shape of our father on his back on the beach as he bicycles his legs in the air. It's the shape of him on his back on the floor of the kitchen as we pile on him for tickles. It's the shape of him on his back in the flower-laden cart pulled by Ernest Rutherford as we turn from our perch high upon the horse's back, in our Magnificent Trousers, waving him goodbye.

We make a raft of driftwood, bind it with seaweed, add a cuttlefish fin at the base for stability (we've done it before, we know the drill). We place the raft on the sand where bubbles and flecks of seaweed tea and tiny shells mark the high tide's line. And on the raft, we place
the lost tail of ernest rutherford
the lost greenstone of the sea

the lost arm of the doll who never was
the all-seeing eye of hermit louis
the holy relic of not-so-saintly minna bloody hofmann
the lost pain of jane deere the cameleer
the lost breath of doctor matti loverock
the lost moons of us
the lost cord of the lost baby whose name we do not know

and last, but not least, we place The Lost Fingerbone of Carnival Charlie Loverock, and when the raft is fully laden, we roll up the legs of our Magnificent Trousers, lift the raft in our six hands and walk it into the ocean. We push it off towards the shape of the hills across the harbour. We let it go.

UNMOORED
Matti

Days crash together, time crinkles and rumples like the sheets on Matti's bed, folds like paper in an envelope. The usual markers of time—work, meals at table, exercise, the sound of Charlie's voice—are missing. The clock on the shelf in the kitchen is only right twice a day.

Wilma Reddy holds the house together. She brings Matti medicines, chlorodyne and Mr Brittain's Tonic, keeps her supplied with dainty food and hearty food and any food at all, and cigarettes and grog. Dear Jane, Jane Deere, does what she can, distracting the children, getting things done. Agnes Bennett comes when she is needed, when her work at the hospital allows, sometimes in the night, sometimes by day. Even the woman—their visitor, the professor—helps to run the house, feed the children; the cared-for has become carer.

Days pass like this. Time slurs, uncertain. Neighbourly pots of soup are left curdling on the doorstep. Outside the door of Matti's bedroom there are steps in the hallway, lowered voices. She lies on her bed, above the cover, curved into herself. She smokes asthma cigarettes all day long. She pisses in a pot under her bed, and the smell of it staling makes her know time has passed. She leaves her room only to go to her daughters, in the dead dark of night. She sleeps the last faint hours of each night in their bed, where the four of them tangle, unmoored, undone.

FATHERLESS
Triplets

Days and days and days of rain follow the bright-sunned day of our father's funeral. Rain batters the windows, spouts from gutters, rivers down the road that leads past our house. Our mother lies in bed all day, each day, as if the rain has washed her feet out from under her.

When finally a day dawns dry-skied, we three burst out into it dry-eyed, rugged up against the cold, gumbooted for splashing, forehead-kissed by Mrs R, barley-sugar-pocketed by Jane Deere the Cameleer (dear Jane Deere, she and Mrs R seem almost never to go home). We stand on the front steps and blink as our eyes adjust to the light, to the new shape of our lives.

We burrow into the hollows of the sand dunes that edge Worser Bay, scraping aside the wet sand to find the almost-dry underneath it, and we lie on our backs on the sand once more. It is not different to lie fatherless on our backs. It is the same, just sadder. Our hands tighten around each other's fatherless hands, and we feel that they feel the same as our fathered hands of before.

What does it mean to be fatherless? We are still getting used to the feel of it, so sometimes we forget the fact. Our father is gone. Our father, who art in heaven, now (if the poem that Minna Hofmann loves to chant is really true). Our father, whose leaving we cannot begin to understand, or even truly to believe.

When will we see our father again? Every night, in our dreams.

On the last morning when our mother won't get up, she lies in our bed, her face turned to the wall, Mrs R in the chair next to her, the two of them muttering low, low (how tired we are of low voices). The three of us sit at the kitchen table, our feet swinging above the floor, our heads resting on our arms crossed on the surface of the table, lulled almost to sleep by the dull ache of their voices.

BREAK
The Lady

I carry my breakfast tray—a teapot, a teacup, a plate with an apple core, my sharp fruit knife—to the kitchen. I stop in the doorway. The three children lie with their heads on their arms on the table, so still and unmoving that I find myself holding my breath until I see them breathe, the movement of their tiny ribs, their narrow backs. I breathe out, and they lift their faces, and smile at me. I set my mouth in a smile, too, but I am not certain it travels as far as my eyes.

Then, 'Well,' I say. 'Well.'

I turn and rummage in the cool safe. I break three eggs into a pint bottle half full of milk, add vanilla essence, three large spoons of sugar, three small shots of brandy. Then I plug the top of the milk bottle with my hand, and shake and shake and shake, until the golden yolks have dispersed, made the whole of the milk butter-coloured, sand-yellow, the colour of a Labrador dog. I pour the thick froth into three teacups, sprinkle the tops with nutmeg powder pinched from a little tin, and hand the cups to the children. They silently take them and drink, and when they take the cups away, they laugh at the milky moustaches on each other's face, and I join them in laughing, and the laughing comes like sun, like the colour of the yolks of the eggs in the bottle. And our laughter brings Miss Deere from the front of the house, and Mrs Reddy from the back, brings all of us together.

THREE WISE'S MEN
Triplets

There's a knock at the door while we are laughing, and Mrs R, still smiling, waves us off to answer it. Our six feet thunder down the hallway, one hand turns the doorknob, our many hands make light work of opening the heavy door. We set our three nutmegged faces in practised solemnity, expecting more soup, a neighbour with stew, perhaps a black-bordered hanky or two.

No neighbour, no stew, no well-meant soup. We are met, instead, by two very shiny black shoes and four big boots, one dark suit in front, two in workmen's blue behind, one short man, two tall, one derby-hatted, two in flat wool caps. The three men together seem to blot out the sun.

A black car is parked on the road, barring our path to the sea. Across the car's flank, in thick white letters, is painted WISE'S.

Ada runs back to the kitchen and returns with Mrs R in tow. Mrs R seems ten feet tall, formidable, storming as we seldom see her storm. She swoops down on us, hugs us in tight, then shoos us away behind her. She turns to face the three Wise's men at the door, grabs the bottom of her jacket and pulls it down firmly, straightening her felted wool armour as if for war. She folds her arms across her big chest, pulls back her shoulders, plants her feet wide. We imagine (though we cannot see it from behind) the set of her face, mouth downturned, eyes wide in challenge.

We huddle behind her in the hallway until, without turning, she shoos us away once more, bidding us with a not-to-be-argued-with wave of her hand to close the kitchen door behind us. So, sighing, we do.

Our mother and Jane Deere are nowhere to be seen. The Lady at the sink, washing teacups and the eggy milk bottle, looks up at us enquiringly. We ignore her and press our ears against the closed door, but all we can hear are rumblings, deep and dark from the Wise's men, low and fierce from Mrs R.

The rumblings don't last long. The front door shuts, the car engine gutters into life. The car roars away with an engine-y bang, the kitchen door opens, and we tumble against Mrs R's trousers as she bursts into the room. She sweeps us up in her arms and collapses us all onto the daybed.

'Oh, the bloody nerve! Those bloody bastards.'

Which bloody? What bastards? Who bloody? Why?

'Never mind. Just some men here to see about some dogs.'

Oho, we think ... men and dogs ... were they the Wonderland men? But where are their dogs?

She soothes her hand over our heads, each in turn. 'Ah, Jesus, Mary and Saint Katie Sheppard. Bloody men and their bloody dogs.' She sighs again. 'Right, where's your mother, d'y'know?'

We tell her that we think she's in the bedroom.

'Off you hop, then,' she says, and we wriggle away as she pushes up from the daybed, no longer formidable. She is suddenly small, and tired, and sad.

The Lady stands, drying her hands, and she and Mrs R share a look over the top of our heads (but we see, oh we see!).

'Ah, perhaps,' says the Lady, 'the girls might benefit from some time in the sunshine? Fresh air, exercise.'

'Yes, yes, go on ratba ...' Mrs R saddens, and shrinks

again. She sighs, plucks her trousers at the knees as she kneels to meet our eyes. 'What say the three of you have a day outside, adventuring?'

Yes, we tell her, yes, yes, and she and the Lady help us make a picnic of cheese and jam sandwiches with apples for afters, and we pack it in a flax kit that Mrs R hoists over Hanna's shoulders, and we head out the back door and around the house past Ernest Rutherford and over the road, watching for bloody dogs and black cars and those bloody men as we cross.

There's a sound like seagulls whining and wheeling up the beach, but we know it's not gulls. It's boys, Worser Bay School boys, a rowdy squawk of them trailing along the shore. One, taller than the others, drags a big stick of driftwood. As we watch from the dunes, he stops and plants the stick in the wet sand, just above the lick of the waves. The stick stands upright, taller than any of them, and all of them stop there as if at a signal. Frank Hofmann (one of Minna Hofmann's many brothers and sisters), the stick-planting boy, stands at the centre of the simmering circle of restless boy legs and sand-kicking shoes. We tune our ears to Frank's whine, all nose and expectation.

'—at Lyall Bay! Another whale! A bloody monster! Hundred foot long—'

The boys shimmer with disbelieving (but wanting to believe) murmurings. Nickers Whittaker breaks away and starts pacing down the beach, counting aloud as he paces. The other boys hem in closer to Frank Hofmann.

'—and it's already started stinkin to high heaven! My brother Bert said—'

Bert Hofmann! Big brother to Minna and Frank and all the other little Hofmanns. Bert Hofmann works with the Tonks's horses, and knows everybody's news, so perhaps this is not just a Frank Hofmann hundred-foot-tall tale after all.

'—Bert said he stood on its back and it wobbled like bloody

jelly and they couldn't move it with ten horses and carts and they're gunna cut it up with pit saws like they cut up a tree and it'll take ten teams of men and they'll have to dig pits beside the whale to fit the men and the saws and then they'll throw the meat and all the sand with blood and stinkin guts and stinkin blubber out to sea but Bert says then they can't bloody swim the bloody horses for a week because of the bloody sharks!'

Frank Hofmann finally takes a breath, and all the boys erupt in a whoop of sharks and pits and blood and saws and horses. Nickers Whittaker waves and shouts, 'A hundred feet!' from halfway down the beach, then starts running back to the other boys.

'I'm gunna go and see it. The whale. And the cutting up. Tomorrow. With Bert.'

The circled boys all thump Frank Hofmann on the back, and they split into twos and threes and orbit the upright stick, bobbing and crouching and pushing, poking and spitting, as boys always do.

The wind swirls and carries their voices away, then it flicks around and lifts their words again and brings them back to us, and we hear the big bad spitting boys are no longer talking of the whale. They say *fireworks* and *fishy* and *funeral* and *fearful* and *funk* and other words that start with eff, and we hear our father's name, and something about jumping, and other accusations too terrible to mention, and we hear *just like the bloody whale, the fat carnival bastard* and *pit saws* and *blubber* and some other words—*black car* and *bay leaf, bank-rubbed* and *broke*—that start with bee.

Oona is first to leap to her feet, her mouth wide in a terrible silent scream, then all three of us are up, standing fierce in the dunes, twenty feet from the terrible boys. Ada and Hanna make enough noise for three, shouting at the boys to stop. The bad boys all turn to look at us and Nickers Whittaker points and shouts, 'Three little Loverock witches!' and we rush from the dunes and charge those big bad boys, wielding between us a great narwhal tusk (though it might just be a stick) that we have somehow, sometime, somewhere collected, though we do not remember the collecting.

We stop and stand, proud and formidable and ten feet tall (like Mrs R), facing the big bad boys. They point and laugh and walk backwards away. Frank Hofmann spits on the sand and, as if the spit is a signal, they all turn their backs on us. Does Frank Hofmann cross his chest as he turns? We can't be sure, but we think he does, and we think we hear *little orphan sideshow freaks* on his breath, then a word that sounds like *poorhouse*. They retreat up the beach in a muttering, spitting, sand-dragging mob, and the wind lifts their voices away out over the harbour so we can't hear the words, just the hum and hurt of the muttering.

Just to make sure, we charge those terrible boys once more, and they scatter and laugh and throw sand and then they are gone, off away up the road, leaving the three of us alone on the beach.

We wonder what it means, what we heard the effing and beeing boys say, about our father and jumping. We only know jumping like stars on the beach, or jumping for joy, though we're not sure that's what they meant. There was spit and hurt in their jumping talk, and we heard the word *sin* (that we know from Minna Hofmann saying it), and it all feels like the sound of something terrible that we do not understand.

Oh yes, we wonder what it all means—the bad boys, the Wise's men, Frank Hofmann's bloody whale tale, and all.

At least with the great dead whale, we can see for our very own selves. We can go through the tunnel, now, and on to the wide ocean bay. There is no one to stop us, now that our father is gone.

It's quite a way, though, to the ocean bay, and all this talk of horses has got us thinking. We run back to the house, to invite dear old Ernest Rutherford to join our adventuring day.

AJAR
Matti

Matti lies on the children's bed, curled on her right side, facing the wall. Her left arm is hooked over her ear, muffling sound to a dull distant murmur.

She had heard them all in the kitchen, before, not their words but their tones: the children quizzical, querulous; Wilma gruff, almost angry; the woman, their visitor, Madame Marya Miranda Skwodovska, sibilant, hesitant. Individual words drifted to her, clear as bells through muffling fog. *Dog. Jesus. Shepherd. Wise men.* Were they telling Bible stories? It made as little sense as anything. *Charlie is gone. I am unmoored.* Nothing makes sense any more.

Then the sound of the children rose, and then there was quiet, and then the sound of the women alone in the kitchen. Teacups and chair legs and low huddled voices, as if in consultation, or retreat.

Soon, soon, Wilma had come to her, bringing tea and a slice of fruitcake as dark as dirt. When Wilma sat on the bed, Matti heard the horsehair in the mattress rustle and shift and shush. Wilma's hand was warm on her shoulder.

'Drink, eat, just a little something, Matti, my dear.'

She had tucked Matti's hair behind her ear, smoothed her hand against her brow, and kissed the top of her head, kissed her hair that smells of sweat and neglect. Wilma had left the door ajar as she left. *Ajar, adrift, asleep, aloft, alone alone alone.*

~ ~ ~

She must have drifted—*adrift, ajar, awake*—to sleep. How long? Not long, she thinks. She lies now between sleep and waking. She can sense daylight, warm and red through the skin of her closed eyelids.

And now, there, there, the sound of the children comes to her, and she opens her eyes, and light pours in. *Too bright, too much, too soon.* She closes her eyes again, and listens.

The creak of a rusty hinge.

The jangle of thin metal rings, light as laughing.

An underbreath hum, the clicking of tongues in unspoken language, animal, easing, calm.

Matti rolls from her side onto her back, levers herself up to sitting. Through the window, she watches her daughters framed in a rectangle of light, in the door of the dark shed. Oona—is it Oona? Can she tell from this far?—points up to the wall as Hanna brings a wooden beer crate, the two of them step up, steadying each other, and they reach and lift down a belt, or a strap, some metal, something tinkling.

Ada stands a step or two in front of her sisters, facing them, watching them. As her sisters step down from the wooden box, Ada turns to face the back of the cottage, towards the window. Matti meets her firstborn daughter's eyes. Ada lifts her hand, waves. Matti lifts her hand, mirroring her daughter's, though she does not wave it, but holds it still, keeping it close to her face. She can see her daughter's mouth make the shape of *mother*. Matti's mouth makes the shape of a smile. Ada turns to join her sisters, and the three girls skip away, disappear around the side of the house.

Matti swings her legs over the side of the bed, lifts herself—heavy as lead, sluggish as mud—to sitting. She lifts the teacup to her lips, sips. The tea is cold. She breaks off a corner of the fruitcake, just a nub the size of her fingertip, and pops it into her mouth, tastes treacle and spice, feels the grit of raisin seeds on her tongue. More tea, sweet, cold. She hears a sound she cannot place, clipped and heavy at once, regular, massive, and the sound of the girls comes with it, and then their old horse appears, led by Hanna and Ada, with Oona walking beside them, and the three children and the dear old horse pass by, crossing the yard in procession, so the last she sees of them, as they disappear around the side of the house, is the old horse's tail lifting, her big arse farting, fruity and cheerful as Christmas.

DOWN THE RABBIT-HOLE
Triplets

Ernest Rutherford's bridle is in the garden shed, where our father has always kept it dubbinned and supple and hanging on a nail, for just-in-case. We fumble as we fit it over her nose and head and behind her ears. Thank goodness for her patience—and for beer boxes to make us taller. We lead her to the front of the house, across the road, and climb up on the fence rail and onto her back. Ada's in front, the rope reins in her guiding hands. Hanna's behind, the lunch kit hooked over her shoulders. Oona is forever in between. Ready? Ready. We all kick with our heels and dear old Ernest Rutherford the Horse sets sail, with all of us aboard.

We ease into her gentle roll and sway, down the now-empty beach. At the Seatoun end of the bay, we steer Ernest off the sand and onto the road, up the gentle rise to the mouth of the tunnel. We stop there, steady ourselves, and look back at the hills lit by sunlight, the fat of the shape of the land lying there, across the water.

Who's in the hills today?

We're not in the mood to play.

We have places to go, people to see, lunch to eat and work to do. We have a whale to investigate, questions to ask, and a horse to ride. We might even see a wise man or three about a dog.

Ada gees on the rope, we all kick our heels and click our tongues, and Ernest Rutherford turns and steps inside the tunnel's mouth. We feel the familiar pull of darkness, and of the light beyond. We hear the echo of our father, *stay this side*, then the echo fades to absence—nothing and no one to stop us now—and a silence broken only by the rhythmic knock of Ernest's hooves.

Ernest steps us through the dark and empty tunnel, one behind the other behind the other on her broad and gentle back. Ada pulls the reins to stop when we get to the middle. Our eyes become accustomed to the strange daylight dark. From high on Ernest's back, we can clearly see the pattern of bricks in the roof of the tunnel. We ponder the impossibility of bricks curving right over the top of our heads, as if they don't know they should fall. Oona shivers, the three of us shiver, and we gee Ernest and she walks on, slowly, straight on until we reach the end and come out on the other side, into brightness.

We feel the slip and slope of the hill take us down down down past the tearooms on Broadway corner, and on we go, following the road that runs straight, all the way to the ocean beach, and the whale, and whatever else we might find.

This midwinter whale day, Lyall Bay is busy with stickybeaks and lollygaggers, holidayers and hoorayers. There's no one bathing, though the ocean sits strangely calm and inviting, milling like a pond in the big broad bay. The peaks of the South Island float distant above the sea, snow-dusted, like cakes in the window of Godber's in Town, or a fairytale castle that cannot be reached.

We stop outside the Bay View Tea Rooms and slide off Ernest's back. No time today—no money either—for Bay View's cakes and warming tea. We find a spot to tie her rope rein to a verandah post. Our father's voice sings in our heads, teaching us our knots, *up through the rabbit-hole, round the big tree, down through the rabbit-hole, off goes she.*

All eyes (and all trails and all noses) lead to the crowd at the far end of the bay, around past the rocks. We head off in that direction, to see what we can see.

We smell the whale before we see it. We've smelled the smell of dead fish a thousand times, and we've smelled dead seagulls on the beach, and once we found a dead penguin, missing his head, poor thing. But this is a dead smell like none we've ever smelled, a terrible stink like the deep bottom of the ocean has been turned inside out and seeped up through all the sewers of the world and up through the tanks and drains of the slaughterhouse and the tannery in the valley of Ngahauranga on the other side of Town.

This deep dead smell is the smell of the whale.

We hurry on towards it.

At first, we can't see past the crowd of people surrounding the stench. We imagine the poor beast lying on the beach like a fat bag, or a stocking, or a tadpole. Or like a teardrop (on its side, going nowhere) that we've imagined before.

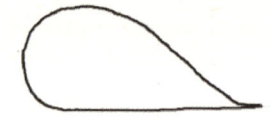

We climb to the crest of the sand dunes, from where we can see the whole sweep of the bay. There we catch our first glimpse of the whale.

It is, as Frank Hofmann reported, bloody enormous. From its fat tip (taller than the men who stand near it, leaning on shovels, handkerchiefs tied around their faces) to its fine tail, it stretches forever down the beach, the size of two tramcars. But it's not the fat teardrop shape we imagined it would be. It's a shape we have seen before, in our memory that is both more and less than memory. The whale lies on the beach as Mr Halley's comet flew across the skies, in that same comet shape we remember. The fat comet push of it at the front. The sleek comet tail of it at the end. Imagine this whale circling our world, crossing oceans, as Mr Halley's comet crossed the skies! (And oh! imagine how our father would love the stink and the shape and the crowd of this, and the great heaving spectacle of it all!)

We make our way closer, losing sight and gaining smell as we drop down from the dune tops to the beach, skirting the edge of the crowd. Taking our lead from the shovelling men, we take our hankies from our pockets and tie them, so they cover our noses and mouths. We duck through the legs of the watching crowd, and suddenly there we are, and there's the whale.

Up close, the smell is overpowering, almost sweet. We take it all in quickly. The whale's great grey-black flank looks like Miss Grimshaw's big blackboard in our classroom, before it's been scrubbed clean at the end of the day. Pale lines and ridges cross its great belly, all coated and gritted with sand. There are cuts and scrapes and holes, the marks of a long ocean life. The smell drives us back again, and we move through the crowd, around and upwind, then closer still. There are letters carved in the skin of the great beast's head, words and names (one of them is Hofmann, there's a surprise). Men in a team at the whale's fat end smoke and lean on shovels. Near them, a photographer fusses out from under the black drape of a camera on a tripod, calls to the shovel men, but they ignore him. A boy runs to the tail end of the whale and steps up onto it, ignoring shouts. Another boy jumps up and past him, and the two of them clamber a yard or three along the whale before the leg of one of them sinks, and a puff of stink erupts. Everyone in the crowd gasps and laughs and gags and jumps back (even the men with shovels), and a man shouts and runs towards them waving his arms and the two boys leap off the whale and away down the beach.

~ ~ ~

There's only so long you can watch a pongy old dead fish, even a great one like this, with words carved upon it, with people standing on it, so we find a pong-free spot in the dunes to eat our lunch. We remove the hankies tied over our noses and mouths and unwrap our jam and cheese sandwiches and, as we eat, we wonder again about the teasing and jeering Worser Bay boys on the beach, and what they said. Though we're fatherless, we know we're not orphans, so the effing and beeing boys got that much wrong. But is it true that we are witches, or sideshow freaks, as those bad boys said? They were right about the whale, and they were right about its smell. What other terrible talk of theirs was true?

Once we've finished our lunch, we head back to Bay View, and Ernest Rutherford. We've saved her an apple from our lunch, and while we untie her, she whinnies it out of Oona's pocket, spittily crunching. We clamber up onto her, and off we walk, clicking our tongues to gee her up.

We head home the long way, this adventuring day. Across the flats and past the Rongotai Knob, around the curve of the inner harbour bay to the big new wharf (no ships there today, no bustle of sails and steam and men and horses for us to stop and watch), then through the cutting that breaks the great humped spine of the Miramar peninsula in two, towering over us as we pass. Down the wide straight of Miramar Avenue, left then right then left and on, until we reach the edge of the great green flat of Miramar Park. The park is edged on its far side by the tall wooden fence that encloses Wonderland. Above the fence rise the turrets of Katzenjammer Castle, the conical roof of the Helter Skelter tower. All is still, all is quiet, but for the sound of Ernest munching grass so loudly we can feel it in our legs, against the side of her great belly. The top of the ramp of the Chute runs straight as a die down the slope of the hillside to where it disappears behind the fence, where we know it meets the lake we cannot see. A pennant hangs limp from a pole at the very top of the Chute, not enough wind to lift it.

We kick our heels into Ernest's sides. She tears one last mouthful of grass, raises her head, and off we go, straight across the park towards Wonderland, as if we don't know we shouldn't.

Ernest Rutherford stops at the front gate of Wonderland and bows her head once more to the grass, as if in prayer, though we know she's just grazing. The WONDERLAND word and the sun that is rising (or perhaps it's setting?), that we know are wrought in iron on the gate, are hidden behind a great sheet of plywood, a sign painted with thick red words covering the gate. One word says CLOSED, and two words say FOR SALE, and there are stranger words we spell out, MORTGAGEE and BANKRUPT and REPOSSESSED, all mysteries.

From the height of Ernest Rutherford's back, we are able to peer over the gate, but all we can see past the wooden sign is closed closed closed. Closed shutters, closed windows, as if the whole of Wonderland has shut its eyes to sleep, or is no more. We sing a song

narwhal amy

down to sleep

that might be prayer—Ada and Hanna sing the words, surrounding Oona's silence—or simply a song of farewell. This Wonderland is not our Wonderland. All the wonder has left, now. It's not the same without our father, Carnival Charlie Loverock. Not the same at all.

We've seen enough.

We turn away, turn for home.

We sway and roll on Ernest's broad back, wondering all the way home if we're somehow to blame. If we hadn't pestered our father (*When can we go to Wonderland?*), if we hadn't begged him (again and again and again), if he hadn't opened Wonderland for the Winter Gala—if if if, well, what then? Would he still be with us? Was it our begging that's to blame? Was it the fault of the dancing red numbers in his big blue counting book, or did our starry sisters winter dance cause the sky to fall?

The hill is too steep for Ernest, so we stick to the flats. Slowly, slowly, as slow as a funeral procession, Ernest walks us all back to Miramar Avenue, down the Old Farm Road and on, to Broadway, up the gentle slope to the tunnel and through the cool echoing dark, and on, all the way home.

    We close the gate behind Ernest Rutherford. Ada slips into the kitchen and brings back a cup full of oats and two carrots. We all take turns feeding them to dear old Ernest, in grateful thanks for her monumental work today. If she were us, we'd tuck her up in bed for a nice sleep, but horses sleep on their legs, so we wish her goodnight and leave her to it. We are inside, hands washed, appetites at the ready, in time for tea, with the events of our adventuring day held safe in our own rememberings.

In the night Ada sings
    and I sing an adventuring song,
    a thanks to ernest rutherford song,
    a great whale of lyall bay song, full voice
    and I sing for my sister, oona,
    magicked silent, and I sing
    the narwhal amy down to sleep song,
    quiet now, quiet,
    and I sing of wonderland, magicked asleep
    by a spell, waiting to be awoken
    with a kiss

And Oona dreams in silence of our father

> *and he is a great grey-black whale,*
> *not beached on the bay*
> *but reimagined in the ocean,*
> *alive and (yes, why not?) soaring*
> *comet-like, brilliant,*
> *through clear oceans*
> *to the very deepest deep,*
> *full fathom five,*
> *what a wonder!*
> *(and I call to him*
> *but he does not hear)*

And Hanna wakes in the night

> *and I go to the lady's room,*
> *but she is not there,*
> *and I go to the window,*
> *and watch the lady walk*
> *on the beach, and I wonder*
> *if she has been magicked*
> *awake,*
> *just like me*

SPEECHLESS
The Lady

I have taken to walking at night, alone, rugged warm against the damp, the salt seep. I breathe deep, and cold air flushes the fog of the grieving house from my lungs, my body, my mind. With each day's passing, each turn of the Earth, I feel my health and strength improving. On nights when the rain is heavy, I stay sheltered on the Miranda, watching the sea across the road, across the dunes, across the shore. There is no one on the beach; there is no one on the streets at night. This is no city for walking and waking. This is no city at all. This town sleeps in the dark; it sleeps, and so I walk, alone, imagining a city, imagining lights where there are none, imagining cafés and people and noise; imagining a house where my two girls sleep, one little, one big, imagining the steps I would take to walk in the night from the house to our old laboratory shed; imagining its rich chemical stink, imagining his marks left in chalk on the blackboard, imagining the smoke-dirtied glass in all the little panes of the windows of the shed, right up to the cold soaring loft of its hole-pocked ceiling; imagining our work and lives held in memory there, lit blue, worshipped, astonishing.

It is time for me to return, to my daughters, my work.
    Soon. Not yet. Soon.
    It is hard to leave when the mother-doctor-widow is still so deeply grieving.

Hard to leave, though it is hard to stay. This house of grief revives my own, older grief, blows stale breath into its mouth, takes it by the hand and leads it into the night, to walk the shore, or stand on the Miranda and face the storm.

There is a face at my window, now, a small someone in my room, looking out at me. I hold the rail, step up to the Miranda, raise my hand in greeting. Inside the room a pale hand rises to the window, forms a fist and knocks on the glass. Tap tap tap. I spy a triplet.

We both open the front door at the same time, she from inside, I from without.

'Hello, Lady,' she stage-whispers, stage-curtseying, her arm out in a flourish of welcome-and-won't-you-please-come-in.

'Hello, Hanna.'

'Couldn't sleep.'

'Nor I. Nor I. Come, we will sit, yes?'

No one in the house stirs while we bustle in the kitchen, heating pans, tinging spoons against china. We settle in my room, she with sweet warm milk and bread for dipping, I with hot tea. I sit on the hard-backed wooden chair by the writing desk. Hanna sits on an ottoman—not much more than a firm cushion, in fact—on the floor at my feet. She balances a tiny tray on her lap. I admire her concentration, tearing bread, dipping, slurping, licking, dropping not a drip of sticky milk. She continues until all the bread is finished, then she sucks one fingertip and taps it on the tray, picking up breadcrumbs, popping them in her mouth. Waste not, want not. I sip my tea, no longer scalding.

Then, 'Lady?'

'Yes, Hanna.'

'It's just. My sister.'

'Yes?'

'It's Oona—'

Hanna bows her head over the half-empty bowl on the tray on her lap. She dips her finger into the bowl, lifts the skin from the surface of the milk. It puckers on her fingertip, a glistening, wrinkled thing, shed. She closes her eyes and pops it into her mouth.

Then as if this action has loosened her tongue she talks, in halting words, about her sister, Oona. Her quiet, her silence. That she smiles but does not speak. That she screams without sound. That she will not, cannot sing. That her body feels tight and bound with words that cannot break her skin. That their mother is too tired and sad for them to talk to.

Hanna shivers, whether from cold, or from the telling, I cannot fathom. I lean forward, lift the light tray from her lap and place it on the desk next to my empty teacup. Then I stand, reach my hand down towards her, not knowing what to say, so—like Oona—saying nothing.

She takes my hand, rising to her feet. She shivers again. I take the fine wool shawl from my own shoulders and drape it around Hanna's. She hunches into it, her eyes closing, murmuring sleepy thanks.

'Rest here, little one,' I say, and I half lift her—she weighs nothing at all—as she steps up into my bed. I raise the covers over her, tuck them tight under her chin. She smiles, eyes closed, and I turn out the low light.

I carry the tray to the kitchen, rinse cup and bowl, leave it for the morning. The door to the girls' room is ajar. There, dark-shadowed, the mother-doctor-widow lies. She sleeps with one dear daughter on each side, between them. She—the mother, the widow—curves a crescent around one child, the woman's back shaped to that of the child, the woman's arms holding her, keeping her. The other child faces away from her mother and her sister, curls in on herself, tight, unmoving. With one hand the girl clenches her own shoulder; the other forms a fist, pressed tight against her mouth.

I ease the door closed, carefully, quietly, and return to my room. Hanna is fully abandoned to sleep. Little sweet snores feather from her. I climb in next to her, ready to sink below consciousness.

TIME

Triplets

Hanna's eyes flutter open in the unfamiliar bed, and there is the Lady
>*beside me, asleep,
>smiling in her dreams,
>and I close my eyes
>and there are numbers
>on the insides of my eyelids
>that I count, and sort, and add,
>returning me to sleep*

Ada rests in the arms of our mother
>*and the smell of my mother is sour
>but sweet to me,
>like bread-and-butter cucumbers,
>and I brush her hair with my hand,
>and breathe her in*

And Oona turns away again, and dreams of our father
>*on a raft on the bay,
>that the wind carries away,
>and I call and call to him
>but he can't hear me,
>and he won't turn back*

~ ~ ~

In our strange and silent house—almost as closed and magicked as Wonderland, almost as silent as Oona—time remains broken. The Lady cooks us porridge for tea, drizzled thick with honey, and we don't like to say that porridge isn't for tea-time, so we eat it just the same. At midnight, she cuts great slabs of bread, butters them thickly, and we huddle at the table, spooning jam into plum-red puddles, feeling the sugar-squeak of it on our teeth. The scrap bucket is full of sweetness. We take the bucket to Ernest Rutherford and press ourselves against her as she eats, feeling the rumble and grind and slick of her teeth on jammy bread heels and apple cores and milk on the turn, custard-thick.

Slowly, surely, as the days unfold, time starts to make sense again. Porridge shifts back to breakfast time, bread-and-butter to lunch. We sit at the table with sausages for tea and try not to notice our father's empty chair. The clock keeps time once more.

Each morning Mrs R picks kawakawa leaves, steeps them in boiling water to make tea for Oona. The more holes the better, she tells us, the stronger the leaves' medicine, but the pale brew doesn't bring back Oona's voice. Give it time, Mrs R says, give it time. After Oona swills and spits, each day, she pokes her tongue out for Mrs R, who takes a good look, sighs a big sigh, and kisses the top of Oona's head.

Our mother dresses each day, though she does not go to work. Sometimes she sits with the Lady at the kitchen table by the blazing stove. The Lady writes inky page upon page, though we don't know what she's writing (letters, notebooks, fanciful stories for curious daughters?). Mrs R sits on the daybed, reading *The Maoriland Worker*. Jane Deere is often here, cooking, smoking. We three lie on our bed, a book open between us, our chins in our hands, watching them all through the open door. And if not watching them, then we are content, knowing they are there, knowing we are safe in this household of women.

School holidays end. We tramp up the hill. Minna Bloody Hofmann comes to us between the bells, with red eyes and a soggy hanky, and she takes our hands and crosses her little flat chest until Second Bell rings, and we scurry into line. At lunchtime we huddle in one of our old favourite spying spots, a twiggy gap in the hedge by Boys Playground, and listen. At first, the boys' talk is of marbles (guttas and oggies, glassies and thumbers and great fat sparkling googs), then of the whale at Lyall Bay, and carving initials in its skin, and how great the stink was, and how Mr Philp the Butcher in Cuba Street sold chunks of whale meat as silverside. Then they talk about Wonderland and sneaking over the fence for the Gala and the sideshow and the fireworks, but when they start to talk about Jumping Charlie Loverock, and the lake, and the Wise's men in their black car, we run away before they say.

Jane Deere cooks us fish for dinner, flour-dredged and fried in the pan, and scrubbed boiled potatoes, everything rich with butter, comforting. We ask her where the fish is from.

'The sea,' she says, then, when we roll our eyes at her, 'the French fisherman.' We store it away, another name for Hermit Louis.

We have other questions for Jane Deere, too, questions we don't know how to ask our mother, or Mrs R, or the Lady. When we have Jane Deere alone, while we're helping with the dishes, we ask her about the Wise's men (without dogs) who came to the door, who made Mrs R formidable.

'Salesmen, such a nuisance,' she says, and she throws Hanna the tea towel to finish the drying.

And what about the sign at Wonderland, and what does BANKRUPT mean? And is it the same as *bank-rubbed* that we heard the bad boys say?

'Never mind, just banking nonsense, not to worry,' she says, and she frowns. Then she makes us hot cocoa, adding an extra spoon of sugar to each cup.

We remember our parents talking, beforetimes, at night, and we remember our father being troubled by the dancing red numbers in his big blue counting book, and we remember knowing that the talking and the worrying and the dancing red numbers and Wonderland being closed before it opened were all, somehow, related. And we want to know more, but no one will tell us, no one will talk. Not about the Wise's men at the door, not about the strange words (the bee words the bad boys said, *bank-rubbed* and *bay leafs*, and the other word—MORTGAGEE—that might be French, or perhaps it means a kind of horse). Not about jumping, whatever that means.

No one talks about our father. No one speaks of him. No one speaks his name. It is almost as if we imagined him, or he has been magicked away.

So we listen to the grownups, to words half-heard but not understood, and try to puzzle it all together. We keep our tales of boys and bays and whales and visits to Wonderland to ourselves.

Oona goes to the beach
>*and I go alone,*
>*leaving my sisters behind,*
>*and I call and call*
>*to our father, my father,*
>*but he does not hear me*
>*and he will not turn back*
>*to me, to us*

While Mrs R is up to her elbows in dirty laundry (scrubbing and soaping and effing and blinding), we ask her why she was so fierce with those men.

'What men?'

The men at the door, the three Wise's men in the shiny black car, you remember, the bloody men and their bloody dogs, we tell her. And what in the name of Saint Katie Sheppard does MORTGAGEE mean, and is it horses?

She shakes her head, wipes her hands down the front of her shirt, and leans down to us (as she did that night, we remember).

'And where did you hear that? Aah, never mind where. It's not for you to concern yourselves,' she says, 'do you hear me?'

But why, we ask her, and what about jumping, and she snaps at us as no one has snapped since that terrible night, 'No, I won't hear it, no more!' Then her voice softens as she adds, 'Curiosity killed the cat! Off you kittens go!' And she plunges her arms back into the grey soapy water, and we know we're dismissed.

We have so many questions, more each day, about banks and rupts and jumps, about men and their dogs, and whales and fishes, and plums and the poorhouse and everything else. But no one answers our questions when we ask them. No one talks to us. No one tells.

So we listen, when they think we are asleep or away from hearing. When the night draws in and the lights are low, and they are sitting together in the quiet, we sneak into dark corners or hold our ears to the crack of a just-open door.

Tonight, our mother and Mrs R sit at the kitchen table, their heads together over the counting book with its leaping red numbers and pencilled question marks. All we hear are whispered fragments.

'—when the sale is complete—'

'—depends on the price—'

'—and who would buy it, for pity's sake?'

'—chance to save it—'

'—the house, at least—'
'If only he hadn't—'
'—if only he had.'

The soft scraps of their speech, that we can't quite stitch together into sense, tangle and lift in the air, as impossible to hold as the smoke from our mother's asthma cigarettes.

FRONT
Matti

Matti ashes her cigarette in the green and white saucer, touching the tip of it on the chip on the saucer's rim, staining the china ash-grey. She takes a deep draw on the cigarette, the paper crackles down to her finger, and she feels the burn of it. She stubs it out on the saucer.

The accounting book is open on the table. The figures swim before Matti's eyes. She pushes the book away, across the kitchen table. Wilma Reddy sits opposite her. Dear Wilma. Dependable Wilma. Wilma, who can be trusted.

The two women calculate and recalculate, and recalculate again, carefully checking each other's figures, suggesting alternative addings and options, but no matter how they try to trim and cut and realign, still the outcome is the same each time.

Wonderland will be sold. They hope the sale brings enough to clear Charlie's debts. Hope, above all, to save the house.

She doesn't blame Charlie. How could she? How can she? He didn't do anything wrong—didn't gamble (except on the success of his Wonderland vision), didn't drink to excess, didn't stray. He followed his dreams, even when they were overambitious. But he didn't do anything wrong. He just failed to do everything right.

Now he's gone, leaving disarray, in matters of money and in all things. It is easier, though, Matti knows, to attend to the unbearable—almost unsolvable—financial mess Charlie has left them in, than to consider for even a moment the question of how he left them, how he died. So, she holds the line: he didn't do anything wrong.

Matti jumps when Wilma slams the book closed on the table. Wilma shrieks her chair back, rubs her hand over her face and through her hair, mutters that there's nothing more to do, it's late, she's done for the night. She leans to embrace Matti, bids her—whispers in her ear, Matti can feel the warmth of her breath—get some sleep, rest, be well, and for heaven's sake eat something, then lets herself out, leaving Matti alone.

The house is utterly silent. No wind tonight to rush and pull. Even the sea is still. Matti lights another cigarette, just to make some noise. The scratch of the match, the flash of phosphor catching, the hiss and crackle of the paper taking flame. She can almost hear the smoke fill her lungs, reach into her, all the branches of her airways, fuming white with smoke, deep, deep, deep.

Matti can feel, some days now, the slip of grief's hold on her. Or the beginnings, at least, of the slip. And so, each day, she dresses, she puts on a front, puts on her face. *More front than Foy's*, Charlie used to say. She can put on a front for her girls, at least.

She has been neglecting the children, she knows this. She cannot bear it, but she cannot be different. She has leant on Ada, held her close, closer, her comfort, her dearest one, her firstborn. She has watched Hanna and their visitor become closer, too, as their visitor has regained her health.

The woman—their visitor, the Professor, Madame Skwodovska—has been a surprising help. Her health and vitality have blossomed, improved, while Matti has sunk low, lower. As if they counter each other, one high, one low, on a teetering seesaw. When one is up, the other is down. When she was up, she was up. And when she was down, she was all the way down.

Matti feels neither up nor down, simply uneven, and without balance.

She draws in, pulls the cigarette down to its last half inch. Crackle, burn, breath, breathe in, breathe out, her own pulse thumps in her ears in the still quiet of the house around her.

And in the silence, she listens.

Oona.

Oona?

She cannot recall the last time she heard dear Oona's voice.

GORSE
The Lady

In addition to my own nocturnal wanderings, I have taken to taking the little girls to the beach, most days, for air and exercise. I have always attached great importance to time outdoors, and to gymnastics, too often neglected in the education of girls—though not that of my own dear daughters, for whom exercise en plein air has always been a priority, and a pleasure, that I have shared with them. I recall that these three girls' father led them in beach exercises each day. They must miss it, as they miss him in all things.

I first suggested this course of action to Mrs Reddy, who deemed it a fine idea.

'No need to bother Matti,' she told me. 'She will be pleased, I know it.'

Indeed, I did not wish to bother the mother-doctor-widow who, poor wretch, is still pitched so very deep in grief. She has Mrs Reddy as her confidante, and the two of them huddle and mutter together. Often the three girls are left to themselves, too often inside, too often lingering in bed, too often listening at doors. It prompts me to wonder: in my own grief in the days and weeks after my husband's death, was I as neglectful of my own dear daughters?

Their mother seems even to ignore the strange recent silence of one of her daughters. Doctor Bennett, I know, has checked the girl thoroughly, medically, found her healthy in body, and has ruled out an organic cause for Oona's silence.

Simply grief, she said, leave her be, in time she'll mend. Mrs Reddy, meanwhile, picks from the wild hillside each day a handful of heart-shaped hole-laced leaves, from which she prepares a fresh tisane for Oona to gargle each morning and night. It seems neither to harm nor heal, and Oona maintains her silence.

So, without bothering their poor grieving mother, now each day I urge the girls outside for exercise. I aim to keep the sessions varied, to maintain their interest: one day, a sequence of stretches and tumbles and leaps; the next, a brisk walk to the wharf and back. Everything on the beach, in the environment, becomes part of their play, a lesson to learn. They climb an upturned boat, progress hand-over-hand all the length of a steel tube fence, walk in careful balance along the wooden frame of the boat ramp high on the beach; we observe creatures in rock pools, plants on the shore, the changing clouds in the sky. The children are inventive, enthusiastic, quick to learn, eager to please. Even the silent sister, Oona, joins in, though when I try to draw her into conversation, comment or song, she resists.

No school to occupy them today, and so, once they have completed their breakfast and their daily tasks—scraping plates, scraps to the horse—and with the morning stretching fine and clear ahead of us, I bid them prepare for an extended session.

'Perhaps you will show me your tumbling routine? We might then botanise.'

While they fetch jerseys and don shoes, I collect my small knife and field glass from my room and slip them into my pocket. We meet at the door and, without further ado, set out, heading north along the liminal strip where salt sand meets grey-green coastal vegetation.

I lead them in a brisk march, arms swinging, deep breathing. They soon outstep me—some days I still tire easily—so I clap my hands to draw their attention, then I challenge them to race each other, down to the wood-and-tin shed on the tip of the bay and back again to me. I stand, resting, breathing in the sharp salt tang, the rich savoury of tidecast. The girls speed back to me, their feet kicking sand up in rooster tails behind them, the three of them falling at my feet in a tangle of lean little limbs.

'Ah, you are all so fast—equally fast—and I cannot tell who reached me first. The only solution is prizes for all.'

I hand each of them a stem of rabbit-tail grass, that I picked from the dunes as they ran. One of them, chattering all the while, tickles another on the cheek with the whiskers of her rabbit-tail; the tickled sister—wordless, so she's Oona, I presume—pushes the stalk of her rabbit-tail through the wool of her jersey, to wear it as a medal. And the other—it is Hanna—tucks the stalk behind one ear, tucks her hair behind the stalk, and smiles a smile that beams from that ear to the other.

'Very good. You all wear them well. Come, come, let's walk.'

'Not just walking,' the chattering one, who must be Ada, says. 'Or racing. You said you wanted to see our tumbling.'

'Quite so,' I say. 'Tumble away, then, do.'

And so we resume our ramshackle procession north along the edge of the beach, variously walking and tumbling and wheeling and dancing. But while two girls—one talkative, one silent—skip and jump ahead, one stays by my side. Hanna reaches up and slips her hand into mine as we walk.

'Brava, brava,' I encourage her tumbling sisters, and Hanna, too, takes up the call.

We slow, Hanna and I, to a botanising pace, a pace not for exercising, but for observing. I encourage her to appreciate what is common, what is all around and everywhere: rabbit-tail grass, sea daisies, dune tussock. We stoop, rest on our haunches, and I draw from my pocket my field glass, pass it into her eager hands. Her curiosity is evident in the intensity of her focus. When she lifts her eyes to mine in wonder—at fine hairs on a sea fig stalk, the pattern of veins on a leaf, the magnification of grass whiskers under the glass, all made magnificent—I am reminded of my dear Big Girl, so far away. A rushing ache goes through my heart.

We come to the edge of the rocks that reach into the harbour to form the northern arm of the bay. The other two girls are crouched by a rock pool, poking fingers, exclaiming, and Hanna goes to them, clambers over rocks to join them in crouching and poking and exclaiming. I turn out of the wind, to push away stray hair that has blown into my eyes. Looking landward, lifting my chin, my sight line follows the slope that rises steep above the houses that dot the coast. Miramar is covered with gorse in flower, stiff crowns buttering the hillside brilliant yellow. Like sunshine. The smell of it comes to me now—sweet, honeyed, overpowering even the sea.

The scent of gorseflower headied the air on the last days that my husband lived, that Easter, six years and half a world away from here. Gorse, brilliant, ringed the pond at the edge of the meadow, where we stopped to rest, to eat, to lie together. I remember.

Pierre, my love, I remember.

I remember the sweet lift of violets, and trembling periwinkles, that you and I picked, and posied, and pinned to my breast. I remember our four bare feet, our four strong hands, our two hearts beating, our two bodies, together. And our two minds. We made ourselves radiant, together.

I am teacher, I am mother, I am scientist and wife.
No, widow.
I am Manya, Marya, I am my daughters' dear sweet Mé.
I am Professor Curie.
I am myself, Marie.

~ ~ ~

In the garden, with our daughters, that last day, you touched my cheek, my fine hair. You told me, life has been sweet with you, Marie. And then you were gone.

My Pierre, I want to tell you that there is gorseflower here. I know this would delight you. I have not seen violets, nor water ranunculus, but there is whiskered rabbit-tail grass—oh, your beard, your perfect little beard!—and succulent sea fig, and narcissus, though surely the season is wrong. And I want to tell you that I have learned again to love the flowers. The sight of them no longer makes me suffer, as it did in the days and months after your death. I have learned again to love the sun, as I could not, then, when I wept on fine days and wanted only dark days, grey, like the drear day of your death.

I want to tell you everything.

I want to tell you about these fatherless girls, here, on this side of the world, and I want to tell these girls that, like our own dear fatherless daughters, they will survive, they will even thrive. I want to tell the silent sister that she will find her voice, in time.

I want to tell their mother, now bereft, that she will learn to love the sun. That life will be sweet again. Not today, but one day.

I want to tell them that they will never forget him, that he will always be with them, as you, my love, are always with me.

Gorseflower, brilliant yellow, sand under my feet. I drop my hand from my forehead, unshade my eyes, and the dark gives way to blinding light. Three girls run to me, all of them waving. Two girls take my hands. One girl runs ahead, and we all run towards the cottage, where a black van has pulled up, WISE'S writ large on its side, legible even from this distance.

BENEFIT

Triplets

We're up to our ankles in a rock pool when we hear car doors slamming. We watch the three Wise's men adjust their hats, roll their shoulders, and walk up the steps to our front door. We see the shape of Mrs R fill the open door, confronting the men.

We run, all three of us—Oona runs ahead, while Hanna and Ada take the Lady by the hand—across the road (watch for motors!), up the steps. The Lady stops on the verandah, hangs back, but we three push between the trousered legs of the three men at the door.

'What, careful, why the blinking—'

We tuck ourselves in behind Mrs R, our arms folded across our chests, standing as she stood that other day, in challenge and defiance, eyes wide, chins up.

Our mother approaches, behind us.

'Girls, girls, please, to your room.'

When we hesitate, she shouts as she has never shouted at us, low and guttural, a sound out of nowhere.

'Go now!'

So we go. There is nothing else to do.

Our mother comes to us, soon after, lies on the bed with us, takes the three of us in her arms, and holds us so tight we think we might stop breathing.

'It's Wonderland, my darlings,' she says, in a voice so quiet it sounds like thought. 'We must sell it, quick-smart. Now that your father—' She gasps and starts again. 'Without your father,' we nestle in and hold tight to her and to her words, 'we cannot. We simply cannot. Hold on.'

We have wondered and wondered what all the talking means, these past weeks, and all the words and all the whisperings and all the red-writ books. After all our wondering and questioning and puzzling, there it is, finally, in plain words we cannot miss. Wonderland must be sold.

The blunt fact of it leaves us feeling upturned. Wonderland, our Wonderland!

And yet we think of how we felt to gaze on Wonderland, the day of our beached-whale adventure, how Wonderland—boarded, blinded, broken—was no longer our own Wonderland, not without our father.

The Wise's men can have that broken Wonderland, if we're honest.

We can go to our Wonderland—Carnival Charlie calls us there, to Miramar's Mecca of Merry Souls—every night, in our dreams.

The appearance of the three Wise's men seems to turn our mother the right way up again. It's as if she's been suddenly shaken awake from her sad magicked slumber. She cooks and sleeps and eats again. She cleans and works and even smiles. She sees us off to school and off to bed and off to feed the dear old horse. But we notice that everything gallops at too brisk a pace, like clock springs wound too tight, as if time is running out. All we can do is try to keep up.

Our mother's pace quickens the closer we get to the day of the Wonderland sale. The date is fixed. The first of the month. On the site. All chattels and fixings must be sold on the day. That's what we know from listening at doors, though we don't know what fixings and chattels might be.

How do they sell a Wonderland, we wonder, and are chattels like camels, and can we ride them? Or are they like tiny cats?

We ask Mrs R, and she frowns and shakes her head. Jane Deere says, 'No, and there's nothing to see, nothing to see,' but we don't think that can be right. We ask the Lady, and she says she couldn't say. Our mother sighs and goes back to scrubbing the stove.

We hear the truck pull up outside our house one fine cold morning while we're out with Ernest Rutherford, stroking her whiskery nose as she finishes the last scraps in the bucket. The horn parps, and Jane Deere's voice calls *Coo-ee*. We wave goodbye to Ernest, and rush towards the sounds.

Jane Deere waits, leaning on her truck. She gathers us around her, all three of us in her arms, and tells us a marvellous thing. Miss Jonassen the Hot-Air Ballooniste is planning a flight in Miramar! Swoon! A dream come true!

'Did you know,' she flips a cigarette into her mouth, scrapes a match to light it, breathes in long then breathes out, blue and fragrant, 'that Nella—Miss Jonassen—is an old and very dear friend of mine?'

We did not! How has she never told us, we wonder, as we clamour and clamber up the front steps, into the house and down the hallway in Jane Deere's smoky wake. We are great admirers of Miss Nella Jonassen, the Hot-Air Ballooniste, the Captainess, the Aerial Queen, the Show-Woman of the Southern Skies. In the year of our birth, she was one of the fabulous features of the opening season of Wonderland, though she's not been back (she's been travelling the world, we hear) in all the years since, so we've never seen her in real life. We do, however, have a swoonworthy picture postcard of her pinned to the wall of our bedroom, *Miss Nella Jonassen at Wonderland, Bound to Rise!* Katzenjammer Castle is in the background, the Aerial Queen herself posed by the basket of her balloon, one hand on the basket, the other on her hip, wearing the white silk flying suit for which she is so famous.

Jane Deere sits down in the empty kitchen. Oona climbs onto her lap, Ada hangs her arms over Jane Deere's shoulders, Hanna clasps her arms around Jane Deere's wool-trousered legs. We beg her to tell us more.

'She'll do one show only. Just the one ascent.'

Our mother and Mrs R enter the room as we leap off Jane Deere, whooping in delight.

'What on Earth—'

'I was just telling the girls,' Jane Deere shouts over our whoops, 'that I told Nell—Nella Jonassen, you remember Nell—about Wonderland.' She looks over our heads at our mother, at Mrs R, and lowers her voice. 'And she's devastated to hear about Ch—'

'—yes, yes,' our mother says.

'—about what's happened, of course. And she's planning a flight here anyway. So she'd like to—'

She stops as the kitchen door opens again, and the Lady enters. Jane Deere nods at her, then turns her head and looks straight into our mother's eyes.

'Matti, dear Matti, she'd like any small earnings from the flight to be to your benefit. For Wonderland. For the girls. For everything.'

Our mother raises both hands to cover her nose and mouth, squeezes her eyes shut tight. She is silent. All of the rest of us watch her. She lowers her hands, thumbs under her chin, palms pressed lightly together, the tips of her pointer fingers light on her lips.

'I cannot say no. Give her my thanks, Jane, dear Jane.'

Our mother walks from the room. Everyone and everything breathes again.

~ ~ ~

And so it's settled. Miss Nella Jonassen's benefit flight will be at the end of the month, the day before the Wonderland auction, Jane Deere tells us.

'And guess where, ratbags?'

We cannot, we cannot guess.

'Right here.'

What's that? Right where?

'On Worser Bay beach.' She flings her arms out wide, towards the bay.

On Worser Bay beach! What a wonder. (How our father would have loved it!)

HOVER
Matti

Matti lies on her bed, trying to still her body, her mind. After those first terrible days—everything slow, too slow, like wading through treacle, breathing mud—she has been too tightly wound, these past weeks. A medication change. Agnes said it should help; the cocktail would bring her energy and oomph—and it has, it has—but she feels jaw-tight, full body clenched. Her teeth grind in the night, leaving her aching-headed each morning. She has no appetite for food. Her mind is chemical-sharp, ice-cold: noticing, but noticing too much, and not enough. Too much, too soon.

She is sharp with the children, too, and with Wilma, and with everyone. Impossible to soften her sharp edges while all this hangs over her. The auction. The reckoning to follow, the endless calculations just to keep them all afloat.

Matti feels weightless, most of the time. More than that; more than empty: incorporeal, unbodied. She feels herself hover above life, above herself, aethereal; above the children, above Wilma, and Jane, and the woman their visitor, as if she is light itself, or spirit.

Everything happens as if not to her.

The children are washed and fed and dressed and schooled and read to. They do not seem to grieve as Matti grieves for Charlie, though she marks Oona's lasting silence, and the quiet space it makes between her sisters. Their visitor, Madame Miranda, no longer needs her care, and instead she helps

Wilma and Jane keep the house and the children in order. Tomorrow is Nella Jonassen's balloon flight, for goodness' sake. The day after that is the Wonderland sale. And the day after that? The fate of it all? Who knows.

She looks down on all of this (she feels as though she looks down on all of this, though her rational mind tells her it can't be so). There she is: Matilda Loverock, Mrs Doctor Matti Loverock, Widow, Doctor, Mother. She can see herself, she can see it all happening, but nothing and no one feels real.

Matti slips back down into her body, feels the bed under her, knows she will not fall. Her teeth grind, her fingers clench and unclench, fist and soften. She slides her legs off the bed, stands. She reaches to the back of the wardrobe, past the spill of clothes, mess, mess, she will clean it up, not now, not now. She retrieves his braided jacket, slips her arms into it. She fills its shape and feels its weight calm her, calm her, hold her close. It anchors her feet to the floor, and through, through, lower, deeper, into the deep of the Earth. She feels her heart slow, slow, approaching normal speed.

BOUND TO RISE
Triplets

The day of Miss Nella Jonassen's flight is with us in a flash. All morning we run between our house and the beach, from the moment the truck pulls up and men start unloading the basket and burners and great bags that will become the balloon. We edge as close as we can before the men shoo us away, then we do it all over again. Dodging in and out of the crowd that starts to build as the morning progresses, looking out for People of Interest, like those big bad boys, or Hermit Louis, or any of the Bloody Hofmanns, makes us almost forget that Wonderland is set for sale tomorrow.

The beach and dunes, the grassy verge, the whole of Worser Bay beach fills with grownups and children, horses and dogs and bicycles, the road crowded with cars and carts, passage now impossible. The crowd spills right up to the steps of our house, and we stand high up on the verandah, at the edge of it all, where we can look down onto the scene.

Miss Nella Jonassen, though, is nowhere to be seen. Her hot air balloon lies on the sand, deflated still, a great empty bag, like a dead jellyfish left by the tide. The crowd circles the balloon bag, watching the dozen men checking the great thick ropes that tether it. Parading the perimeter, a megaphone to his mouth, is a man in a bright white uniform hung with golden chains and medals, swaggering, spruiking the show.

'These very flammable materials are made safe only by the most careful and precise handling, in a scientific way, to achieve the inflation of Miss Nella Jonassen's magnificent balloon. The wonder and danger, ladies and gents, of Gases, Aeriality and the Science of Flight.'

He's not nearly as talented at working the crowd as our own dear father. Nonetheless, the crowd mills, people push closer, craning to see.

'Not too close now! Keep a safe distance as you make your donations, ladies and gentlemen, boys and girls, good people of the Borough of Miramar, your donations, please, to the marquee by the boat shed here. Without your donations we cannot keep the balloon and the ballooniste safe, nor make it safe for you, our audience. In addition, we can benefit, in some small way,' he coughs to clear his throat, 'the family of the recently deceased, your great local entrepreneur and showman, Carnival Charlie Loverock!'

There's a smattering of applause, and a muttering of voices, but all is drowned out by the man's shout, 'Light the burners!' and the noise that follows, *crump* and *whoomp*, then a hot harsh roar.

The balloon bag puffs at first, then bulges, bigger, no longer a jellyfish cast on the tide, more like the shape of a whale, but a cartoon whale, or one drawn by a child (or, yes, a teardrop on its side, going nowhere). The whale shape bellows and blows, it writhes on the sand, lifts and settles, growing all the while. As the swaggering uniformed man tends the flame, we hear the hot rush of the burners. And then the balloon is no longer a whale on its side on the beach, but has become itself, has become a balloon. We can tell it by its shape and its roundness and its lift, upright as a balloon should be, the great ropes straining to hold it down, and the men straining, too, surrounding it and stopping its flight. It finally looks just like the balloon on our postcard, from the banner (*Bound to Rise!*) on the side of it to the basket at the base of it. A gentle breath of wind shifts and the balloon surges and lifts, the ropes and men strain, the crowd oohs and ahs. The wind settles, passes. The balloon rests, ready. But where is Miss Nella Jonassen?

The crowd surges as the balloon did, and there she is, at the base of the balloon, just like the postcard, standing by the basket in her white silk suit, her white headscarf, both hands on her hips, then both hands waving in the air at the crowd. She circumnavigates the basket, touching the great thick ropes with her hands as she passes underneath, ducking and rising, waving at the crowd, to great cheering and whistling and applause, so loud that no one can hear the announcing man or what he says (but we've recited it in our heads and we reckon we know it by heart, *the Daredevil Captainess! The Aerial Queen! Our very own Show-Woman of the Southern Skies!*). We join in the applause, stamping and jumping on the wooden boards of the verandah.

Our mother joins us, and the Lady joins us, too, and we all watch as Miss Nella Jonassen steps onto a stool and up and over and into the basket. She waves again to the crowd, facing each side of the basket in turn. Then she raises her hand, a white silk hanky held in it.

The crowd draws in on a single breath, as if all of us are breathing with the same lungs.

And for a moment there is silence.

No roar from the burners.

Even the gulls and the waves seem to still, and stop, and wait.

And then Miss Nella Jonassen drops her white hanky, and at her signal the burners roar once more, the great straining ropes are released, the men step back, and the balloon and the great wicker basket with Miss Nella Jonassen in it lift up from the beach, as if drawn upwards by a cord strung from the moon or the sun or the stars. And the crowd roars, too, louder than the roaring gas burners that heat the air on the inside of the balloon, and as Miss Nella Jonassen and her basket and her balloon lift up up up, so our faces lift up with her, following her ascent.

All but one of us lift our faces upwards. Only Ada looks to the side
I look at our mother,
my mother,
and see tears on her upturned cheeks,
and I move to her side
and take her hand and she
squeezes it so tightly
in her hand
that I draw a gasping breath

The Bound to Rise balloon rises, rises, and stops when the great binding ropes reach their full extent. The balloon hovers, high, so high, as high as the top of the Wonderland Chute. We see a flash of white, Miss Nella Jonassen's headscarf waving from the basket of the hovering balloon.

The burners roar, and over the side of the basket tumbles a rope-and-rod ladder. Then the burners roar again, and over the side of the basket tumbles Miss Nella Jonassen, stepping lightly down the ladder, until she reaches the bottom rung. And she lets go with one hand, raising her arm high above her head and arching back, back, and the crowd breathes in as one. And she lifts one foot from the ladder, reaching her leg out behind her, and the crowd holds their breath, hands go to mouths, hands cover eyes. And she hovers the outstretched arm, the reached back leg, the one back, the other forward, the one forward, the other back, with grace and agility, as though she is walking or gliding on air, defying gravity (as if she does not know what it is to fall), and all of us watching below regain our breath and we all applaud and hoot and whistle as she climbs back up the ladder, hauls the ladder up behind her, and waves and waves and waves to the crowd, though it feels as if she is waving just to us, only to us.

She stays aloft for only a few minutes more. She pulls ropes, and the fabric of the balloon bag lifts here and there, and the great straining ropes slacken, and men on the ground pull on those ropes and haul her in slowly, slowly, like hauling in a great hooked fish, or a whale, to land it. And so, Miss Nella Jonassen's basket touches down on the sand, and twelve strong men hold the basket down, and Miss Nella Jonassen steps from the basket, steps away from it to take her bows and bouquets. The sun makes her white silk flying suit glow, so she looks like a ghost, or a cuttlefish, or like a saint on one of Minna Bloody Hofmann's holy prayer cards, as the great fabric bag of the balloon descends and deflates behind her, on the silver sand, spent, empty. The great fat balloon in the sky is only a memory.

Our mother's head is in her hands, and she weeps, loud, long, deep. The Lady stands beside her, one arm around our mother's back, one hand patting our mother's arm. There there, come come, there there, she coos. They both face in the same direction, past the balloon and the crowds and the mêlée, to the sea, and the hills, and the sky.

Our father is fireworks, comet, whale, a teardrop tipped on its side (what a wonder!). He's the hot-air balloon of Miss Nella Jonassen (Aerial Queen, Captainess, Show-Woman of the Southern Skies) at the point of touching down, not aloft, but not yet *not* aloft, lying on its side on Worser Bay beach, but still just holding shape, holding breath, halfway up, halfway down. Holding.

The next day—the day of the Wonderland sale—we sleep late. We stumble out of bed, eye-rubbing and sleepyheaded, to find our mother already buttoning her coat, fixing her hat in place. Our father's shoeshine box with its Radium polish, horsehair brush and buffing rags, is open on the table, the smell of it leathery, rich and heavy in the air. The back door opens, and for just one sleep-nodding mouth-yawning eye-rubbing boot-polishing moment we forget and think it might be him. Mrs R steps through the door, breaks the spell.

Mrs R reaches out to our mother, straightens the collar of her coat. She lifts one hand to our mother's cheek. Our mother rests her head against Mrs R's hand, and her eyes drift closed for a long moment. We run to her—to both of them—and hold tight around their skirts.

Mrs R untangles herself from the cluster of Loverocks, and our mother leans to kiss our heads, kiss kiss kiss. She picks up her bag and starts to follow Mrs R. In the doorway she turns, and hovers, one leg behind her, the other forward, her arm outstretched.

'Back soon, my darlings. Back soon. All will be well. All will be well.'

She waves, waving only to us, and then she is gone. Off to the Wonderland sale.

RISEN
The Lady

A knock, soft but insistent, distracts me from my thoughts, my work. I shake my head to come back to the world, place my pen in the furrow of the notebook, ease myself to standing, brushing my skirt into place, call out, 'Please, yes, come in,' as Mrs Reddy takes two steps into the room. Doctor Loverock is behind her in the hallway, standing by the front door but facing back into the house, her spine—indeed, her whole body—in an awkward twist, her focus fixed on something I cannot see.

'We're going now, getting the ferry to Town. For the auction. Wonderland,' Mrs Reddy tells me.

'Is it time already?' I lift my hand to the watch that is pinned to my breast, as if to check it by touch. 'Of course, of course, I had lost track of the morning.'

'The girls are in the kitchen, just risen. If you would be so kind? Breakfast and such?'

'Yes, yes, of course.'

'We may be hours. I don't know how long an auction takes. This auction.' She steps towards me, her voice lower, harsh, caught in her throat. 'To sell off a life. Christ. This, after everything. Matti wants to be there. I tried to dissuade her, but no, she insists.' She shrugs, shakes her head, looks back over her shoulder to her friend. 'Thank you, Prof,' she says, resting her hand on my forearm. 'Come on Matti, love,' she says, turning, and then they are gone.

TORSION
Matti

The taste of her daughters' hair is on her lips, soap, vanilla, the souring milk of sleep. She can feel the torsion of her spine. She twists against it, straightens herself, prepares to meet the day. This day to be endured. This day will bring an end. *All shall be well, and all shall be well, and all manner of things shall be well.*

She hears a sound, soft, animal, and she realises it comes from her, deep in her voice box, unleashed, unmeant.

Wilma Reddy turns to her.

Their visitor—Madame Miranda Marya Skwodovska, the Professor—is behind Wilma, her face concerned.

She puts her hand to her mouth, as if to cough, clears her throat. She nods her head. 'We should go.'

All manner of things shall be well.

Wilma takes Matti's arm, and they step out, across the verandah, down three steps to the path, and onto the road, towards the wharf.

LIKE SUNSHINE
The Lady

I stand at the open door and watch the two women make their way down the road, their gait, together, unbalanced, uneven, so they almost seem to stagger. The ferry is steaming across the bay; the women and the ferry will converge on the wharf. I clench my hands at my throat to cinch in the blanket draped across my shoulders for warmth, but the cold of the day soon breaches that barrier, so I close the door and turn towards the kitchen, that I know will be warm.

There is only one little girl, not the three I was expecting. She looks up at me from the book open in front of her on the table.

'Good morning, Hanna.'

She beams at me, returns my greeting, and before I can ask it, she answers my question: her sisters are dressing and washing, they are not far away.

'Your book,' I say, pointing. 'What are you reading?'

She props it at an angle to show me.

'I can read the whole story and almost all the words,' she says. 'But my favourite word of all to read is this one.'

With the tip of her finger, she follows the familiar serifs on the cover of the book. *Alice's Adventures.*

'Won-der-land,' she says, drawing the syllables out as her finger traces gilt.

Because today is a Wonderland day, she tells me. The end-of-Wonderland day. The all-shall-be-well-after-today day.

Did I know, she asks, that their mother and Mrs Reddy have gone to watch Wonderland sale away?

Before I can answer, the two other girls come running into the room. They stop short when they see me, smiling good morning as they join their sister at the table. Soon all three dark heads are bent with studious intent over the book on the table between them. I start to gather fixings for breakfast, turn towards the stove. I hear them whispering and tittering, then a voice pipes up.

'Hey, Lady.'

'Yes, Hanna?'

More tittering, then, 'There's radium on the table, Lady.'

It sounds like *wadium* when she says it. I smile, turn away from the porridge pot to face the three of them. 'Is there indeed?'

'Yes, yes,' Hanna says, and she points across the table to a small wooden box, hinged at the top. 'In there.'

'Oho, I see. Well, is it safe for me to lift the lid and reveal the radium?'

The three of them clap, yes, yes! I flick the bent nail that acts as a latch and lift the lid, to reveal rags and a brush, the sharp smell of boot black, waxy, chemical.

'Alas, no radium, simply boot wax,' I shrug in mock sadness.

One of them runs around the table, stands on tiptoes and peers then reaches into the box. She pulls out a small tin, round, flat, disc-like, and places it in my hand, a perfect fit. Its lid is enamelled black and deep blood red, RADIUM emblazoned white and gold and bold across it, and below that, WATERPROOF BOOT POLISH. I start, first at the sight of RADIUM, my radium, then at the oddly pleasing resonance of the word—POLISH—that in English describes me, my origins, my homeland. *I am Marya Skłodowska, I am Manya, I am Marie, Madame Curie. I am my father's daughter, I am my daughters' dear Sweet Mé, I am Pierre's*

Little Student. I am I am I am I am, but who in the world am I?

The little girls are watching me, waiting for a response. 'Ah, you were right! Radium, indeed,' I say, 'and this radium is, I see, *free from injurious matter*. How very lucky.'

The three of them laugh with delight, and two of them say in unison, 'Radium shines like sunshine!'

'Our father always says that,' Hanna says, 'every time he shines his shoes. *Radium shines like sunshine!*'

I replace the tin in the wooden box, close the lid, gently latch it shut.

'Radium shines like sunshine,' I repeat. 'So it does. So it does.'

After breakfast, we walk on the beach, the three sisters as animated as ever, in their element. They do not seem dimmed, nor overly perturbed, by today's auction of their beloved Wonderland. Perhaps the loss of Wonderland, after the deeper loss of their father, is too much to comprehend. I think of Hanna's words, this morning, at the kitchen table. *Today is a Wonderland day, the end-of-Wonderland day, the all-shall-be-well-after-today day.* There's hope, I suppose—or is it denial, or delusion?—in that notion that all shall be well.

The girls review and relive yesterday's ballooning display as we walk, and I seize upon the teaching opportunity. I tell them of gases and expansion, of heating and cooling, Brownian motion and Gay-Lussac's law. I draw in the sand the diagrams and equations that somersault through my mind. All three are initially engaged, but two little girls soon wander off, tumbling, cartwheeling, leaving Hanna, only Hanna, crouched on the sand, figuring with me, questioning, responding.

The weather, crisp and bracing all morning, turns suddenly grey while we're on the beach, the wind whipping sand into the air, tearing hair loose from its bounds. I realise that we are not dressed for the fresh chill, and so I call the two tumbling girls, and the three girls and I turn towards the house. We are level with the front door, just about to cross the road, when a familiar black car rolls down the road, cruising—it seems—towards the same destination.

One man jumps out of the front of the car, almost before it has stopped. He opens the rear door, and Mrs Reddy steps down from the car. She turns, offers her arm, and the mother-doctor-widow emerges. The children run to her and cling to her legs. Mrs Reddy herds them all up the path, up the steps, and in through the front door of their home, supporting her friend all the way.

Two men, meanwhile, linger by the car, one of them, the elder, giving orders to the other.

'Good day, gentlemen,' I say, and they start at my address, the younger man touching his hand to the peak of his cap, the other man tipping his hat.

'Afternoon, Missus.'

I nod at them and sweep past into the house.

Mrs Reddy stands at the stove, heating water, clattering the tea caddy. The mother-doctor-widow sits on the chaise longue, with the three little girls by her side. The doctor strokes the hair of one of her daughters, with an absence that is chilling. The girls—all three of them, not just the one—are preternaturally quiet.

At the unmistakably masculine sound of a throat being cleared, I step aside, turn. The two men are framed in the doorway, cap and hat, respectively, in hand at belt height. The hatted man has a notebook under one arm. The capped man carries a folding rule, a pencil tucked behind his ear. A throat clears again; the hatted man speaks.

'If it's all the same, we'll start in the front and work through—'

The mother-doctor-widow looks through them, past them, above them, strokes her daughter's hair. Mrs Reddy bustles past me, 'Come on, come along then,' shuffles the men away down the hall. I follow them at a remove. She directs the men into the doctor's bedroom, then stands in the doorway, arms folded, watching them.

She sees me. 'Ah!' she says, 'yes. I'm sorry, these jokers, these gentlemen, will need to go into your room. To measure. To take an inventory.'

'Of course, but whyever ...?'

She lowers her voice, keeps her eyes fixed on the men as she speaks.

'The auction. It wasn't—that is, it didn't—'

'Was the auction not successful? Did Wonderland not sell?'

'No, it did. It sold. Everything sold. The Tea House, the Chute, the front gate, the ticket house, Katzenjammer bloody Castle. All of it. Every lock, all the stock, every stinking beer barrel. But not for enough. Just,' she unfolds one arm, flags her hand in the air, 'not enough money was made. I don't know ...' She breaks off, raises a hand as if to bat away what she does not know, shakes her head.

It is—I discover—no surprise to me. I think of that day of the Gala, when finally I saw Wonderland. I had somehow expected, from the little girls' descriptions and their father's excitements, something approaching the greatness of the Paris Exposition, its celebration of science and industry—the Palace of Illusions! the Great Telescope!—and all the very world; or at least some echo, if not the grand scale we'd seen in Paris at this century's dawn. But Wonderland was not great or grand, oh, no, it was not. It was not. Even the children, in that strange and empty fernery, seemed to see the down-at-heel-ness of it all, the very smallness, the peeling paint, the sad neglect. Barely a wonder at all.

'And so—what is this, what is happening?' I gesture towards the men.

She sighs. 'The house will have to be sold. To cover the full extent of the debts that Charlie left. Bless him, his heart was in the right place, the silly bugger. He wasn't foolish, or careless. Just,' she shrugs, 'unlucky. And too good a man, truth be told. Too kind. Ever the bloody optimist. A great showman, but not ruthless enough for business. So. It has come to this. Oh, they'll be fine. They don't owe much—just more than the auction returned. Nella raised a little from her balloon flight, so that helps. And the house should fetch plenty to clear the weight of the debt. Matti and the girls can move in with Jane and me, until they get back on their feet. These bloody jokers,' she nods her head in the direction of the men, one measuring and calling numbers under his breath, the other licking his pencil and noting, licking and noting, both working efficiently, in rhythm. 'These jokers, they're preparing an inventory. There'll be an auction.' She shakes her head, her shoulders sag. 'Jesus, Mary and Saint Katie Sheppard. Another bloody auction.'

'I—I had no idea it was—'

'I know. I know. And she hasn't told the girls. Not yet. So—'

'Of course, of course. When will—?'

'The house? End of this month, maybe sooner. As soon as Wise's have done the inventory.'

'And is there any chance, any prospect—?'

'Another option? Saving the house?' She shrugs. 'This is it. Unless a bag of money falls from the sky. This is it.'

She takes her eyes off the men, turns to me, puts a hand on my arm. 'It's all going to come right. Never mind. It's all going to come right. And you're welcome, of course, to come too, to our house, if you are still, that is, if you need—'

'Ah, you are so kind. But,' I hesitate, then continue in a rush, 'I'll be gone. I hope to book my passage, to return home. Perhaps within the week. My work. My daughters—'

'Of course, of course.'

'Now that I am well. Thanks to you, and the doctor. All of your care. Your kindness.'

Her hand grasps my hand. Her grip is fierce, strong, calm.

'I hope to go to Town—I was going to ask you or Miss Deere if you would be so kind as to help me in this—to book my passage.'

'Of course, we can go to Town, whenever you wish. Just ask. But do know that you will be missed.' She pulls me into an embrace. 'Madame. Professor. Marie.' How sweet it is, and how strange, to be called by my own name. 'You will be missed. By all of us.'

MEASURED
Matti

The hammer knock, once, twice, sold, echoes in her ears. *All shall be well, all shall be well.* Ada sits on her lap, presses into her front, like a newborn seeking succour that Matti cannot give. *All shall be well. All shall be well.* Two men prowl the house, measuring, minding, poking, prying, noting, adding so they can subtract. *All manner of things shall be well.* Wilma Reddy is in the hallway, muttering with Madame Miranda Marya Skwodovska. *Be well. Be well.* Matti lifts above herself, she rises, she rises, her three daughters hold her down. *All manner of things. All shall be.* The men walk through the kitchen, the children freeze, like animals caught in bright light. *All manner. Things shall be.* Matti feels measured, as if for a casket or coffin, for a costume of burial clothes. *Well.*

GIFTED
The Lady

Long after the Wise's men have gone, their presence lingers in the house. Everything is out of place, though only just perceptibly. I move around the room, restoring my possessions to order, straightening bedclothes, closing a just-open drawer. The whiff of the men remains, cigarette smoke and something sour.

I sit with my back to the writing desk, facing into the room, this room that has held me fast through my recuperation, returned me to the relative health—and quiet peace—I now enjoy. This family. Their welcome, their sanctuary, their nursing; their great and small kindnesses, bestowed without fuss. Their recognition of my need, and their response, without question. Their immeasurable gift, when they have so little.

That even the little they have left—their home, this haven—will be lost, now, after the unbearable loss they have already borne, is simply unimaginable.

Can I, then, imagine another outcome? And, once imagined, make it so?

I turn the chair to face the desk, and in my mind's eye I see another desk, in my home on the other side of this great Earth. I see the small wooden box that lies upon it. There: my phial of radium. There, in its little glass prison. It has cost me everything. It has given me everything. The misery of fame; the dream of discovery made a reality. I carry it with me always, in the marks on my skin, and in my thoughts.

There is money, still, from the Swedish prize. Mrs Reddy will know how much the doctor-woman-widow needs to save their house. I need not ask the doctor herself. She need not even know.

'A bag of money, fallen from the sky,' Mrs Reddy might tell her, or gold at the end of the rainbow. Or radium, that shines like sunshine.

A knock at the door, a creak as it opens, her sweet face appears in the gap.

'Hello, Lady.'

'Hello, Hanna.'

'Are you writing?'

'No, no, just thinking.'

She takes a step into the room. I nod, smile, and she comes to me, stands by my side, puts her hand on my knee to push herself up so she can see the empty surface of the desk.

'Is the thinking about your little lamp?'

'Radium. My radium. Yes.'

'Radium shines like sunshine.' She reaches her hand towards my own, that rests on the desk, that holds the imagined phial. 'The darling light,' she says, as though she can see it, as though she can feel it. She pulls at my sleeve. 'Lady, do you know—?'

'What, Hanna dear?'

'Do you know? Did our mother tell you?'

'Tell me?'

'About Wonderland. And the sale. She didn't say. She won't say. And Mrs R won't tell.'

I can see no reason to withhold the information. 'Your Wonderland is sold,' I tell her. 'The sale went through, and all will be well.'

Hanna nods, and sighs, then pulls again at my sleeve.

'And Lady?'

'Yes, Hanna.'

'It's about our father, and his going.'

'Ah, my dear, go on.'

She is quiet for a long moment, her head bowed low. When she starts to speak, she lifts her eyes to mine, and words rush and tumble from her, unstoppable once they start. 'Why did he leave us? Was it something that we did? Was it something that we are? Was it something we shouldn't have done, or something we forgot? Was it our fault? Why, oh why, did he die?'

I think I can hear the thud of her heart, though it may be the thud of my own.

'Hanna, dear Hanna,' I begin, not knowing how to go on. I answer her unanswerable questions with murmuring mothering talk, tell her that she and her sisters were never to blame. No one was at fault. Murmuring, mothering, soothing words. She is sad, I say. She and her sisters are grieving.

As she listens, her breathing slows, relaxes. She leans both elbows on my leg, and I can feel her bones. I imagine their imprint on me. I imagine the look of the bones under her skin, revealed by radiation, thin, sharp, strong, like the wings of a small bird. I imagine her able to fly. (What a wonder!)

I speak softly—as if I am telling myself—of my dear daughters losing their father, that he was lost—as Hanna's dear father was—in a moment of simple distraction, an accident, a random event, no one's fault. 'I was as sad as your mother, as sad as you,' I tell her, 'and I am as sad today, still. And my daughters were as sad, are sad still. My Big Girl was just a little older than you when her father died. My Little One, just a toddling infant, never knew him, not really. But my Big Girl. My Big Girl. She remembers her dear father, as you will remember your dear father, forever.'

'Did they cry?' she asks me. 'Did your daughters cry? And why can't I?'

'We all find our own way of remembering,' I tell her, 'and our own way of grieving.'

I lean down, lift her onto my lap. She seems almost weightless. She leans into me, her back against my front, her hands on the desk, resting between my hands.

'All will be well,' I tell her again. 'I promise you.'

I hold her hand in mine, and feel her mesmerised.

WINKING, BRINKING, INKLING
Triplets

On this new day, in this new week, our house feels on the brink. Of what? We do not know. No one will tell us, no one will say, but the Lady says all will be well. Our mother pastes a bright mask to her face for the world, and for us. But she folds herself into herself when she thinks we cannot see.

This new day, though, this brinkish day! While we ready ourselves for school, Mrs R and the Lady are off to Town, where the Lady will book her passage home. They are dressed in best coats and polished shoes (Radium shines like sunshine!), hats pinned in place, all ready to meet the morning ferry.

Mrs R and the Lady huddle in the hallway, whispering. We creep towards them, but all we hear is *bank* and *pounds* and *gift* and *save* and *sign*, before Mrs R shoos us away (her specialism, she says—she is the very best at shooing).

'It's money business, for adults, not for ratbags, off you trot!'

Mrs R and the Lady smile at each other in the hallway.

'We're off to the ferry now, Matti,' Mrs R knocks then calls through the closed door to our mother's bedroom. 'And Oona, little ratbag,' she shouts towards us, 'don't you forget to gargle! I've left your tea in a cup on the table.'

Mrs R adjusts the Lady's hat, steps back to inspect it, then nods at her, and the Lady nods back. We think we see the Lady wink at Mrs R before they link arms and depart.

Winking, brinking, what a day! We have an inkling all will be well.

SAVED
Matti

All manner of things pivot with a knock on the door. Wilma and Madame Miranda Marie left in the morning, for Madame is sailing away, some day soon. Matti slept and smoked and wept and smoked and slept all morning long, as she has every day since the Wonderland sale. She hears them return, now, hears a knock on the bedroom door. Wilma Reddy enters, kneels on the floor by Matti's bed, brushes her hand—its touch like balm, like rescue—over her forehead, her cheek, brushes the hair from her eyes. Everything is going to be all right, Wilma Reddy tells her. The house is saved. You can stay, stay forever if you wish. A bag of gold from the sky, shines like sunshine, a Swedish prize, a gift. *All manner of things*. What a wonder.

DISMANTLED
Triplets

A horn toots, truck grunts to a stop, a door slams, a voice shouts *hi!* and Jane Deere judders in through the kitchen door.

'Hi! She's sailing! Wonderland is sailing!'

We leap towards her. What can she mean?

'There you are, girls! Where are they all? Matti! Wil! Prof,' she shouts to the house, 'Come on, you'll miss it!'

Our mother and Mrs R appear from the laundry, the Lady from her room.

'What on Earth—'

'It's Wonderland! Dismantled and packed, all done in a day, ahead of schedule, and all aboard the schooner *Amelia Sims*, sails set for Auckland.' We leap and dance and whoop around Jane Deere. 'She's come round the bays already, heading for the heads. Come on! Let's see her off!'

Mrs R wipes her hands down the front of her trousers, reaches for her jacket that's draped on a chair. The Lady has just come in from a walk, so she's already dressed for outside. Our mother stands with her hands to her face, as if she's alone in the room. We run to her, reach our arms around her, surround her with us, hold her close. Her arms drop and reach to ours, and she says, 'Ah, well, it has come to this. Come then, let's see the old dear off.'

We all bustle out of the house in a crowd, and pile into Jane Deere's truck. Mrs R's in the front with Jane Deere, the Lady between them. The three of us and our mother squeeze into the back, and Jane Deere whoops, and all of us whoop and cry, as she releases the brake and the truck lurches around the bay.

'Look! Look back now, she's just coming into view!'

We stand on the seat and look through the gap in the side of the truck canopy and there, we can see the schooner, sitting low in the water, her two great masts towering, men in the rigging. With just four of her sails set, still she's hurling along at pace.

'That's her!'

'*Amelia Sims*!'

'Ah, she's a beauty!'

'Look at her go!'

'What a bloody wonder!'

'Come on, she'll be out of the harbour in no time at this rate!'

Jane Deere guns the engine, and we all cheer her on. She lurches the truck around the curve of the bay and drives out as close as she can to the southern point, away past the army camp, pushing on once the road becomes a track, only stopping when the track becomes a path unfit even for rabbits. We all pile out of the truck and push through flax and tussock onto the beach, shale crunching under our feet, gentle waves pushing in.

Out here on the point, *Amelia Sims* seems so close we could reach out and touch her. And there, look, she's crammed to the gunwales with Wonderland, our Wonderland, set sail! The turrets of Katzenjammer Castle jut proud between her great main masts. There's the cone of the Helter Skelter tower, unroofed, propped like a haystack near her prow. The curve-tipped pagoda roof of the Japanese Tea Kiosk (we can almost smell the iced buns) is unmistakeable, even though it's lying on its side, smaller than we remember. The Eiffel Tower sprouts like a third mast, unsailed. The great iron gate, ⱭꞐAⱢᴚƎⱭꞐOW spelled out like nonsense above the wrought-iron rays of the rising sun (no, the sun is surely setting, now), is strapped to the side of a wooden crate on the deck.

We stand on the beach, all of us in a line, and watch this apparition, this procession, moving bright against the backdrop of the dark hills across the harbour.

There's a sound like *wump!* as another sail unfurls, and the shape of it, the silken fall of it, makes us think of Miss Nella Jonassen's balloon, and the whale, and the comet, and a teardrop finally falling, going somewhere. Then another *wump!* and another great fall, and the wind picks her up as *Amelia Sims* breaks out of the lee of the point, and she lifts, she lifts, rising on the waves, and Wonderland sails away.

Hanna stands next to the Lady
> *and as wonderland*
> *—our wonderland, unmade—*
> *sails, I take the lady's hand,*
> *knowing she will sail away,*
> *as wonderland has sailed,*
> *and I start to sing*
> *a goodbye song,*
> *a wonderland song,*
> *a lady song,*
> *a sister song,*
> *and I sing them all full voice*

Ada takes our mother's hand
> *and as wonderland*
> *—our wonderland, unmoored—*
> *moves on,*
> *I feel the pressure of my mother's*
> *hand on mine,*
> *and I join my sister hanna in song,*

another song,
a mother song,
careful, smoky, sweet

And Oona stands apart, alone
and I watch as wonderland
—our wonderland, no more—
passes through the harbour heads,
and on, and on, and away,
carrying what our father left behind,
and with a wump! here is my voice,
as if back from the dead
—silenced no more—
released, like the sails,
and I raise my voice,
soft at first, then louder, louder,
keening, strong,
I join my sisters' song, singing,
adding a final song,
a father song,
high and bright and beautiful

FITTING
Matti

There's a crack: the sound of the sails as they unfurl, fill with wind. There is the look of it, the sails as they take shape, fattening against the sky. There are the shapes, too, of Wonderland—their Wonderland, no more—unmade, muddled, topsy-turvy on the sea. The hairs on the back of her neck prickle, as her mind's eye draws the shape of Charlie, her Charlie, on the deck among the Wonderland fittings, fitting in, a fitting end. There is another sound: a cry, a sound from deep within her. Matti flicks her tongue and catches tears, tastes her own warm brine.

There is another sound, a sweet, soft sound. Matti feels Ada's hand—tiny and warm as a little mouse, though not as timid—and she presses her precious daughter's hand, and then she kneels by Ada's side and raises her daughter's hand and kisses it, holds it tight to her. She stumbles, both of them tumble together—what does it mean to fall?—and folds to her knees on the sharp shale of the beach, and Ada folds into her and onto her lap, and the two of them press together, warm, and together they face the harbour, and the hills, and Wonderland's beautiful departure.

And there, another sound, much missed, long silent. There is the sound of Oona's voice, returned to them, raised, arisen.

UNIVERSE
The Lady

I did not expect this departure by sea, Wonderland tumbled like an unsolvable puzzle, upended as all of us are upended, on this beach, in the cold, at the edge of the universe. Only the broad hills across the water anchor the sky to the Earth; all else is excited, uplifted, brilliant. The three little girls cry and shout—even Oona, the silent sister, shouts—and their cries join and lift into the air and turn into a kind of song. They sing into the salt spray, the glow of sun on their faces. The woman-doctor-widow is on her knees, tears flowing freely, sobbing, released. Mrs Reddy and Miss Deere hold each other in close embrace. Hanna—dear Johanna—holds my hand in hers. Her voice joins her to her sisters, the three of them radiant. Sunlight beams off the water, off the precious cargo, sailing away. I am mesmerised.

WHAT IT HOLDS
Triplets

On the morning of the last day before the Lady leaves, we're up bright and early, bustling in the kitchen. Our mother has gone to work. The Lady has gone to walk one last time on the beach. We heard the front door creak open, then close with a click of the latch.

Now, the house is empty apart from the three of us. Only us.

We slip into the Lady's room. On the bed is her satchel, and next to it her suitcase, that she spent last evening packing. In her suitcase are clothes (one black dress, one blue, one grey skirt, one black, three shirts of bright white, shoes wrapped in brown paper, their toes stuffed with stockings). In her leather satchel are books (three notebooks, wrapped in cloth) and bundled letters.

Hanna takes one of the notebooks

> *and I slip it under my arm*
> *slip under the blanket of the*
> *lady's bed*
> *and in the dark and fug*
> *I open the notebook*
> *and see the glow of her in it*
> *and I know what it holds*
> *of her*
> *I hold it in my hands, and feel*
> *the heat of it*

*(or perhaps the heat is from my
hands?)
I know the beauty of it
the knowledge of it
the power, its gift
not mine to keep, but mine
to hold, to be held
and to remember
this book, this knowledge,
this science
that somehow holds her pain
and its absence
that somehow holds her power
that somehow holds her loss
and holds her husband
that somehow holds radium
(her radium)
and holds me in it, too*

Ada turns away from the Lady's things on the bed
*and I move across the room
to my mother's cabinet
her cabinet of wonders
I turn the little key in the lock
and the front drops
revealing
everything that is hidden away
every treasure
every little thing
I trace my finger
over hanks of silken hair
touch eyeballs of glass
and cool china foreheads
and I remember
I remember*

and I imagine
the lost breath
the lost cord
every terrible thing
and every beauty
every untold secret
and every wonder
that was ever within

Oona slips from the room
and I leave my sisters there
and go to my mother's room
that she shared with my father
charlie
I drag the chair to the wardrobe
stretch and climb
and reach to the very top
to the very back
and pull my father's jacket to me
heavy
too heavy
not heavy enough
and I slip my arms into his arms
and feel the weight on my shoulders
trace my fingers on the braids
metallic, bold as brass
good as gold
large as life

Hanna slips out from under the blankets and returns the notebook to the satchel, wrapping it as it was wrapped, replacing it with care. Ada lifts the front of the cabinet, clicks it into place, turns the little key to lock it all away. Oona shrugs out of the jacket and leaves it on our mother's bed, in the careful shape of our father, Carnival Charlie Loverock.

~ ~ ~

We have a gift for the Lady. Three tiny dolls we've made from three tiny bottles, each one of them bound with a tie of colour, one violet, one white and one green, scraps from the making of our Magnificent Trousers. We leave them in the top of her satchel, so she knows we've been. We leave her these three little beauties, made with love, for her and for her fatherless daughters, so she will not forget us, as we will not forget her, and her gift.

For the Lady's last night, Jane Deere roasts one of their dear old chickens with spuds and pumpkin for all seven of us (our mother and the Lady, Jane Deere and Mrs R, and the three of us, all around our kitchen table once more). We drink a toast—whisky for the grownups, ginger beer for us—to the Lady, wish her good health and safe travels and *bon boy-arch*, and she drinks a toast to all of us, and thanks us for our care, for safe haven. And we all drink a final toast, but it is quiet, without words, just raised glasses and shining eyes. Jane Deere has brought chocolate wrapped in silver paper for pudding, and we finish it all at the table, then there is more whisky for the grownups, but only milk for us.

Before Mrs R and Jane Deere leave for the night, to return to Karaka Bay, Jane Deere carries the Lady's big suitcase from her room and leaves it by the front door.

Mrs R says to the Lady, 'I'll come with you into Town, on the ferry. No, no,' she waves away arguments, 'I insist. We'll be here in the morning. Sleep tight.'

Mrs R blows us kisses as they leave, and our mother sighs and insists it's time to sleep, so off we scurry to our bed.

And in our bed, before we sleep, we dream a waking dream of the Lady's satchel, and what it holds. We have seen inside it. We have watched her pack and unpack and repack it, until we know it off by heart, and until everything fits, snug as a bug in a rug. We know that there are travel papers, a velvet purse for coins, and a clip holding paper money. There are pencils, and her little knife (with the silver bee on its handle) to sharpen them. There is her pen made of tortoiseshell, and a travelling bottle of ink to fill it. There are handkerchiefs, and bottles of medicine, and a bouquet of herbs from Jane Deere the Cameleer, bound with a tie of flax. There is a piece of dark-blue kohl-eyed sea-bright shell, that we think might have come from Hermit Louis. There are three notebooks, one of them imprinted on the cover with the shapes of letters (an M, a P, we think we see), with a photograph in it of a man with a neat little beard, of her standing behind him, with her hand on his shoulder, with her long fingers aligned (pointing strong and true) towards his heart. There is a postcard, *Four Views of Wonderland*, the Eiffel Tower, the Kiosk, the Chute, Three Little Miramar Maids. There are the three tiny dolls we made her, bound with our starry trouser silk. There is a photograph of her daughters, their high foreheads like her own, one dark, one pale, both left behind, and to whom she is returning.

BRAID
Matti

Wilma and Jane have left for the night. The girls are tucked up in bed, all their whispering finally quiet. Matti wipes the iron roasting pan, places it into the dying oven to dry. She folds the tea towel, hangs it over the rail by the stove. Everything is shipshape. All well.

She tips a cigarette from the tin, taps its end on the table, scratches a match to life and lights the smoke. She lies on the daybed, balances on the splay of her chest a saucer for ash, and inhales, deep, deep. The saucer rises, rises, rises, then falls. Above her, high above, tiny flowers pattern the pressed tin of the ceiling, mark out its perimeter. Always there, rarely noticed. *Hello, flowers.* She smiles, picks a strand of tobacco from her lip, flicks it into the night, breathes in deep, deep, nearly time to sleep. The woman, their visitor, leaves tomorrow. Leaves them with her gift, unimaginable, but quite real. Wilma had told Matti, showed her the bank note. All well. All well. Matti had wept, melted into the weeping, tears drawn deep from her, letting it go.

She had gone to the woman, the professor, Marie. She had taken her hands, but she could not speak her thanks. The woman had nodded at her, grasped her meaning without words. Their clasped hands gripped each other, holding on for dear life. Two women, two widows, two mothers.

Matti stubs her cigarette in the saucer, swings her legs to the floor, places the saucer on the table and goes to her daughters' door, inches it open. The three of them nest, one behind the other behind the other, in the dark. The pale skin of them. The sweet whistle of their breath. Well. All well.

She moves through the kitchen, down the hall, to her room, stepping her hands down the wall, feeling her way in the dark. Her head spins, from whisky, from smoke, from relief. In her room. His jacket on the bed. Still in the shape of Charlie. The girls. They must have. If only they. Why would. If he had. Why did he. Why didn't. All well. Bound to rise. Cures all ills. She had found the jacket on her bed, last night, slipped under it, slept with it, felt it weighing her down, felt him on her, about her. She had run her hand down its arms, its back, felt its hard brass cold on her skin.

She raises the jacket's arm to her cheek, to her lips, kisses the twist of the braid at its wrist. Bound to rise. All well. She steps out of her clothes, and into their bed, and feels his weight upon her. One more night. Just one more night, she promises herself, then she'll pack the jacket away, safekept.

FARE WELL
The Lady

On the morning of my departure, I wake before it is light. All is still and cold outside. All is quiet in the house. I rise. I fold quilt, blanket, sheets, plump pillows, pile them neatly at the head of the stripped bed. I perform my ablutions—pot, jug, cloth—and dress, ready for travel. I place my satchel on the bed. My large valise stands ready in the hall. I open it just enough to tuck my night-dress inside. No need to unpack, to check and repack. I am ready.

    I open the door of my room, listen to the house—still quiet—then open the front door. Once more to the admired Miranda. I stand at the rail and watch the water shimmering dark against heavy hills. The subtlest light, the faintest radiance shivers, and starts to warm the sky. I draw my jacket close around my neck and step down, across the road, to walk on the beach, one more time, as the sun rises on this farewell day.

I am halfway to the rocks at the point when I hear her, and I turn, and she rushes to me, and takes my hand with her little hand.

    'Lady, Lady,' she huffs.
    'Hello, Hanna.'
    We stand together and watch the sun rise above the gentle-tempered sea, the precious glow warm on our upturned faces. Then we turn, together, and follow the shellcrush tideline

along the beach. Hanna picks up sea-glass, amber, rounded, a window into time and its passing. We imagine its origins: the crossing of oceans, or merely of harbours. This glass from Africa, or from Italy, or from America (*Amehdika* is the way she says it, *Ahhh-MEH-Di-Kah!*).

She asks me about my journey here by sea, those few short months ago that feel like a lifetime (or its loss). I tell her how ill I was and recall and describe the rocking of the waves, intolerable, unforgiving.

'And now, the return journey,' I tell her. 'Going home is always easier. Sweeter.'

'We thought you might stay forever.'

I tell her I have to return to my work, then I give a better reason. 'My daughters need me to return. I need to return to them, now that I am well, thanks to this place.' I sweep my arm out, to take in all of the bay, all of the hills across the harbour, and the little cottage behind us. 'This place, and your mother, and all of you.'

'But you help us. You help me. And you help our mother.'

'You do not need me. And your mother is stronger every day. She will be well, she will be well. She has her work. And she has the three of you. And you all have Mrs Reddy and Miss Deere. All will be well. Yes?'

'Yes,' she echoes.

We walk on, quiet for a time, along the beach towards the cottage. The bay is radiant now, and blue and beautiful, in the clear light of the fresh-risen sun.

Hanna rests her hand in mine. It flutters, almost weightless.

'Lady.'

'Dear Hanna.'

AWAY
Triplets

On the day the Lady leaves us, we all walk together the three hundred yards from our house, around the bay, to the wharf. Jane Deere the Cameleer carries the Lady's suitcase, and Mrs R carries her satchel. Our mother and the Lady walk beside them, leaning lightly on each other. The three of us walk behind the four of them. We take turns walking backwards, to watch the *Duchess* come towards us across the water, from the city, getting bigger, and bigger, starting toy-sized, becoming child-sized, now life-sized, rising and falling lightly on the day's small waves.

We move, all seven of us, in procession onto the wharf, and out to the end as the *Duchess* bumps in. The captain waves from the wheelhouse, and we all wave back to him. The deckhand steps from the boat and onto the wharf, takes the suitcase from Jane Deere's hand, steps back on the *Duchess* to stow it aboard.

The Lady moves towards Jane Deere, and they clasp each other's hands, and speak a few words, and Jane Deere takes the dark glasses from her pocket and hands them to the Lady, who nods at her, and smiles. Then the Lady turns to our mother and kisses her cheek (first this cheek, then the other, then the first cheek again) and we hear them murmur in the sweet foreign language that we do not understand, *mare-sea, mare-sea*. Then the Lady bends to each of us—first Ada, then Oona, then last of all Hanna—and gives each of us, in turn, a single kiss and a whispered *goodbye*. Then she pulls the three of us to her, all of us together, and she kisses us again, then lets us go.

She turns to Mrs R and places her arm gently atop hers, taking her hand, and they step up—as if they're about to dance—onto the deck of the *Duchess*. And now the Lady stands there, on the ferry's deck, both hands on the railing. Her suitcase is stashed in the wheelhouse, but her leather satchel stays with her, close by her side.

We stand on the wharf with Jane Deere and our mother, as the deckhand casts off the rope and Mrs R joins the Lady at the rail and the captain chugs the *Duchess* off and away. We all wave and shout goodbye from the wharf, and Hanna takes three steps forward and cries out to the Lady, and the seagulls lift in the air and match her cry, and the Lady tries to lift her hand from the rail to wave but perhaps the sea unsettles her, so her hands stay where they are, somewhere in between resting and gripping tightly. The white-painted rail, stark against the deep blue of her dress, seems almost to cut her in two. The dark glasses on her pale face hide her eyes, though we know they're there, and we know the depths of their kindness.

As the *Duchess* pushes away and punches into the water, we three break from our mother and take off at a sprint back down the wharf and on to the road, and we run on the road and then the beach, then back on the road and the beach again, following the *Duchess* but never catching her. We stop on the beach, our lungs tight with running and the wind and the air and the salt, and we watch as the Lady becomes a tiny dark blue line on the *Duchess* in the distance, and we watch until the *Duchess* shrinks, becomes tiny, until we cannot see her, though we know she is there.

And we link our hands again (Ada's hand in Oona's, Oona's hand in Hanna's) and again we start to run. And we run, and we keep running, always running, not away from, but towards. The three of us together, always and ever together, bright and beautiful.

Coda

TIME PASSES
Triplets

We three sisters sit, leaning our heads on our hands, watching the rising sun. We begin dreaming after a fashion, and this is our dream.

First, we dream of the Lady, and we hear the very tones of her voice, and we see her grey eyes and her wandering flyaway hair, and finally we see her little light, the precious phial, and we hold it in our hands, and we meet her two daughters, and we dance with them on the beach. Jane Deere rolls by leading her camels, all four of them in a line—we hear the rattle of the teacups in the kitchen as our mother and Mrs R and all the Cronies share their never-ending drinks and smokes—once more the great whale lies on the beach—once more Ernest Rutherford nuzzles our necks and leaves her beautiful horse smell on our hands—once more Miss Nella Jonassen is aloft above Worser Bay in her Bound to Rise balloon. Once more Hermit Louis sells fish on the beach, from a dripping wet sack, a penny a piece. Once more the shriek of the wind up the hill to our school, the squeaking of Miss Grimshaw's chalk, the insistence of Second Bell, all of these sounds fill the air, mixed up with the distant sobs of Minna Bloody Hofmann, with yet another bloody nose.

We sit with closed eyes, and half believe ourselves in Wonderland, though we know we have but to open our eyes again, and all will change to dull reality. We know that Wonderland has closed forever, sailed away for good. We know that the Lady has left. We know that our father will still be gone, though we can conjure him to join us, we can see his belly in the hills, his face in the waves, hear his carnival voice in the wind.

This is our story, seen with our own six eyes, heard with our own six shell-like ears, held in our very own six hands. We've told you (oh yes, we've told you).

The story does not end with Wonderland's sailing, nor does it end when the Lady leaves, as it did not end with our father's loss. The story continues, as stories do, sometimes in soft focus, gauze-draped, indistinct, other times crystalline, sharp-edged, clear and bright as daytime in our minds' eyes. We remember backwards, and we remember forwards, not waiting for the future to show, but following the knots and strings of memory wherever and whenever they take us.

We remember the time before this time.

We remember the after-time.

We remember everything in between, from all the different beginnings, and alternate imaginings.

We remember together, the three of us.

And each of us remembers on our own.

After the Lady leaves us, our house shifts, resettles. Our mother moves into the front room, all the better for creeping out of the house without disturbing the rest of us, for night-time baby hospitalling. The three of us move into the bedroom our mother and father once shared. When we open the doors of the wardrobe and climb inside behind the hanging winter clothes, our father is there in the smell at the back, wool and wood, salt beach sweat and sweet worn leather.

The buckles in the tramlines by the Rongotai Knob are finally fixed, just after the Lady sails away, as if her leaving has straightened them out. The tram strike ends, and the trams start running again, to Miramar, and through the

Seatoun tunnel. The school year ends, and another passes. Ernest Rutherford the Gentleman Scientist is knighted on the other side of the world, and that very same week, in our side paddock, our own dear old Ernest Rutherford the Horse dies, poor thing, she just lies down one day and never gets back up.

Ernest Rutherford the Gentleman Scientist comes to visit just as the war begins. He brings his gold Nobel medal (which we all admire), and his wife and his daughter (we are less keen on them).

The war rolls on. On half-holidays we go with our mother and Mrs R and Jane Deere to the parades and marches at Newtown Park, and through the Town from the Railway Station to the wharf, where the Quakers hand out PEACE pamphlets.

Our mother and Mrs R work twice as hard as ever, if that's possible, with so many doctors (including Doctor B) and nurses gone off to the war, and just as many babies to deliver, and general doctoring to boot. We all do what we can, our mother says, and what we must. The Lady writes from France that she is twice as busy, too, that she and her Big Girl drive X-ray trucks to treat the troops and see their bones. There's a steady stream of nurses, sometimes two or three at once, in and out of our back bedroom, staying for a few nights, a month, sometimes more. Our house is full of women, and full of music, smoke and dancing, and we love this time of war for the party that it seems to bring.

Mrs R bakes a magnificent cake when the suffrage law passes in London, ices it violet, white and green, and we all toast Votes for Some Women, and Mrs R says she supposes Some is better than None, though there's work still to be done.

Our lives lock down when the virus comes, and we barely notice the war ending. School stops. We cannot play. We stay home to stay safe, wash hands to save lives. Our mother goes from house to house, curing and failing to cure, attending all the while. Our days become smaller, our lives draw in. Go home. Stay home. We don't understand, but our mother says it's contagion, pure and simple, biology and mathematics (and luck, good and bad, says Mrs R) determining the spread, person to person to person. Mrs R sews little blocks of camphor into tiny muslin bags that she loops around each of our necks on strings of thick wool, to tuck inside our undershirts, ice-hot and sharp-scented against our skin. Our mother makes beef broth, pours it into tins, leaves it to cool to jelly. We help her deliver it to families with the sickness, leaving teacloth-wrapped tins on doorsteps with a shouted 'Soup ahoy!' and three alerting knocks on the door. We wave at pale faces in windows, then scarper to make the next delivery.

Hermit Louis gets the virus and moves into our back room. It's touch and go for a while, but our mother doctors and nurses him better. We grow accustomed to his presence, and learn his name is really Léopold, though we still and always call him Louis, and we think he doesn't mind. The summer after, when he is entirely well, Hermit Louis moves into a shack around the coast, all the way out in Mākara, where the fishing is better, he says.

The Lady sends letters to our mother, and to Hanna, with news of her daughters, and their trip to America (*Ahhh-MEH-Di-Kah!*). Travel is tiring, she writes, though my girls are great companions. President Harding welcomed us to the White House, she says, and gifted me with one gramme of radium, more valuable than gold.

The year we turn fifteen, each of us falls in love. Ada's and Hanna's affections are unrequited and soon forgotten. Oona's first love—head over heels—is Minna Hofmann. They moon and fawn together for months, until the next summer, when we all turn sixteen, and Minna is sent off to live in Levin, as home help for her aunt.

Hanna enters university early, barely seventeen, thanks in

part to a good word or three from our mother's old friend Ernest Rutherford the Gentleman Scientist to his alma mater. When Hanna moves to Christchurch, we each, for once in our lives, have a room of our own. Oona stays in the middle room; Ada returns to the back room the three of us shared long ago. It takes us all a little while to learn to sleep alone.

The Lady writes to Hanna, tells her that her daughter—the Lady's Big Girl, Irène—is working towards her doctorate, and encourages Hanna to do the same. She tells her she has the ability, it's clear, and that she—the Lady—would like to help, with travel and so on, and a position in Paris, in her laboratory. The Lady sends Hanna's fare, the term she graduates from Canterbury. Before she steams off to Paris (swoon!), Hanna spends the summer at home in Worser Bay, all three of us sharing the back bedroom once more, practising our schoolgirl French, walking the beach, watching the hills across the harbour. We try to encourage our mother to talk—to talk about our father—but without success.

Mrs R talks, though, one night in her cups, when our mother is at work. She talks of vile rumours. No truth to it, there cannot be, she says. Charlie in no way contributed to, let alone intended, his own demise. Let the record show, she says, raising her glass in emphasis and salute, that Charlie Loverock died as the result of a tragic and unavoidable accident. A slip. A mis-step. A moment of inattention that could happen to anyone. He was a big man with a big heart, and it is unclear where and when, in the order of events that night, his big heart stopped beating. Cause and effect, that is to say, remain unclear. Electricity may or may not have been involved. Or so it was reported. Entirely unconnected, she says, it's true that Wonderland was in debt—nothing Charlie had done wrong, not even especially bad management, just bad luck. Other men might have gambled money away, but not Carnival Charlie. Unless, that is, bad luck and misplaced optimism can be considered gambling. The rumours? Pfff, nothing but rumours. A good man, felled by bad luck and a big heart.

Hanna (who goes by Johanna, now) sends long letters from Paris, tales of the Lady and of the Institute named for her and her late husband, and of her work in the laboratory of the Lady's daughter, Irène. Ada takes a job at the *Dom*, writing for the women's pages, dancing and tennis and dresses and lipstick and bobbed hairdos, slipping in hygiene tips and higher thoughts (Mrs R is always feeding her ideas), when she thinks she can get away with it. Oona works as a projectionist in King's Theatre on Dixon Street in Town, beaming light and stories onto the screen.

Here, we turn twenty-one, Ada on the last day of the year that's been, Hanna on the first day of the brand new year—and in France, so it's a day behind for Ada and Oona at home—and Oona celebrating, as she always does, on both those days. It's a birthday festival for the three of us, to see out one year and see in the next, looking back and looking forward all at once. We clink glasses with our mother and Jane Deere and Mrs R, toasting our lives.

Ada moves into a flat in Newtown, closer to work. Sometimes Oona stays with her in the Newtown flat and, later, a bigger flat in Miramar. Hanna sends letters regularly, though they're shorter now, telegraphing news (Irène and Fred have had a baby, she's a corker little thing; the Lady is in good form), glossing over work that's going well but, she suspects, will not be understood.

Time passes. Months roll by. Another birthday season spans the turning of the year. And what a year this year will be.

What a time.

What a wonder!

1928
Hanna

In Paris, I am Johanna.
Here, back here, back home for now, I am
and always will be Hanna, no matter what
I call myself or how the world knows me.
I am my own woman, apart from my sisters,
away, abroad. You cannot confuse or
confound us, now, at twenty-three, as you
could when we were seven. No longer
indistinguishable, we three have grown
our bodies and faces apart from one another.
But here we are, together again, now.
We again, three again, the three of us here again.

I'd left for Europe nearly three years earlier, with a somewhat precocious science degree under my belt and an invitation from the Lady to visit her laboratory, and Irène's, to see if research suited me. And it did, it did. I settled quickly, easily into Irène Joliot-Curie's laboratory, immersing myself in the work, versing myself in the intimacies of the atom, finding in nuclear instability my own firm and fixed place in the world. I hummed with the excitement of my new life's launching.

My first trip home was planned with careful timing. I could spare just one month there, but what a precious month it would be. I arranged my leave to coincide with the long summer break in Paris and, more critically, the forthcoming addition to our little Loverock family on the other side of the world. I spent the voyage alternating between seasickness and health and, when in health, tried to keep up with the writing and reading my studies demanded.

On the day the ship finally steamed into Town, a strange rain pelted sideways, from the north, drenching everything, turning everything and everyone on the dock the same shade of dark grey. They were almost indistinguishable in that milling damp dark crowd, yet I saw them, plain as day: my sisters, my mother, Mrs R, Jane Deere. I was first off the ship and onto the wharf, dropping my suitcase, running to them, my arms held wide.

We three sisters fell together, as tight as we could around the mound of Ada's belly, the first time we'd been us, all together, since I'd left for Europe.

The three of us fell easily into old rhythms. We walked on the beach, lay in the shallow dips of the dunes and stared at the colours in the sky, looked for shapes in the hills. We told each other stories, of love and love lost, of small pleasures—the smell of hot ink on new paper, the flicker of filmlight telling tales in the dark, the cry of love wrought by the touch of a hand—and worldly excitements. I spoke of my work, the wonder of science, the awe, the power of understanding the mysteries and the many beauties of the elements. And at night, and long into the morning, we slept together in our old bed, curved perfectly into the shapes of each other, even though my sister's shape had changed.

Our mother was busier than ever, still leading a topsy-turvy life, delivering babies at all hours. Mrs R was still our mother's right-hand woman, confidante, best friend, and she and dear Jane Deere were often with us at the little house in Worser Bay.

In this household of women—our family—we all prepared for the imminent birth of Ada's child.

In this in-between time, the three of us talked, too, of our father, and of his death. One particular day, as we walked on the bright-lit beach where we'd farewelled him, we talked of the haunting of our not understanding, of our never really understanding, and of the shadow it had cast.

I could have lived my life forever in that shadow, looking for cause and effect, for certainty. But I'd taken to heart the late-night words of Mrs R, that drinking night of years ago, and the longer-ago words of the Lady. There was no reason. There was no purpose. No one—not us, not our father himself—was to blame. The rumours were nothing but rumours. There was no explanation, no neat tying up. There was just the world and what happened. Our father was there, and then he was not. A good man, felled (as I knew the Lady's husband had been felled) by bad luck, by accident, by random chance.

I had vowed, I told my sisters, to make my own luck, to live my life not in the shadow of our father's death, but in the light of his life. I had vowed, I told them, to hold him as we three had always held him: his big heart, his big voice, his big life near and dear in my heart and my mind, a way of remembering.

I broke into slow cartwheels down the beach, that day, and Oona caught my feet and steered me wheelbarrowlike along the sand, while Ada put her hands to her mouth and parped a pretend trumpet, the three of us (and Ada's child, tumbling belly-borne) in delicious procession, all the way home.

We were all eager for the child to come, ready to welcome and care and celebrate, all of us together. Mrs R had woven a flax basket for a crib, and filled it with flannelette nappies, muslin cloths, wraps and gowns of winceyette, a tiny cap knit from fine wool. Already enormous, Ada grew unbelievably, marvellously bigger.

An expectant calm settled on our household. Ada still

refused to speak of the child's father, even to Oona and me. Though he was not with her, our sister was not facing the birth on her own. She had us, all of us, around her, surrounding her.

1928

Ada

My sisters and I are three again,
we again, the three of us, here again.
One and one and one makes three,
and I'm about to add another.
My daughter tumbles in me, cartwheeling,
wheel-barrowing, parping. I'm as big as
Miss Nella Jonassen's hot-air balloon
at the point of touching down,
as big as a great grey-black whale
soaring through clear oceans, as big as
our father in life. I'm the shape
in the hills. I'm a comet fattened.
I'm a teardrop, not tipped on its side,
yet still going nowhere (for now).

My daughter was born on my mother's bed, my sisters by my side, my mother at my head. Mrs R presided at the business end, urging her birth, making it right, delivering my dear daughter, as she had delivered me and my sisters twenty-three years before. Mrs R tied three ribbons to my daughter's ankle, three ribbons braided, violet, white and green.

    I named her Tilda for her grandmother, our dear mother, Matti Matilda. I alone chose her name; she does not have a father to speak of—she does not need him, and anyway he is in Sydney now with his good lady wife and their upright young sons, and good luck to them.

(I know what it is to fall, not under the force of gravity, but under suspicion, and contempt.)

My daughter filled my days and nights, my every minute, every hour, every thought. Thank Saint Katie Sheppard for Mrs R, who brought me rich treats—buttery creamed potatoes, fresh cracked nuts, dark stout—and reminded me to eat. My sisters took turns keeping me company, but in truth I had eyes only for my daughter, ears only for her, love only for her. All else around me happened in a blur, barely noticed— there, my mother going back and forth to work; there, Oona greedily reading a letter; there, my sisters whispering; there, a small packed bag in the hallway, by the front door—while I slipped through those first ill-slept milk-slick days and nights of motherhood.

Midnight, clear and cold, my daughter fed and sleeping, the house quiet, and yet I could not sleep. In the kitchen I found Hanna, books and papers spread before her on the table as she smoked. She looked up from her writing, tamped her cigarette in the ashtray and asked me what I needed. Mrs R's malt extract in warm milk had helped the night before, I told her, so Hanna bustled at the stove, poured and stirred and heated, placed the mug by my hand.

She returned to her seat at the table, lit a fresh cigarette.

'I have news.' She spoke in a low voice, smoky, night-time. 'Guess what?

'Oh, I cannot. Just tell.'

And she told me that Oona, our sister, was gone.

'It's Minna,' Hanna said. 'Minna's coming, from Levin. Oona's gone to Mākara, to meet her.'

~ ~ ~

The road to Mākara isn't much more than a cart track after the turnoff at the end of the Karori Road. The car judders over dirt and corrugations, pulls hard towards the bush that flanks the road. It takes concentration to stay on track, a strong grip on the steering wheel, and my hands are clumsy in the cold. Wind leaks in through the angled glass of the little side window that never quite closes.

The road lifts up and over a bend, the bush still close, not yet opening up to the coast. The car shudders around a bend and I ease off the accelerator. Checking the mirror, I see Hanna's face—just the side of it, in profile, as she smokes out the side window—and I smile at her, as she smiles at me.

'All good in the driver's seat?' Hanna asks.

Tilda—remarkably, and for the first time—slept through the night last night, so I am feeling fit to drive (luckily, as Hanna has never learned).

'Very fine,' I say.

I shift the angle of my gaze, until the face in the mirror is my own. My hair is long, plaited and coiled and wound crown-like on top of my head. My cheeks have plumped to apple, matching my body, curved now, full, as unlike both my sisters as I have ever been.

I catch myself again in the mirror, and the mirror reflects in the window. One and one and one makes three.

I reach my hand out to my left. On the front seat of the car, in the flax basket that Mrs R wove for her, sleeps my daughter. Tilda mine. Her blanket moves and shifts, and Tilda's tiny fist punches the air, and her eyes open, and in that moment I meet her fierce stare: my daughter's eyes, my sisters' eyes, my mother's eyes, mine. Then her little fist lowers, and her eyes close, the car's rocking settling her once more in sleep. I can see clear sky ahead, as the road approaches the coast and the trees thin, everything low-growing, salt-stunted, windswept.

I hear the ocean, smell it, before I see it. The road curves one last time and the land opens out and the bay is there, the ocean, looking north, towards and connected with the rest of the world. Waves thump into the shore, push rocks up from the deep, turning them, smoothing them, changing them, moving them.

There's the smell of smokehouses, rich and sweet and savoury, sugar and fire and oil and fish. There's petrol and diesel from boats and generators, steam from a tar-coated shack. There are tractors on the beach, and boats, and in between them, higher on the beach, there are spread fishnets and woven willow craypots, ropes coiled, canvas drying.

I leave the car at the end of the track. I lift Tilda—still sleeping—in her basket. On the car's back seat is a wooden crate that holds a bottle of wine, a tin of Grimault's asthma cigarettes, a box of matches, a loaf of Mrs R's good bread, a slab of butter wrapped in waxed paper. These supplies can wait; there's time. Instead, Hanna fills her arms with a quilt our mother stitched long ago. It's for Oona and Minna, our mother said this morning, when she brought it to the car, folded it onto the back seat with care. A loving quilt.

There is our sister, Oona. She lifts her hand, waves. Hanna lifts the bundled quilt in colourful salute. I lift Tilda and her basket, and we walk towards Oona, towards the sea.

1928

Oona

*Our mother has lived all her days
in the wake of grief, since our father's death.
But I found my voice after my father died,
and I never lost it again. My mother's grief—
and the echo of my own—opened my heart,
made it keen for love, as deep and true
as the love my parents shared
(but longer, oh, let it be longer!).
I live, now, not in the wake of grief,
but in the wake of love. No, not in love's wake,
but in the centre of its fury, this maelstrom,
this tempest. Here, at this wild ocean beach,
I can abandon myself to love's storm.
To its wonder.*

I first came here with my mother. It has long been her habit to drive out to Mākara every month, bringing supplies for Hermit Louis, bread and good coffee, tins of milk and peaches and jam. She does the rounds of all the fisherfolk, distributing tobacco and medical attention, tending lingering coughs and weeping sores that the damp and salt water do not allow to heal. I lack my mother's medical skills. I lack even her sense of care. All I can do is tell stories—in the dark at the cinema, spilling light—the stories not even my own. Is there any earthly good in telling other people's stories? I can only hope.

Hermit Louis lives down the beach from this shack I have borrowed from one of the fisherfolk, who has—Louis assures me—gone north for the winter. I arrived here at sundown two days ago, having cadged a lift most of the way, then walked the last mile, a pilgrimage to the ocean. Louis sat by his door in the last of that day's weak winter sun, red cardigan buttoned over his shirt, blue trousers bright against grey weathered boards and the black of tar-sealed wood. I waved to him, shouted *hallooo!* and *bone-jaw*, as we used to do. He welcomed me without question, fed me toheroa soup from a tin, and showed me to this shack.

This tarred shack is one room, one window, one door, one verandah fronting the shore like the prow of a ship. I can succumb to my love, here, in this wild place, I can keen and sway and moan. I am made small by love, and I rise and rise to it, become large in the eye of its storm.

Minna will join me, here, soon, her precious letter promises. We've met here before. She knows the way.

In this tarred shack on the waves, I sing, I dance, alone (for now). I dance a once upon a time long ago starry sisters dance, marvellous, wondrous. I spin, a whirling dervish.

I fall into exhausted sleep, and dream of Minna Hofmann (her silver hair, her pale skin, her beautiful eyes), and of love.

In the morning I step off the prow of the tarred-shack-ship and walk into the wind. I pick treasures from the beach: an egg-shaped stone, green as moss; a mermaid's purse bleached silver-white; a bottle, blue glass, sea-smoothed, that fits in the palm of my hand. I pick soft catkins from the top of the beach, where the land meets the sea. I fill my pockets and whistle in the wind, the Loverock whistle, unmistakeable, the first note low and long, then I trip three quick notes above it.

There is the sound of tyres on gravel. I turn and see—not Minna, not yet—my mother's car, my sister's face behind the wheel. There is Hanna, a pile of fabric in her arms, as though she carries a flag. There is Ada, with her daughter in the basket of flax. I lift my hand, and Hanna calls my name, and Ada and Hanna walk towards me, and I run to them, and we meet on the steep curve of the beach.

What a wonder!

AFTER-TIME

Triplets

                    and I run to my sisters
                    and their endless embrace
and I stand with my sisters
and hold tight my daughter
                    and I skip to the beat of
                    my sisters' hearts, mine
together   we dance   on the beach
for Tilda   for love   and also and always for us

and as we dance our very selves form, conjured in triple-sun-starred ocean spray, three great bursts of magnificence

    green first   bone-white   then rich
    iridescent   chalk-bright   deep-dark
    seaweed-green lit white   violet bloom
    for Ada   for Oona   for Hanna

and all this colour lifts on the sound of the boom of the surf, thunderous in our ears and our bellies and right down through the soles of our dancing feet, and it echoes in us, and radiates out beyond us, from this beach, across the ocean, to the world.

In the after-time, grown women grown old, we will keep, through all our years, the dancing times and curious puzzling minds of our childhood. And we will gather together, with ourselves and with little children in the after-time, and back in the time before time, and make *their* eyes bright and eager and curious with stories, and dances, and dreams, perhaps even with the dream of Wonderland of now and long ago. And we will feel all life's simple sorrows, and the sorrows of loss and mourning, and we will find pleasure in all life's simple joys, remembering our own child-life, and all the days of the sad winter of the Lady, and of time before, and of the after-time.

But not now. Not yet. We're ahead of ourselves, again, time and memory muddling, again. We remember forward to the time long after the winter of the Lady's visit, forward to the time when our father is long dead, and Wonderland long gone, forward to the time after this time of Tilda's birth. We remember a time to come, when the Lady dies, and the year after that, her daughter wins the Swedish prize. Remember forward, further still, to the time when Ernest Rutherford the Gentleman Scientist dies, and is buried in Westminster Abbey. We remember all our many loves, some fleeting, a precious few constant. We remember the births of all our babies, and our babies' babies. We remember (of course we do) our own full-lived lives, our many accomplishments. And we remember forward, to the gentle deaths—all three, remarkably, within a single year—of Mrs R, then dear Jane Deere, then finally our own beloved mother, Matti, aged ninety-three, the year we three turn sixty.

Imagine these, and other memories, all the might-have-beens and maybes of our radiant lives.

But not yet, not now.

Now there is only this: a beach with three women dancing, a baby held close; and a fourth woman walking towards them, one hand lifted to shade her eyes against the brightness.

We'll end, again, here at this different beginning.

THE END

AUTHOR'S NOTE

So many books and artworks helped me create the characters and events in this book, with some listed over the page. Any inaccuracies or deviations from historical fact or chronology are mine alone; this is an alternative history, a fiction.

It seems particularly important to note that Marie Curie did not visit Aotearoa. In 1912, Curie did travel in mainland Europe and England, mostly incognito and mostly without her daughters, with the support of family and friends (including Hertha Ayrton) and colleagues such as Ernest Rutherford. Some of the words I've given to Marie Curie draw from her own writing, or from the biography written by her younger daughter, Ève, or as reported in other biographies.

Wonderland amusement park in Miramar, Wellington, ran from 1907 to 1912, and it was managed in real life by PP Bigwood rather than my fictional Charlie Loverock. The Loverocks are entirely my own invention. In the Coda, the triplets echo fragments from the closing pages of Lewis Carroll's *Alice's Adventures in Wonderland*.

Some incidental characters in the novel—including Ernest Rutherford, Hertha Ayrton, Agnes Bennett, Mr Bickerton and Dr Couney—are drawn loosely from historical records, with fictional versions embroidered by me. Hermit Louis is a fiction, but the character draws from two Wellingtonians of the early twentieth century, known as French Louis (Leopold Haupois, a Mākara fisherman, originally from Normandy) and the Hermit of Houghton Bay. Others—Mrs R, Jane Deere and Nella Jonassen—are purely fictional.

Bibliography

Denis Brian, *The Curies*, Wiley, 2005

John Campbell, *Rutherford: Scientist Supreme*, AAAS Publications, 1999

Lewis Carroll, *Alice's Adventures in Wonderland*, 1865

Ève Curie, *Madame Curie*, transl. Vincent Sheean, Doubleday, 1938

Marie Curie, *Pierre Curie*, transl. C. & V. Kellogg, Macmillan, 1923

Delahunty & Schulz (eds), *Alice in Wonderland: Through the Visual Arts*, Tate Publishing, 2011

Stephanie de Montalk, *How does it hurt?*, VUP, 2014

Shelley Emling, *Marie Curie and her Daughters*, Macmillan, 2012

Barbara Goldsmith, *Obsessive Genius: The Inner World of Marie Curie*, WW Norton & Co., 2005

Robin Hyde, *The Godwits Fly*, Hurst and Blackett, 1938

McRae & He (eds), *Wonderland: Alice on Screen*, Thames & Hudson, 2018

Bob O'Brien, *Waka, Ferry, Tram: Seatoun and the bays before 1958*, 2001

Rebecca Priestley, *Mad on Radium*, AUP, 2012

Susan Quinn, *Marie Curie: A Life*, Radcliffe Biography Series, 1996

Lauren Redniss, *Radioactive: Marie & Pierre Curie, A Tale of Love and Fallout*, Harper Collins, 2010

Adrienne Rich, 'Power', in *The Dream of a Common Language: Poems 1974–1977*, WW Norton & Co., 1978

Ian Wedde, *The Grass Catcher: A Digression about Home*, VUP, 2014

David Wilson, *Rutherford: Simple Genius*, Hodder and Stoughton, 1983

Films

Alice in Wonderland (1966), dir. Jonathan Miller (music Ravi Shankar)

Blue (1993), dir. Derek Jarman

Artworks and exhibitions

Candice Breitz, *Factum* (2010), video installation, in exhibition of works by Candice Breitz at City Gallery, Wellington, 2015

Wonderland, exhibition at ACMI, Melbourne, 2018

ACKNOWLEDGEMENTS

This novel has made its way into the world as a result of winning the NZSA Laura Solomon Cuba Press Prize. I am sincerely grateful to prize judges Anne Kennedy, Cassie Hart, Mary McCallum, Denika Mead and Nicky Solomon; to New Zealand Society of Authors Te Puni Kaituhi o Aotearoa for their support; and especially to Nicky and the Solomon family for this prize that honours the life and creative legacy of novelist, short-story writer, poet and playwright Laura Solomon.

Enormous thanks to The Cuba Press—to Mary McCallum, Paul Stewart and Tara Malone for their patience, collegiality, care and enthusiasm, and to Siân Robyns for thoughtful and insightful editing. It's been such a pleasure to work with you all. Look what we've made together!

I am grateful to all involved in awarding funding and support through the long (long!) process of writing this novel: Creative New Zealand (for an Arts Grant and an Arts Continuity Grant); Fellowship of Australian Writers Western Australia and Copyright Agency Cultural Fund (Australia) for FAWWA Established Writer Residency (2017); Michael King Writers Centre for the 2018 Spring Residency; Bundanon Trust (for an Artist Residency in 2019); and Varuna, The National Writers' House (for a Residency Fellowship in 2019). The very first glimmers of this novel were scribbled in 2015, while I held the inaugural Mildura Writers Festival Residency.

I owe huge thanks to those who, whether they knew it or not, helped me write this book, helped me stay the distance, helped me stay sane(-ish). Here's to all of you (including the many I have missed listing here by name): to writers, artists, friends—Fiona Kidman, Chloe Stevens, Jenny Ackland, Yvette Walker, Rachael King, Junichiro Iwase, Donata Carrazza, Kenney-Jean Sidwell, Antoinette Ratcliffe, Enid Flannery, Georgia Richter, Shelley Lewis—who gave feedback, support, inspiration, advice, or asked the right question at the right time; to Joe Hubmann and Michele Morris for a place to stay, early in the writing of this work; to India Flint for workshops that, in letting me look away from my writing work, have helped me see it more clearly; to Alison Manning for saving my (writing) life; to Virginia Lloyd and Carol Major for advice and insight; and to Susan Armstrong and Leah Woodburn for their support of, belief in and suggestions for this novel. Deepest thanks, as always, to my family for supporting me, and for their forbearance (when I've been all-but-unbearable). Ngā mihi nui, thank you, thank you, thank you all. What a wonder!